Without w
Wade gathered her up in his warm,
protective embrace.

"What am I gonna do with you?" he sighed into her hair. "You're as bighearted and pigheaded as they come. And while that's a tempting combination, I can't be—"

"So who asked you to be my protector? I told you, I can take—"

"—care of yourself," he finished for her. "I never meant to insult you. It's just that, for some reason, you worry me."

Patrice couldn't help admitting that she was touched by his concern. "There's no need for that. I'm fine."

"Something is happening here," he whispered, lifting her chin. "And I don't know whether to run from it or straight at it."

Patrice trembled in his arms. *If he isn't the guy for me, Lord,* she prayed, *speak now or forever hold Your peace....*

Books by Loree Lough

Love Inspired

*Suddenly Daddy #28
*Suddenly Mommy #34
*Suddenly Married #52
*Suddenly Reunited #107
*Suddenly Home #130
His Healing Touch #163
Out of the Shadows #179

*Suddenly!

LOREE LOUGH

A full-time writer for nearly fifteen years, Loree Lough has produced more than two thousand articles, dozens of short stories and novels for the young (and young at heart), and all have been published here and abroad. Author of thirty-seven award-winning romances, Loree also writes as Cara McCormack and Aleesha Carter.

A comedic teacher and conference speaker, Loree loves sharing in classrooms what she's learned the hard way. The mother of two grown daughters, she lives in Maryland with her husband and a fourteen-year-old cat named Mouser (who, until this year—when she caught and killed her first mouse—had no idea what a rodent was).

Out of the Shadows
Loree Lough

♥ *Love Inspired*

Published by Steeple Hill Books™

STEEPLE HILL BOOKS

Steeple Hill™

ISBN 0-373-87186-4

OUT OF THE SHADOWS

Copyright © 2002 by Loree Lough

Visit us at www.steeplehill.com

Printed in U.S.A.

...yea, in the shadow of Thy wings
will I make my refuge....

—*Psalms* 57:1

Out of the Shadows is dedicated to all the "real" Patrices out there who dedicatedly devote themselves to children in hospitals all over the globe; my hat's off to you all!

Prologue

Fifteen years ago, Halloween Night

If not for that lousy D on his last report card, he'd have a car to protect him from the biting late-October wind. His mother's stern lecture echoed in his head: "If you're not responsible enough to get decent grades in school, Wade Michael Cameron, you're not responsible enough to maneuver two tons of steel on the road!"

Angry—at his mom for making the stupid "C Average Required to Get a Driver's License" rule, at Mr. Woodley for giving him the low grade in Biology, at himself for not turning in the report that would've earned him that C—Wade dug his hands deeper into the pockets of his windbreaker.

Scowling, he hunched his shoulders and walked faster. Why hadn't he grabbed a heavier jacket when his mom suggested it? Well, another block and he'd be home. And hopefully when he got there, there'd be leftover lasagna in the fridge…

Ear-piercing sirens and the red-and-white strobes of fire trucks and ambulances shattered his train of thought. Sounded to Wade as though the commotion was coming from the cemetery.

His get-home-quick pace stalled as the turmoil near the railroad tracks mounted. He ran for a closer look.

The blades of a helicopter whipped dry leaves and grit round and round him, making Wade feel like he'd been trapped in a minitornado. Forearm shielding his eyes, he ducked behind the trunk of a massive oak.

To the adventure-hungry sixteen-year-old, it looked like a movie set, what with the headlights of a dozen cop cars crisscrossing against the revolving strobes of emergency vehicles. Dark-uniformed policemen bolted up and down the polished railroad tracks, hollering and yelling, some aiming flashlights into the woods, others marching through the underbrush looking for...

Looking for *what?* Wade wondered, suddenly forgetting how cold he'd been a moment ago.

"Found a boot over here," one cop shouted above the whirlybird's rotors.

"Got me a flannel sleeve," bellowed another.

A boot? A shirt sleeve? Wade's pulse pounded in his ears.

"Hey! Get a gurney over here, *stat!*" shouted a female paramedic. "The engineer is in full cardiac arrest!"

All activity now concentrated on the front of the freight train. Men and women who'd been searching on and around the tracks moved in. Soon, Wade couldn't see a thing past broad-shouldered cops, EMTs and firefighters.

Surely these guys didn't think the pumpkin-headed dummy Wade and his pals made had been *real*.... He leaned left and right, wishing for a better look. He soon discovered it wasn't the boys' Halloween dummy on the stretcher, but a real-life human being. The man's face, contorted with pain, was white as the fleecy blanket covering him.

He and the guys had made the dummy, then thrown it onto the tracks to see how far the train would drag it. Evidently, the engineer had mistaken it for a real person, and radioed for help to find the "man" who was missing after he hit him.

Wade found it difficult to swallow past the hard, dry knot in his throat. His breath came in short, harsh gasps and he knuckled his eyes. Wade and his pals Luke, Travis, Buddy and Adam had done some pretty outrageous things in the past, but nothing so terrible as this!

A flurry of activity captured his attention as several men lifted the gurney and ran, full steam ahead, toward the waiting helicopter. Seconds later, the machine shot straight up into the black sky.

"Lord," he whispered, "let that guy be okay...."

Not much chance God would listen to someone like him—especially considering.... Still, Wade repeated his prayer, just in case.

"The engineer told me he saw a guy on the tracks," he heard a cop say to a firefighter. "Said he braked for all he was worth, but couldn't stop in time."

Wade squeezed his eyes shut, admitting the obvious. What the engineer had mistaken for a homeless man was nothing but an assemblage of items Buddy had ordered the guys to bring to the cemetery—an old shirt, tattered trousers, beaten-up boots—stuffed with week-old newspapers and topped by a jack-o'-lantern head, and a ragtag fedora.

Swallowing, he stepped out from behind the shrubs and walked up to the nearest emergency vehicle. Assuming his best curious-kid expression, he said, "Hey, mister, what's goin' on?"

The paramedic looked up from his gear and frowned. "What're you doin' out this time of night, son?"

Wade shrugged. "I live right over there. So what happened?"

The paramedic went back to stuffing equipment into the side of his ambulance. "Engineer had himself one doozy of a heart attack."

Heart attack.

Wade's heart thudded wildly. Slapping a palm over his eyes, he groaned.

"Aw, don't get your britches in a knot over it," the paramedic said. "Stuff like that happens hundreds of times a day." He shrugged. "Hard as we try to save 'em, there's nothing we can do about it sometimes."

Maybe so, Wade thought as guilt swirled in his gut. But sometimes, they *did* save people. "Y'think he'll be okay?"

"Hard to say." He slammed the compartment door. "Doesn't look too good, though."

Wade swallowed. "So where will they take him?"

The paramedic slid behind the steering wheel. "University Hospital." He fired up the truck, then met Wade's eyes. "Now go home and get to bed. That's what I'm gonna do."

Nodding, Wade dug his hands deep into his jacket pockets. "Yessir."

And the instant the man was out of sight, Wade stuck out his thumb, intent on hitching a ride into Baltimore with the first driver headed for the city.

Wade waved his thanks to the truck driver who'd dropped him off at the hospital, and shoved through the emergency room doors.

The silence was almost eerie, and the reception area was illuminated only by the dim, flickering fluorescent lights above the nurses' station. In the waiting area, a man flapped the pages of his raggedy newspaper, and directly across from him, a young girl sat on the edge of her chair, hands clasped tightly on her knees and eyes glued to the doors that read No Admittance: Staff Only.

Wade walked up to the nurses' station. A nurse met his eyes. "Can I help you?"

"I, uh, I'm here to see how that guy is doing…the one they just brought in on the helicopter?"

She raised one eyebrow. "You a relative of Mr. Delaney?"

Wade gulped. So the engineer had a name: Mr. Delaney. "N-no, I'm a—"

"Friend of the family?"

Hardly, Wade thought, but he nodded, anyway.

"Wait over there," the nurse said, using her chin as a pointer. "Lemme see what I can find out."

Wade slumped into a chair, two down from the young girl. He leaned forward, scrubbed both hands over his face and shook his head.

"Who are you waiting for?" the girl asked.

From between his fingers, Wade looked over at her. She appeared to be ten or twelve years old, wearing a faded pink sweat suit and fuzzy bunny slippers. "Just some guy." Elbows on knees, he laced his fingers together. "You?"

"My little brother, Timmy." Her big eyes fixed on the No Admittance doors. "He's been in there for*ever*."

Wade sat back, propped an ankle on a knee. "What's wrong with him?"

She sighed, kicked one foot until the bunny ears flopped. "He was born with this weird heart condition. We have to bring him in here two or three times a month, usually in the middle of the night." Another sigh. "I'll bet he's slept here a couple hundred times."

"That stinks." Wade didn't think he'd ever seen a sadder face. He wished he had enough change in his pocket to buy her a soda, maybe a package of chips or a candy bar. "You always wait out here alone when your folks bring him in?"

She nodded. "It doesn't usually take this long, though." She glanced at the big double doors again. "Something's wrong."

He noticed that one of her bunnies had just one eye, the other was missing an ear. "What makes you say that?"

Tears welled in her big, dark eyes, and her lower lip trembled. "Usually, somebody comes to tell me something by now." She glanced at the clock on the wall. "I've been here nearly three hours and—"

Wade leaped to his feet. "I'll be right back."

He knocked on the nurses' station desk. "Um, excuse me…I hate to bother you, but that little girl over there," he said, gesturing with his thumb over his shoulder, "has been waiting three hours to hear about her brother. Do you have any idea what's going on back there?"

The lady he'd talked to earlier leaned to the right and peered around him. "Poor li'l thing," she said, clucking her tongue.

"She's getting to be a regular fixture around this place," the woman said. She looked at Wade. "Let me see what I can find out." Then, "Say, Marsha, why don't you see if you can scare up an o.j. or something for these kids.'' She winked at Wade and hurried into the ER.

Marsha rooted around in a small refrigerator. ''Here y'go,'' she said, handing him two tiny cartons of chocolate milk. ''Need straws?''

Wade accepted the milk. ''I don't,'' he said, glancing toward the waiting room, ''but she might like one.''

''You're a nice boy,'' Marsha said when he took it from her.

Nice. Yeah, right, he thought, remembering what had happened to the engineer. But ''Thanks'' is what he said.

Sitting beside the girl, Wade peeled back the spout of one carton and slid a straw into its opening. ''You want me to see if I can get 'em to cough up some doughnuts or something?''

She sent him a hint of a smile. ''No, I'm not hungry.'' After taking a tiny sip, she looked straight into his eyes and said, ''You're very nice. Thank you.''

Wade nearly choked on his chocolate milk. All his life, he'd been hearing what a loser he was, and twice in as many minutes, two people had told him the exact opposite. What a joke, he thought, because if they knew him…if they'd seen him earlier tonight, at the cemetery, they wouldn't think he was so nice!

''What's your name?'' the girl asked.

''Wade,'' he said, nervously opening and closing the milk carton. ''Yours?''

''Patrice McKenzie.'' She tilted her head slightly. ''Do you live near the hospital?''

He shook his head. ''Ellicott City. How 'bout you?''

''I live in Freeland, on a farm.''

''A farm? With cows and pigs and horses and stuff?'' He grinned. ''No kiddin'.''

That made her laugh—just a little—but it made Wade feel good to have brightened her mood, even slightly.

The ER doors swooshed open, interrupting his thoughts. "Patrice?" a woman wailed. "Patrice, baby, where are you?"

The girl jumped up so fast, she nearly spilled her chocolate milk down the front of her pink sweatshirt. "Right here, Mom."

Wade figured the man and woman who bundled her into a group hug must be her parents. From the looks of them, the news about her brother wasn't good. Then Patrice started to cry. The misery seemed to start deep in the core of her, ebbing out one dry, hacking sob at a time and racking her tiny body.

As Patrice's family trudged out of the ER arm in arm, Wade realized little Timmy must have died. He hung his head. Maybe he should've tried to scare up something sweet for her to eat, even though she'd said she hadn't wanted anything. Because the way things looked, no telling how long it might be before—

"Hey, kid."

Wade got to his feet. "Yeah?"

"Sorry, but we lost Mr. Delaney, 'bout fifteen minutes ago."

Wade pinched the bridge of his nose between thumb and forefinger.

The nurse he'd spoken to earlier put a hand on Wade's shoulder. "The cops are on their way now, to tell the family. You might want to get over first chance you get, see if there's anything you can do for 'em…since you're a friend of the family and all."

Friend. Shame burned hot in Wade's gut. Funny, he thought, that until the nurse said "friend," he hadn't understood what the word *hypocrite* meant.

"How'd you get here?"

"Walked," he fibbed, knowing if he said "hitch-hiked," he'd probably be in for a safety sermon. The nurse seemed like a nice enough woman, but Wade was in no mood for a lecture, no matter how well intended.

"So, how you gettin' home?"

Wade shrugged. "Same way, I guess."

"I could call you a cab...."

Shaking his head, Wade got to his feet. "Nah. I'll walk. It's not far." *You're gettin' awful good at fibbin',* he told himself. *Better watch it.*

Truth was, there were thirty miles between here and his house, but he'd walk every step of it. It'd do him good, having all that time to think.

The nurse frowned. "This isn't the best neighborhood, so you keep your eyes peeled, y'hear?"

Wade fought the impulse to exhale a sarcastic snicker. Nothing was going to happen to him; bad things only happened to good people.

"Okay, then, if you're sure...."

He nodded, and the nurse headed back into the ER, leaving Wade alone in the waiting room.

Alone, and feeling more lost than he'd ever felt in his life.

Chapter One

Present day, Halloween Eve

As he stepped off the elevator, Wade glanced at his watch, then ran a hand nervously through his hair. He'd never honed the ability to keep an emotional distance from his patients; especially when the patient was a kid.

Knowing it would be the toughest visit of his rounds, he'd saved this patient for last. Just outside her hospital room, he took a moment to get his head on straight. Then, one hand on the door handle, he froze as a whisper-soft voice from inside the room said, "And may God bless Emily and speed her recovery."

Wade grimaced. *Fat lot of good your prayers are gonna do,* he silently scolded this patient's mother, *'cause if the Big Guy exists, He ain't listening.*

Only yesterday, Wade had spent nearly eleven hours in the OR with little Emily Kirkpatrick. He couldn't help but wonder what kind of God would stand idly by as a six-year-old endured such intense and constant pain.

Now, shaking his head, he forced a bright smile and shoved his way into the child's room.

"Dr. Cameron," Emily's mom said, hands still clasped in prayer, "how good to see you."

Humbled by the gratitude on the mother's weary face, Wade felt himself blush. "How goes it, Mrs. Kirkpatrick?" He grabbed Emily's chart from the plastic slot attached to her door, tucking it under his arm as he met the woman's eyes. "Get any sleep last night?"

"Oh, I managed to catch a few winks. How about you? You're the one who spent eleven hours in the operating room."

Long ago, he'd accepted that now and then, he'd run across someone who seemed to have turned nurturing into an art form. Mrs. Kirkpatrick was one of those people. "Slept like a baby," he answered.

Laughing, Emily's mom grabbed her purse. "If you don't mind, I'll run down the hall and grab a quick cup of coffee while you're examining Emily."

"Take your time," Wade said, dragging a chair closer to Emily's bed.

Emily opened sleepy eyes. "Hi, Doc."

He perched on the edge of the chair. "Hi, yourself, kiddo. How y'doin'?"

Emily managed a wan smile. "Hurts," she said, pointing to her chest.

"Sorry to hear that, sweetie." Gently, Wade laid her chart beside her on the mattress. "You're due for a little medicine soon, so by suppertime, you'll be feeling much better."

She gave a weak nod.

"So how'd you sleep?" Gently, he touched a finger to the end of her upturned nose. "Did those busybody nurses keep you awake, taking your temperature and stuff?''

Her smile broadened a bit. "Yeah, but it's okay. Mommy says they're just trying to help me get better.''

He took her tiny hand in his. "What's this?'' Wade asked, grinning.

"A ladybug, crawling on a daisy,'' she said. "This nice man came in and painted it on me.'' Her blue eyes darted around, then settled on something across the room. "Miss Patrice brought him here.''

Wade followed Emily's gaze to where "Miss Patrice'' stood, entertaining Emily's roommate. If the young woman had seen him enter, she gave no sign of it; her attention was fixed on her one-child audience.

Which was fine by Wade; volunteers had good intentions, what with their puppets and face paints and musical instruments, but in his opinion, their main contribution was to wear out his patients and generally get in the way.

"And if Nurse Joan tells me you don't eat your supper again tonight,'' Miss Patrice made her monkey puppet say, *"I'm going to tell my best friend.''*

The child snickered. "Yeah?'' the girl demanded, grinning. "Who's your best friend?''

"Why, Santa Claus, of course!'' Miss Patrice manipulated the sticks controlling the puppet, making it tousle the child's hair. Wade would have bet the kid's peals of laughter could be heard all the way to the bank of elevators down the hall. He couldn't help but notice that her merriment had crept to Emily's side of the room, too.

"If Santa finds out you're not taking proper care of yourself,'' said the puppet's gravelly voice, *"there's gonna be T-R-O-U-B-L-E.''* She made the monkey wig-

gle a hairy finger under the girl's nose. *"And you know what that spells!"*

"Trouble!" Emily answered, grinning from ear to ear. For the moment, at least, she appeared to have forgotten her pain.

Patrice whirled around, eyes wide and smiling, and, puppet balanced on her forearm, stepped up to Emily's bed. *"And just who do you think you are, li'l missy, the Spelling Bee Queen?"*

"No, silly," she giggled, "I'm Emily Kirkpatrick."

"Pleased t'meetcha, Emily Kirkpatrick!" The monkey tickled her chin. *"My name is Mortimer Mohammad Mastriani McMonkey."*

"That's a long name!"

Mort did a little jig on the edge of Emily's bed, then tapped a paw to his chin. *"Yes, it is a bit of a mouthful, isn't it. Tell you what…you can call me Mort."* The monkey's hands rested on its hips. *"Now tell me, cutie, how're you doin'?"*

"I had a op'ration yesterday." She gave Wade an adoring look. "Dr. Cameron fixed the hole in my heart."

The puppeteer met Wade's eyes. For a moment, no one spoke…not even Mort McMonkey.

"Yes, so I heard," Miss Patrice said at last.

The puppeteer had the most expressive face Wade had ever seen. The short, reddish-brown curls topping her pretty head reminded him of the elves on those cookie packages. He wondered why she allowed it to cover one eye; it seemed to him those big brown eyes were so warm, they could thaw an igloo.

She looked vaguely familiar, and he was about to admit it when she moved Mort aside enough to expose her name badge. Patrice McKenzie, it said.

"Will you be having supper with us tonight, Emily?" Mort asked.

Wade was too stunned to hear Emily's response. He'd met a Patrice or two since that night, but how many Patrice McKenzies could there be? *Can't be that Patrice,* he told himself.

Could it?

She blinked, confused, he presumed, by his scrutiny.

It had been fifteen years since he'd shared a bleak ER waiting room with a teary, terrified girl, but he'd recognize those big brown eyes anywhere. If the young woman on the other side of Emily's bed *wasn't* the same Patrice, he'd eat his stethoscope.

Mort started hip-hopping again. *"Well, well, well,"* the monkey said, *"it looks to me like your Dr. Cameron is a real live hero, Emily Kirkpatrick!"*

The girl's mother stepped into the room just then. "Yes, yes he is," she said, standing beside him.

Hero? The very idea was laughable! Wade wanted to warn them all that, in the first place, though Emily's condition was much better than it had been at this time yesterday, she was far from out of the woods. And in the second place...

The train fiasco that had sent him to the ER all those years ago flashed through his memory. Heart pounding, Wade checked his watch. "So, are you ready to show me your incision, Em?"

She nodded. "Okay, I guess."

Because of her heart condition, Emily wasn't as big as other girls her age. The operation made her seem even smaller, frail, vulnerable. Wade finger-combed golden locks from her forehead. "Say goodbye to Mort," he said gently, "'cause we need to close the curtain."

She shook the monkey's tiny, hairy hand. "G'bye, Mort. See you later?"

"*You betcha!*" The puppet waved at Emily, at the child in the next bed, at Mrs. Kirkpatrick, then at Wade. "*See yas later, 'gators!*"

As Patrice started for the door, Wade grabbed her elbow. "Mind hanging around a minute? I have something to ask you."

Her dark brows rose slightly, as if to say, *What could you possibly want to ask me?*

"*Okay,*" Mort answered in Patrice's stead, "*but it's gonna cost ya, Doc.*"

For a reason he couldn't explain, Wade abandoned his all-business demeanor. "Name your price, monkey face."

The kids and Mrs. Kirkpatrick laughed as Mort slapped both fuzzy hands over his mouth. "*Monkey face? Well, I never!*" He shook a furry finger at the doctor. "*It was gonna be just a cup of coffee, but after that remark, you'll hafta throw in a slice of pie, too!*"

Small price to pay, Wade thought, for a private session with Mortimer Mohammad Mastriani McMonkey… and his handler.

"I'll be in my office," Patrice said.

For the second time in as many minutes, she'd used her own voice. Like everything else about her, it was adorable.

But wait—had she said her *office?* "Since when do hospital volunteers have offices?"

Patrice laughed, the sound reminding him of the small copper bells that used to hang on his mom's back porch.

"Technically I'm not a volunteer," she explained, walking backward toward the hall, "But I am the person who makes sure there *are* volunteers for the children.

I'm the pediatric social worker who heads up Child Services.'' She opened the door. ''You know where the Zoo Lobby is?''

Wade didn't like admitting that he hadn't a clue. ''Ellicott General is like a small city, and I've spent most of my time in the 'heart' of town, if you'll pardon the pun.''

Mort came to life again. *''I get it, Doc,''* the monkey said. *''Cardiologist…heart…. Ha-ha-ha.''* Mort patted Wade's shoulder. *''First-floor elevators to the giant stuffed animal cages, left down the hall, office on the right.''* Clapping, the monkey added, *''The sign above the door says Child Services. Got it?''*

Wade was about to echo ''Got it,'' when Patrice winked and ducked into the hall.

''She spreads such joy wherever she goes,'' Mrs. Kirkpatrick said as Wade pulled the curtain around her daughter's bed. ''And isn't she just the cutest thing?''

''Yeah, cute,'' he muttered halfheartedly, opening Emily's file. He'd never been a big advocate of nonfamily members meandering in and out of the hospital, overstaying their welcome, leaving behind their germs. And Patrice McKenzie had built a career of *inviting* them to do just that.

He wondered how much joy she'd feel like spreading if he gave her his two cents worth on the subject.

He pictured the long-lashed, dark eyes, heard her lilting voice in his memory, and found himself fighting an urge to rush through Emily's examination so he could make his way past the Zoo Lobby to the Child Services office…

…and the lovely lady who'd breathed life into Mortimer Mohammad Mastriani McMonkey.

* * *

She caught sight of her reflection in the silver frame that held a photo of her father, taken before the fiery car crash. Instinctively, she fluffed her hair, effectively hiding the scar. The hideous, horrible welt coiled from just below her right earlobe to the corner of her eye, like a rope that tied her, permanently, to the accident that had paralyzed her father.

Patrice sat back and squeezed her eyes shut. It wasn't until her knuckles began to ache that she realized how tightly she'd been gripping the chair's wooden armrests. It had taken several sessions with her pastor to realize why she refused to get rid of the picture…and the scar. Flexing her fingers, she sighed. "Someday," Pete Phillips had counseled, "you'll give them both to God. Until then—"

Footsteps, just outside her office door, cut short the memory. Grabbing a pen, she hunched over the papers piled high on her desk and feigned hard work.

"Knock, knock…."

She recognized the charming baritone: Dr. Wade Cameron.

Patrice looked up and smiled. "Hi," she said, standing "Come on in."

He placed a partitioned cardboard tray on one of the chrome-and-blue upholstered chairs in front of her desk, then sat in the other. "All they had was cherry," he said, handing her a plastic-wrapped slice of pie. "Hope that's okay."

A nervous giggle popped from her lips. "Oh. Wow. I, um, I was only kidding," she said, as he put a disposable cup on the corner of her desk. "About the pie, I mean."

He held up one hand. "We had a deal." Grinning, he

glanced at the puppet, leaning on the silver picture frame. "Well, the monkey and I had a deal, anyway."

She liked his smile. Liked his eyes, too. There was something familiar about him. No big surprise; thousands of medical professionals made up the Ellicott staff. She'd probably passed him in the halls, or shared an elevator, or stood in the cafeteria line with—

"Your directions were great," he said. "I found your office just like that." He snapped his fingers, then glanced around the room. "Kinda dim in here. You want me to hit the lights?"

She lifted her chin. "No. Thank you. Fluorescent light..." Pausing, Patrice folded both hands on the file folders stacked on the blotter. "It's...it's hard on my eyes." Not quite a lie, but not exactly the truth, either. She found the incandescent glow of the sixty-watt light-bulb in her desk lamp more than adequate to work by, and it prevented people from seeing her scar.

"Well," Wade said, pointing at the mess on her desk, "I can see you're busy, so I'll get right to the point." He leaned forward, balancing both elbows on his knees. "I think we've met before."

She put her hands in her lap. "Really?"

He nodded. "Fifteen years ago, in the ER at University Hospital."

Patrice swallowed. Hard. Because fifteen years ago today, her brother had died. She felt her mouth drop open. "So *that's* why you look so familiar. You're the nice boy who bought me chocolate milk."

One shoulder lifted in a slight shrug. "I didn't buy it—the nurse at the reception desk gave it to me."

"I stand corrected. You're the nice boy who *brought* me chocolate milk."

Wade stared at his clenched fists.

Patrice peeled the lid off her cup of coffee. When the puff of steam evaporated, she realized it wasn't coffee, after all, but hot chocolate. Smiling, she said, "So you're still a nice boy, I see."

Even in the dim light, she could see him flush, reminding her of an innocent boy.

"So how're your folks?" he asked. "I remember seeing them, too, that night."

She swallowed again. "They're..." Shaking her head, she cleared her throat. Since it wasn't likely she'd be seeing him again, except maybe in passing, Patrice saw no point in telling him all the gory details. "We never quite got around to talking about why *you* were in the ER that night."

His gaze darting from her face to Mort to his own clasped hands, Wade frowned. "I was checking on the condition of a—" his frown deepened "—a friend."

"How'd he make out?"

He looked up. "Huh?"

"Your, uh, friend. How is he?"

"He, um, he died that night."

Patrice leaned forward. "Oh, Dr. Cameron—"

"Hey, we're old pals, so call me Wade, okay?"

"Sorry to hear about your friend," she said. "Guess that was a pretty dismal night for both of us, wasn't it."

Something was happening behind those sparkling, hazel eyes. Something that made Patrice wish she had the ability to read minds.

Wade got to his feet. "Anyway," he said, neatly sidestepping the question, "you're busy, so..."

Patrice stood, too. Somewhere deep in her heart, she'd hoped that maybe the handsome Dr. Cameron's interest in her was inspired by more than mere curiosity. She checked to make sure her scar was still hidden. Thankfully, it was. But maybe he'd seen it in Emily's hospital room, where the lights were much brighter than in her office. "Thanks for the hot chocolate," she said. "And the pie."

He waved her thanks away. "Well…"

Well, *what?* she wanted to demand. He'd gotten the information he'd wanted. If he had more to say…or ask…why didn't he just come out with it?

Wade clapped one hand to the back of his neck. "I, um, I was wondering if, uh, maybe you'd, um, like to have dinner with me sometime." He pocketed both hands and stood there, a half grin on his face, waiting for her answer.

"Um, well, sure," she began, "I, uh, I guess so."

Wade began to laugh. It started slow and quiet, and escalated to a pleasant rumble. Soon, Patrice was laughing with him.

"Maybe we oughta join Toastmasters," he joked.

"Oh, sure. Like anybody would hire the Um-Uh-Er-Uh Duo to give a speech!"

His smile and laughter dulled. "I'd rather hear you stutter and stammer than listen to…just about anything."

In the seconds that followed, Patrice stood in silence, unsure what to make of his probing, penetrating gaze.

"So what do you say?"

About their mutual stuttering? she wondered. Or his dinner invitation? Suddenly aware that she was clasping and unclasping her hands, Patrice stuffed her fingertips into the back pockets of her jean skirt. "I—"

"What's your preference? Italian? French? Asian?"

Her cheeks were hot, and she hugged herself, hoping the low lighting had kept him from seeing her blush. "I'm not fussy," she said, shrugging. "Food's food."

"How do you feel about tacos, enchiladas, chimichangas, quesadillas?"

"Long as lima beans aren't part of the recipe, I'll eat just about anything."

His eyes lit up. "Great, 'cause I know this terrific little Mexican place and—"

"Tonight?"

He shrugged. "Well, sure." The sparkle dimmed as he exhaled. "Aw, man...I should've known you'd already have a date."

Another nervous giggle popped from her. "Now, really, how could you have known a thing like—"

He interrupted with "You're gorgeous, for starters!"

When he slapped the back of his neck again, Patrice realized Wade probably regretted the compliment.

Well, *she* didn't; it was nice to hear, even if she didn't believe a word of it.

"I'm not busy tonight," Patrice blurted.

The glint returned to his eyes and he said, "How about scribbling your address and phone number for me on one of those business cards, there." He pointed at the plastic holder on her desk.

After grabbing a card and a pen, she printed the information he'd requested. Their fingers touched when he took the card from her extended hand, sending a tremor of warm tingles up her arm and straight to her heart. He was everything she'd ever dreamed about—tall and handsome, with muscles in all the right places and a dimple beside his generous mouth.

Uh-oh, she thought, it was happening already.

Every time she allowed herself to fall boots over bonnet for some good-looking hunk, all she ended up with was another heartache. *Well, not this time!* she decided, straightening her back.

Wade tucked the card into the side pocket of his white lab coat. "I'll pick you up at six, okay?"

Patrice nodded. He sounded slightly uncertain, which only added to his charm.

"Dress casual," he said, "'cause this isn't a fancy place."

Another nod. Most guys wouldn't have thought to share a thing like that, meaning that in addition to everything else, Wade was considerate. "Casual," she echoed. "Thanks."

Grinning, Wade snapped off a smart salute and headed for the elevators, whistling an off-key rendition of *West Side Story*'s "Tonight."

Not knowing what to make of any of it, Patrice flopped onto the seat of her chair, leaned her elbows on the desk and pressed both palms to her face. "Not this time, Lord," she prayed aloud, "'cause I don't think I can survive another heartbreak."

Wade frowned at a black-framed photo hanging on his office wall, taken when he was voted Baltimore's Bachelor of the Year by *The City Magazine* readers last year. On its left, another picture, snapped when he won a similar award at the Heart Association Ball two years ago; on the right, a certificate naming him this year's Most Loveable Doctor.

His participation in the contests and events helped to raise money for one worthy cause or another—the only reason Wade agreed to accept the invites. When the awards arrived, Wade gave them the attention he thought they deserved...by stuffing each into the trash can. If his secretary, Tara, hadn't fished them out to mat and frame as Christmas gifts, they'd be buried deep in a Maryland landfill by now.

He pushed back from his desk, swiveled the chair around so that it faced the windows and propped his shoes on the credenza. Here, where other doctors kept pictures of their wives, their children and grandchildren, were more reminders of Wade's bachelor-for-life status.

Wade stared past his certificates and awards, across the sea of cars in the parking lot below his window. Was it his imagination, or were there colorful baby seats and booster chairs in nearly half of them?

What would it be like, he wondered, hearing the words his best friend had so recently heard: "Honey, we're going to have a baby!"? He'd never seen Adam that happy, and he'd known him nearly twenty years. Well, that wasn't entirely true; the guy had practically done handstands on the day he married Kasey. If Adam Thorne, of all people, could make his life over, find lasting love and a life mate and the whole ball of wax, might there be hope for Wade, too?

He let out a bitter snicker. *Not likely, Cameron, since you seem incapable of getting past a second date*. Not that he didn't want a lasting relationship....

"And what *do* you want?" he whispered to himself.

Moments passed, but no answer came. Not surprising. He'd failed to puzzle this one out, though he'd tried, dozens of times before.

Dropping both feet to the floor, Wade stood and grabbed the miniblind's wand. After several angry twists, he effectively shut out the parking lot...and every child-toting vehicle.

His office door creaked open, and Tara said, "See you Monday, Wade."

"You bet," he answered. "Say hi to Matt and the kids for me."

"Sure thing." She started out the door, then poked her head back in. "Do me a favor?"

"If I can."

"Get some sleep this weekend, will ya? You're beginning to worry me."

"Careful, or I'll move in so you can mother me full time."

"Yeah, yeah," Tara said, waving away the comment. "Just what a guy like you wants—an infant and a toddler and mountains of diapers to come home to every night."

He was about to say *better than my one-room apartment,* when he replayed what she'd said: A guy like him?

"If you're gonna stay much longer, you might want to turn on a light in here. Eyestrain, y'know."

He forced a grin. "Old wives' tale," he said, grabbing his sports jacket. "Besides, I'm right behind you."

They walked side by side to the elevator. "Hot date?" Tara asked, pressing the down button.

He pictured Patrice, with her mop of auburn curls, doe eyes, sweet smile.... "Yeah, I guess you could say that."

The car whooshed them to the garage level. "Well, don't burn yourself." She patted his hand. "'Cause those babies are miracle workers."

He resisted the impulse to pocket both hands. "You have one of those baby-carrying gizmos?"

"An infant seat, you mean?"

Nodding, he said, "Yeah. Infant seat. You have one in your car?"

"As a matter of fact, I have two of them. One for each of the kids. What kind of mother would I be if I—" She stopped talking mid-sentence and narrowed one eye. "Why?"

Wade pretended he hadn't heard the suspicion in her voice. Truth was, he had no earthly idea *why* he'd asked the question. "Just wondering, is all."

"Boy-oh-boy," she said, giggling, "I'd give anything to meet the woman who has Dr. Nevermarry thinkin' about baby seats!" She hopped out of the elevator.

And she was still giggling when the doors hissed shut.

Patrice stood in front of the foyer mirror and adjusted the earrings dangling from her lobes. "You sure you'll be okay for a couple of hours?"

"Sure I'm sure." Gus fiddled with the controls of his wheelchair. "I'm okay while you're at work all day, aren't I?"

Hands on her hips, she faced him. "Yes, Dad, but Molly is here with you while I'm at work."

"Yeah, well, I'd go hoarse trying to convince you I don't need her."

"Save the tough-guy routine for somebody who'll fall for it," she teased. "Molly, for instance." She winked. "I know you like having her around."

He shrugged. "She's okay."

"Okay? Who else would let you beat them at board games the way she does!"

Gus grinned. "You make a good point." He sniffed the air. "You smell pretty."

"It's the perfume you gave me last Christmas." She leaned closer. "He said casual. I didn't go overboard, did I?"

Gus inspected her outfit: black flats, blue jeans, a pale pink turtleneck. "So who's 'he' and where's 'he' taking you?"

She went back to fussing with her hair. "To a Mexican restaurant, somewhere here in Ellicott City."

"And where'd you meet him?"

"His name is Wade Cameron, and I met him at the hospital." She paused, wishing she didn't have to say it. "He's a cardiologist."

"Oh-h-h, no-o-o," Gus groaned. "Not another doctor!" He shook his head. "Every time you get involved with one of those pompous know-it-alls, you get your teeth kicked in. When are you gonna learn, Treecie?"

Patrice couldn't very well argue with him. But she didn't have to agree with him, either. "It's a meal, Dad." *Besides,* she added silently, *it's going to be different this time. This time I'm not going to fall crazy in love on the first date.* "So please, when he gets here, be nice?"

Gus raised both eyebrows and feigned innocence. "I'm always nice."

"True." Bending, she kissed his cheek. "So be extra nice, then, for me, okay?"

"Well, I'll—" The doorbell rang, interrupting his promise.

Patrice took a deep breath, then opened the door. Earlier, Wade had looked incredible in his lab coat and stethoscope. He looked even better now in khaki trousers and a fisherman's knit sweater.

"Hey," he said, smiling. "How goes it?"

"It goes pretty well. Come in. I'd like you to meet my father." Patrice watched carefully, studying his reaction to the man in the wheelchair. If she'd learned this trick years ago, she might have spared herself a heartache...or two. "Dad, this is—"

"Wade Cameron," he broke in, grasping Gus's hand. "Pleased to meet you, Mr. McKenzie."

"Good to meet you, too," Gus said. "Treecie, here, tells me you're a cardiologist."

He shrugged as if to say "no big deal," then glanced around. "Nice place."

"Awright, enough with the pleasantries," Gus said. "Get on out of here, you two."

Wade chuckled and Patrice smiled. "Honestly, Dad, if I didn't know better, I'd say you had a hot date planned for tonight."

"Matter of fact, I *do* have a hot date—with the television set."

"Well," Wade said, "are you ready, Patrice?"

She grabbed her jacket from the hall tree, hung it over her forearm. "I'll have my cell phone on," she said, patting her purse, "in case—"

"I won't need you. There's a boxing match on cable." He winked. "That oughta keep me out of trouble for a couple of hours."

She kissed his other cheek. "All right, but if you get hungry—"

"Are you kidding? You fed me enough supper to last till *tomorrow* night!" He laughed. "Now get a move on, or I'll miss the first round."

"We won't be long," Wade told Gus

"Take your time…*please*." And snickering over his shoulder, he rolled into the family room.

"He's quite a guy," Wade said as she locked up.

She nodded. "Did you have any trouble finding the place?"

"Nah. I was a volunteer firefighter during my senior year in high school." He opened the car door for her. "Got to know the area pretty well."

She slid onto the passenger seat. "So doing good deeds and saving lives has always been in your blood?"

He slammed the door, hard. Routine? she wondered. Or in response to what she'd asked? Something told her it was the latter. But why would the question bother him?

"How long has your dad been in the wheelchair?" he asked, revving the motor.

She sighed. It was his turn, it seemed, to ask hard-to-answer questions. "Long time."

"Accident?"

Nodding, she whispered, "Yes."

"Automobile? Or work related?"

Patrice forced a sigh. "You're off duty, Doc, so just relax, okay?"

He shot a glance her way, and she could see by the puzzlement in his eyes that he didn't understand her reluctance to talk about her father's condition. She didn't *mind* talking about that, exactly…it was how he got into the chair in the first place that she minded talking about.

"So do you live near the hospital?"

He shook his head. "I live a few minutes from here. Plumtree Apartments."

"How long?"

"Little over a year."

"Wow. Amazing."

"That I live nearby?"

"Well, that, and the fact that we haven't run into one another in the grocery story, or at the pharmacy."

"So how'd it happen?"

"That we haven't run into one another?" Maybe playing dumb would get him off track.

"Okay, I can take a hint." He looked at her again. "Not your favorite subject, I take it."

She breathed a sigh of relief—

"So what's your mom up to tonight?"

—and the breath caught in her throat. She hadn't prepared for this eventuality.

"Is she a boxing fan, too?"

"Mom hated boxing," Patrice blurted.

"Hated? Past tense?" He shot a stunned look in her direction. "Oh, man. I'm sorry, Patrice. I had no idea...."

She leaned against the headrest and closed her eyes. "Some fun date this is starting out to be, huh?"

Wade reached over and took her hand. "If it was fun I wanted, I wouldn't have asked you out."

That snapped her to attention! "Ex*cuse* me?"

"Oh, wow. Oh, man. I, uh, I didn't mean it that way. I only meant—"

Laughing, she squeezed his hand. "It's okay, Wade. I know what you meant." She paused. "I think—"

"After that crack, I feel I owe you something better than the dinner I'd planned."

"Don't be silly. The Mexican place is just fine." She smacked her lips. "In fact, I've been craving soft tacos all evening."

"Soft tacos? No foolin'?"

She nodded.

"My favorite," they said in unison.

This time, Wade squeezed Patrice's hand. "Say, maybe this night is gonna turn out all right, after all."

Maybe, she thought. *And maybe I'd better be* real *careful with this one.*

Because already, she felt the oh-so-familiar tugs at her heartstrings.

Chapter Two

His hand on the small of her back, Wade led her into the restaurant. She seemed so small, so vulnerable beside him. If he had to guess, he would've said Patrice was five feet tall, not a fraction of an inch more.

The instant they stepped into the restaurant, an elderly woman hollered, "Dr. Cameron!" She hurried toward them, arms outstretched. "It's been too long. We've missed you!"

"Nice to see you, too, Mrs. Gomez," he said as she wrapped him in a grandmotherly hug. "How are you?"

She pressed a hand to his cheek. "Fine, thanks to you."

"And where *is* Mr. Gomez?"

Her eyes twinkled with mischief when she released him. "In the kitchen," she whispered, "telling Juan how to do his job."

"That's a good sign."

Suddenly, she faced Patrice. "And who is your lady friend?"

It seemed the most natural thing in the world to slide

an arm around her waist. "Patrice," Wade drawled, pulling her close to his side, "ah'd like you to meet Corrinne Gomez, sweetest li'l gal east of the Rio Grande."

Mrs. Gomez took Patrice's hands in her own, then drew her into an embrace. Wade watched as Patrice returned the woman's warm gesture, seemingly unperturbed by the uninvited physical contact.

"Ah, theese one," Mrs. Gomez said, "theese one, she's a keeper." She grabbed two menus from the hostess stand. "Come with me. I'll find you a nice quiet booth in the back, where you'll have some privacy."

As Patrice slid onto the burgundy leather seat, Mrs. Gomez winked. "I'll send Enrique right over with tortillas and salsa," she said, handing them each a menu. After whipping a book of matches from her apron pocket, she lit the candle in the middle of their table. "*Suerte grande!*" she said, winking again before hurrying away.

Patrice's gaze followed until Mrs. Gomez disappeared into the kitchen. She rested both arms on the table and leaned closer to Wade. "Lots o' luck?" she translated, grinning as her eyes bore into his.

Wade always brought women to *Mi Casa* for a first date. If they passed the Gomezes' muster, he made a second attempt. So far, no woman had eaten here more than twice. He felt more than a little guilty, putting Patrice through her paces this way. For one thing, she hadn't been the aggressor, like the others. For another, he genuinely *liked* her.

He felt the heat of a blush, ran a finger under his collar.

"And what was with that conspiratorial little wink?" she added, winking herself.

He couldn't very well tell her the truth, and for some

reason, didn't want to tell the usual first-date fibs. So he grinned, shook his head and said, "That Mrs. Gomez. Quite a card, isn't she."

Wade prepared himself for a sassy retort, and likely would have heard one—if Juan hadn't blustered up to the table just then.

"Dr. Cameron! We were worried you'd fallen off the horse." He laid a beefy hand on Wade's shoulder "It isn't Friday night unless Baltimore's Bachelor of the Year brings a pretty girl here to eat!" His hearty laughter thundered as he gave Wade a playful slap on the back. "Glad to see you're still in the saddle, m'boy!"

Wade squirmed under Patrice's level gaze. *Yeah,* he thought, *still in the saddle.*

"Theese," he said to Patrice, "eese one special man."

One well-arched brow rose a bit as Patrice made a feeble attempt to smile. She met Wade's eyes. "I'm beginning to get the picture," she said carefully.

"He has a heart the size of his head, theese one." Juan glanced at Wade. "Shall I tell her thee story?"

Wade held up a hand, traffic cop style. "No. Really. Juan, we'd like a basket of tortillas, if you don't mind, and some—"

Juan shoved his bulk onto the seat beside Patrice. "Four years ago," he continued, slinging an arm over her shoulders, "I was a telephone repairman. I was high on a pole when the ol' ticker gave out. Thank the good Lord for safety harnesses!"

Normally, the Gomezes teased Wade about his exploits. He couldn't remember a time when either of them had mentioned Juan's surgery. "Juan," he began, "Patrice, here has to get back because—"

"Patrice." Juan faced her. "Pretty girl, pretty name,"

he said, beaming. Then he aimed his dark-eyed stare at Wade. "Maybe theese time, you peek a winner?"

Wade covered his eyes with one hand. "Juan—"

"You think because you're a big-shot doctor you can interrupt an old man's story?" Another round of rumbling laughter filled the booth. He turned to Patrice again. "As I was saying, I had a heart attack up there, hanging from the telephone pole. And it would have killed me, if not for the good doctor, here." He reached across the table, squeezed Wade's forearm. "I thank the good Lord for him every day of my life."

A moment of silence ticked by before she said, "Maybe *I'm* the one who picked a winner."

Was she kidding?

Wade came out of hiding in time to see the merry gleam in her eyes. So she'd decided to play along, he realized as his blush intensified.

Juan held a forefinger aloft. "But you haven't heard the half of it!"

She tilted her head—a bit flirtatiously, Wade thought. "There's more?"

He figured Juan was gearing up to tell her about the loan, and he didn't want that. Didn't know why, exactly, he just didn't. Pinching the bridge of his nose between thumb and forefinger, he tried to think of a way to divert Juan's attention. He saw Enrique just then, having an animated conversation with a diner. "Looks like your boy could use some help," Wade said, pointing.

Juan didn't so much as glance in his son's direction. "After the operation," he went on, "I couldn't go back to climbing poles, and I wasn't trained to do anything else." His voice softened. "For as long as I could remember, I took care of my own. Not being able to work was—"

"Juan, enough. You're—"

"My condition began to worry the good doctor, here. And months after the surgery, after a checkup, he came to our house. I was making soft tacos, he agreed to join us for supper…and he gave me the idea for *Mi Casa,* right there at our kitchen table."

Patrice blinked and sighed. If she said "my hero!" like an actress in some *B* movie, he'd dump the sugar bowl into Juan's lap.

"We had spent all our savings, keeping the bills up to date while I was out of work. One bill we didn't have to pay was Dr. Cameron's. He didn't charge a penny for his services. What do you think of that, Patrice?"

She looked from Wade to Juan and back again. "I honestly don't know what to say."

"Well, what would you say about this. He also gave me the down payment to buy this place."

Wade could only exhale the breath he'd been holding and shake his head, hoping for the best.

A few seconds ticked by before she said, "I guess I'd have to say you're right to call him a hero."

The entire Gomez clan had been calling him that for years. Patients and their families routinely dubbed him a hero, too. His sister's kids had never said the word, but he could see in their eyes that they thought the world of their Uncle Wade. Despite it all, he hadn't felt the least bit heroic—until Patrice said it.

But, sure as he was sitting here, looking into her gorgeous face, the truth would come along sooner or later, and change her opinion of him. So for as long as this feeling lasted, Wade decided, he may as well go ahead and enjoy it.

She thought it was charming, the way Wade blushed like a schoolboy under Juan's obvious admiration. Horse and saddle references aside, she admired him, too. And so Patrice made a concerted effort to ease his discomfort.

She introduced dozens of topics, from the philosophical to the political. The interchange of opinions and ideas taught them they had a lot more in common than Ellicott General. They voted for the same man in the last election, became enraged at the mere mention of flag burning, loved kids and dogs and apple pie.

"Dessert?" Enrique said, rolling the dessert cart to their table. Patrice smiled as Wade rubbed his palms together.

"I'll take an order of the flan," he said, grinning. "Patrice, what'll you have?"

She couldn't remember her name ever sounding quite so lyrical. "I'm stuffed," she admitted. "Maybe I'll just have a bite of yours?"

His grin made her stomach flip and her heart lurch. He turned to the waiter, held up one finger, then two. "One flan, two spoons," he said. And when Enrique rolled his cart to the next table, Wade blanketed her left hand with his. "You're awfully quiet all of a sudden. Worried about your dad?"

"Maybe." With thumb and forefinger, she measured a centimeter of air. "Just a little."

He gave her hand a gentle pat. "I'm sure he's fine."

She nodded. "I know. And I know it's silly, worrying about him, because he's really quite capable."

"Well, we'll be through here in no time. Then you can see for yourself."

Another nod. "Thanks, Wade, for understanding."

He gave a shrug, as if it was no big deal that he'd cued in to her fears…and hadn't made her feel ridiculous for them, as other men had.

"So how'd it happen?"

Patrice took a sip of her decaf. "Car wreck."

His hold on her hand tightened slightly.

She'd learned a ton about him tonight; why not even the score a bit?

"It was my fault."

Silence was his response. She wondered if his caring expression was sincere, or something practiced and mastered in med school. "It was raining that night...*teeming* is more like it. I wanted to go to a party, and talked him into driving me."

Patrice tried to wriggle her hand free of his grasp, but Wade wouldn't allow it. Absently, her right forefinger picked at its neighboring thumbnail. If she were a betting woman, she'd say his concern was genuine. "He slammed the car into a big brick wall after he picked me up from the party. He's been paralyzed from the waist down ever since."

He nodded, and she could almost read his mind. *No wonder you're such a devoted daughter—you blame yourself.*

"I'm sure you've heard this before, hundreds of times, no doubt," Wade said, "but accidents happen, Patrice." His hazel eyes darkened and his lips thinned when he added, "*Usually,* they're nobody's fault."

Usually? The fact that he'd stressed the word made her wonder if Wade blamed himself for an accident in his own past.

"I didn't have to go out that night, but I didn't want to miss Marcy's party." If she didn't shut up, and quick, she was going to cry. Why had she opened this Pandora's box!

"And your dad didn't have to take you." He sandwiched her hand between his own. "If you insist on laying blame, lay half of it on his shoulders. You were a kid, he was a grown-up. He made the final decision, after all.''

She shook her head. ''Not really. He hadn't been himself at all since the—'' *Lord,* she prayed, *please help me deal with this!*

''Since the what? C'mon. You've told me this much. What's the point in holding back the rest?''

''Suicide.''

His brows dipped low on his forehead. ''Sui—*What?*''

Nodding now, she sighed. ''A year after Timmy died—almost to the day—my mom killed herself. She knew Dad would take it hard, said so in her note.'' She closed her eyes. *Okay to shut up now, Lord? Or is this my penance…telling a total stranger about what happened to my mother and that I'm responsible for my father's paralysis?*

''You were a kid,'' he repeated. ''Just a kid, for cryin' out loud. Give yourself a break!''

She was about to say ''My dad didn't get a break, why should I?'' when Enrique returned, a serving of flan resting on one palm, two spoons wrapped in the other. He placed each on the table.

''More coffee?'' he asked.

''Make it decaf, okay?''

''Sure thing. And the lady?''

''Same,'' Patrice said, her voice still trembling slightly. ''Thanks.''

Wade seemed in no hurry to eat the dessert. Instead, he changed the mood from confessional to conversational. He talked about the weather, the last movie he'd seen, an article he'd read in the newspaper about certain brands of bottled water that came straight from kitchen taps. She had to admit, he had a real knack for making people feel relaxed, comfortable. At least, he had that talent with *her*.

Suddenly, Wade picked up one of the spoons and carefully cut off a piece of the custard. Holding it in front of Patrice's face he said, "You first."

Calmer now, she laughed at the suggestion. She'd seen this in the movies, and now hesitated, afraid she might open too wide, or not wide enough, and the dessert would end up all over her face—or worse, in her lap. "This is silly," she admitted.

Yet she went along with the suggestion. Wade skillfully slid the bite past her teeth, his own lips parting slightly as he watched her accept his offering. "Thwnkym," she said around it.

He'd already popped a sizable chunk into his mouth. "Ywr wrlcm."

Their laughter brought inquisitive stares from nearby diners. They seemed to share one thought: All dressed up like respectable adults, but talking with their mouths full, like a couple of kids.

"I do believe," he said between snickers, "we're making public spectacles of ourselves."

He chose that exact moment to reach out and remove a tiny drop of caramel syrup from her lower lip. The pressure of his thumb lingering there, seemed natural and normal. Their eyes fused on a sizzling current.

She began searching for things to dislike about this man, because having some negative character traits sure would make it easier not to fall for him! But try as she might, so far Patrice couldn't come up with a single thing. In fact, she felt as though she'd known him for years.

"I can't believe how much I talked tonight," he said

as they crossed the darkened parking lot to his car. "I don't think I've bumped my gums this much, all at one time, ever in my life." He slipped an arm around her waist. "I hope you won't think I'm a total boor for dominating the conversation all evening."

She remembered her confession. He'd hardly controlled the discussion. Would've been a lot better for her if he had!

Teasing and flirting had never been part of Patrice's personality. Yet with Wade, the two seemed to go hand in hand as naturally as the stars went with the inky sky. "Well, you're not a *complete* oaf, anyway," she said, blinking up at him.

"Keep looking at me that way," he said, one hand on either side of her face, "and you're gonna find out real fast what a barbarian I can be."

Immediately, Patrice tensed, for his left palm was touching her scar. She tried to wriggle free of his embrace, but he held tight.

"No need to pretend it isn't there, Patrice. I saw it in your office and again in your foyer. I'm a cardiologist, remember? I've seen thousands of scars. I've *made* thousands of scars."

She bit her lower lip, closed her eyes. *Please, Lord,* she prayed, *make him—*

He wove his fingers into her hair, combing it back and exposing the scar, then pressed his lips to the gnarled, angry flesh on her cheek, her temple, the corner of her eye. Slowly, he made his way to her forehead, her chin, the tip of her nose.

This wasn't what she'd meant when, seconds ago, she'd asked for Divine intervention...

...but when Wade's lips found hers, she realized it was exactly what she'd been wanting.

The familiar flutter of fear rolled in her gut. Too much too soon had brought her nothing but pain in the past.

Well, a girl can hope, she quickly tacked on.

The pleasant chatter they'd enjoyed during those last minutes in the restaurant continued during the drive home. Wade chose a collection of old country and western tunes to entertain them this time, and now and again, sang a line or two with Willie Nelson or Patsy Kline. Patrice enjoyed every note, even though his singing voice reminded her more of a rusty hinge than any melody she'd ever heard.

When he parked in front of her house, he turned in his seat and placed a big hand on her shoulder. "Since you already know what a clod I am, I guess it won't do any harm to invite myself in for a cup of coffee...."

Her heart fluttered. She could barely make out his features in the darkness, yet somehow she knew those bright hazel eyes were boring into her, hoping for an affirmative answer. As she'd dressed for dinner, she'd determined to be pleasant and polite, nothing more, no matter what he said. But things had taken an odd turn somewhere along the way. There didn't seem to be much point in pretending she wasn't...interested.

"High-test or decaf?" she asked.

His quiet chuckle warmed her, right down to her toes. "Decaf, if you have it."

As they walked up the flagstone path, he casually draped an arm across her shoulders. Patrice liked the way it felt, and resisted the urge to lace her fingers with his.

"Let me just check on Dad," she whispered, locking the door. "Meanwhile, make yourself at home in the kitchen. I baked chocolate chip cookies this morning. Do me a favor and have a few.''

Wade nodded as she headed for the back of the house. She knocked softly and called, ''Dad?''

''Come on in, Treecie.''

She opened the door a bit, poked her head through the opening. ''So who won the boxing match?''

He chuckled. ''I haven't the foggiest idea. Fell asleep before the first round ended.''

''Hungry?'' she asked, stepping into the room.

''Not in the slightest.'' He indicated the half-empty plate of cookies on his bedside table. ''If you don't stop doin' stuff like that, I'm gonna be big as a house.''

She fluffed his pillows, smoothed the line-dried sheet over his blanket. ''How about a nice cup of chamomile tea?''

''Thanks, but I'm about ready to turn out the light.'' He winked. ''You get back to your doctor. Just be careful, y'hear?''

The accident hadn't dulled his paternal senses one whit. ''Don't worry. Things are going to be different this time.''

''Oh, really?'' He inclined his head. ''How so?''

Truthfully, she didn't know, exactly. ''Well, I'm taking my time, for starters.''

''Good girl.'' He gave in to an enormous yawn. ''Now give your old man a good-night kiss.''

One hand on either side of his whiskered face, she pressed her lips to his forehead.

''Don't stay up too late, now. Tomorrow is Halloween and we have *plans* to make!''

''How could I forget?'' she teased. ''There must be a dozen scarecrows and pumpkins on the front porch!''

"Yeah, well, you ain't seen nuttin' yet. I made a tape today while you were at work."

"Did Molly help?"

"I should say so. That woman has the most ear-piercing scream I ever heard. She oughta rent that voice out to the movie stars, for the scary parts of monster movies!"

Laughing, Patrice turned out the lights. "G'night, Dad. I love you."

"Love you, too," he was saying as she closed his door.

"Hope you don't mind," Wade said when she entered the kitchen. "I rooted around in your cupboards until I found the coffee, got a nice head start on the brew."

With the back of his hand, he brushed chocolate chip cookie crumbs from his lips, then took a swallow of milk. "These are great," he said, using a half-eaten cookie as a pointer. "So you're a good cook, I see."

"I'm no gourmet," she said, taking two mugs from the cabinet, "but I can whip up a respectable meat-and-potatoes meal when the situation calls for it."

He nodded approvingly. "Most professional women I've known seem scared of kitchens."

She wondered what it was about him that brought out this outrageously flirtatious side of her. Grinning, she said, "There's not a gadget in this room that scares me, mister."

Suddenly, the friendly light in his eyes dimmed. "Yeah. You're all kinds of brave, aren't you."

Patrice had no idea what he was talking about, and said so.

He held up his hands in mock surrender. "Far be it for me to tell you how to run your life. Seems to me, though, you'd live a lot longer if you'd stop blaming yourself for something that wasn't your fault.''

She could see by the caring expression on his face that he meant well, could hear the concern in his voice, too. Still, the advice irked her. "I've been on my own for a long time, Wade. I can take care of myself."

He took another bite of the cookie. "Well, you won't starve to death, that's for sure."

At least the mischievous grin was back. Patrice hadn't realized how much she enjoyed looking at it until it disappeared. Finally, the pot hissed, signaling that the coffee was ready. "You take yours black, right?"

He turned a kitchen chair around, straddled it and rested his forearms on its back. "Brave as a lion, memory like an elephant. Maybe you should've been a veterinarian."

She chose to ignore the remark, pouring milk into the creamer, instead. Wade took his time drinking the first cup of coffee, then helped himself to a second. For the next twenty minutes, he talked nonstop about guilt and blame and personal responsibility. Finally, lectured out, he stood and put his mug into the sink. "Promise me you'll at least think about what I've said."

She did her best not to reply in a bored monotone. "I'll pray on it."

His eyebrows rose high on his forehead. "Pray on it? What good do you think that'll do? Religion, prayer, guilt—tools used by organized religion to make us feel beholden."

She'd pray, all right, but not about whose fault the accident was. She'd ask God to give her the strength, the wisdom, the words that would turn Wade's heart toward Christ.

He placed both hands on her shoulders. "I'm serious,

Patrice. You're a terrific woman. You should be living a full, happy life. How are you gonna do that if you're emotionally exhausted from lugging around guilt that isn't yours?''

Narrowing her eyes, she regarded him with sudden suspicion. *I'll live a full, happy life—as long as I keep a safe distance from romance!* she thought. If only she could back up the tape, erase this whole episode.

With no warning, he gathered her to him in a warm, protective embrace. Automatically, her arms went around him.

''What am I gonna do with you?'' he sighed into her hair. ''You're as bighearted and pigheaded as they come,'' he added, kissing the top of her head, ''and while that's a tempting combination, I have a practice to run. I can't be—''

She broke free of his hold and stood, hands forming fists at her sides. ''So who asked you to be my protector? I told you, I can take—''

''—care of yourself,'' he finished for her. ''I know, I know.'' He opened the door, then clicked it shut again. ''I never meant to insult you. I hope you know that. It's just that, for some reason, you worry me.''

Patrice couldn't help admitting that she was touched by his concern. ''There's no need for that. I'm fine.''

Wade grabbed her wrist and pulled her to him, his lips a fraction of an inch from hers. In the dim light of the foyer lamp, his eyes glittered like amber as his gaze flicked from her mouth to her throat to her eyes. She wondered what that thick, dark hair would feel like beneath her fingertips, and held her breath as she waited for his kiss.

He inhaled sharply and stepped back. ''Take care of yourself, you hear? Because...''

Because *what?* she wondered. What did he care if her guilt was deserved or not? During the pause, Patrice thought maybe he'd changed his mind. Maybe he didn't intend to kiss her, after all.

He cupped her chin with one trembling hand, brushed the hair from her face with the other. "Do you have any idea how beautiful you are, how much I want to—"

"I had a lovely time."

Wade blinked several times before a low chuckle began bubbling deep in his chest. "That was the general idea," he said. "And for your information, so did I."

"Well, that's a relief," she teased, "because I'd hate to add *that* to my guilt burden, too."

His soft laughter wafted through her hair as he hugged her. "You're something else, you know that?" He sighed into her ear. "You're in big trouble now, missy."

She looked up at him, into his sparkling hazel eyes, willing him to kiss her.

"Something is happening here," he whispered, lifting her chin, "and I don't know whether to run from it or straight at it."

Patrice trembled as his muscular body pinned her to the wall. She inhaled crisp aftershave and sweet cookie breath. *If he isn't the guy for me, Lord,* she prayed, *speak now or forever hold Your peace.*

When his lips touched hers, Patrice gasped. The soul-stirring taste of him sent silent shock waves straight to her heart. Weak-kneed and light-headed, she felt his arms encircle her, providing surefooted and much-needed support. Slowly, his fingers combed through her hair, traced down her shoulders and back, gently caressed her cheeks. His lips skimmed, light as feathers, from her earlobes to her throat to her forehead, before sliding back to her slightly parted, waiting lips.

Between kisses, he stammered and stuttered, and his words made no sense to her. "It's been…never thought I'd…you're like…Patrice, oh Patrice…."

When he said her name, it was a soft spring breeze, rustling the pines and sending dogwood petals floating gently through the air. Liking the way he'd warmed her lonely heart, she wanted to learn more about this strong-willed man—until her decision to keep a safe distance echoed in her head.

He seemed to sense her sudden mood swing and gradually ended the delicious kiss. "I—I don't know what's gotten into me," he murmured shakily. He kept her close, though, and looked deep into her eyes. "That's a lie. I know exactly what's gotten into me."

A tightrope walker could have balanced on the taut thread that linked their gazes. Wade stood back slightly, his eyes sliding over her features, reminding Patrice where his lips had been mere seconds ago. She waited for him to tell her exactly what had gotten into him.

"I sure could use another cup of coffee," he said instead.

Small talk over the minimountain of chocolate chip cookies was companionable, and when he stood to leave the next time, she wanted to stop him. Wanted to feel his big, protective arms around her again, making her forget the horrible nightmares that disturbed her sleep. Wanted him to prove to her that the guilt and remorse she'd heaped onto her shoulders all these years truly *was* misplaced.

"Wait," she said.

He'd made a stack of cookies while they talked, and now he was straightening a teetering column. "For what?"

He sounded pleased, even happy, that she'd asked him

to stay. "Let me pack a few of these for you to take home."

Grinning, he said, "Do you do this often?" Wade gestured toward the cookie pile.

"Only when I'm upset. Baking…soothes me."

Wade chuckled softly. "From the looks of things, something had you *real* upset."

She was stuffing a small grocery sack with sweet treats when he bent to kiss her temple—the one with the scar. Her hands froze.

"Beautiful," he rasped.

Her heart raced as she clutched the bag to her.

"Well," Wade said, "guess I'd better get home." He hugged her and a cookie crumbled between them. He kissed the top of her head. "Lock up tight when I'm gone, you hear?"

Nodding against his hard chest, she wondered about the myriad of sensations spiraling through her. What she felt with Wade was nothing like what she'd felt all those other times. If that had been love, what was *this?*

Chapter Three

Wade never really paid much attention to his home, such as it was, but those few hours at Patrice's house made him see it differently. "Not your stereotypical bachelor pad," his sister had said, the one and only time she'd seen it.

He'd laughed along with Anna—and quickly dismissed her opinion. What did he need with suede sofas, an intricate stereo system, and sophisticated lighting designed to romance a woman? His beat-up foldout bed and mismatched lamps suited him just fine. The only females who'd ever seen them were Anna and his cleaning lady. If anyone had asked him, he would have said that's how it would stay—until he saw the way Patrice lived.

Dozens of times, he'd been invited to women's houses. Except for the blond nurse whose town house resembled the sty of a certain Muppets character, his other lady friends had lived in organized style.

So why did Patrice's place seem so...*different?*
Like a home.

Wade blew a stream of air through his teeth. *Home is more than a place to store your clothes, eat TV dinners, spend the night,* he thought dismally. *It's where a man goes to be with his kids…and the love of his life.*

Things he'd never have.

A year ago this time, he would have been heading out the door in a tux and shiny black shoes, on his way to one gala or another. Either that, or rushing to pick up some model wannabe for dinner and dancing.

Wade put the soda bottle on the end table, aimed the remote at the TV and hit the on button. He tucked one hand under his head and squinted at the screen, determined to block Patrice's pixie face and sweet voice and cozy home from his thoughts. He scrolled through the channels, but nothing—not even the super-sucker vacuum cleaner on the shopping station or the lion-hyena war on the science station—could take his attention from Patrice.

It was the chocolate chips, he thought, grinning to himself. But when he closed his eyes and licked his lips, cookies were the last thing on his mind.

After that McMonkey display in Emily Kirkpatrick's room, he should've known she'd be animated, funny, sweeter even than those homemade cookies. Even if the shenanigans with the sick kids hadn't told him a thing or two about her personality, the visit to her office should have.

Black-and-white photos of hospitalized kids lined the walls. Numerous illnesses kept them tethered to their beds by plastic tubes, slouching weakly in wheelchairs, leaning on IV poles—yet every child in the pictures had one thing in common: a Patrice-induced smile. On her bookshelves, she'd proudly displayed lumpy animals, flower vases, and candy dishes made of modeling clay—

mementos for the young woman they'd lovingly dubbed Monkey Lady.

She'd been caring for her father for more than a decade, but Wade hadn't noticed a trace of distress in her demeanor, hadn't heard a hint of bitterness in her voice. Her dad's cheerful attitude seemed proof that not even *he* had detected so much as a note of regret or resentment.

Wade started counting Patrice's qualities on his fingers: smart, good sense of humor, a big heart... The spotless house told him she was an "attention to detail" kind of gal, and the tasty cookies she'd baked from scratch said she enjoyed the sweet things of life, too. With all that going for her, who'd expect her to have eyes that would inspire poetry, a figure like the porcelain ballerinas his mom used to collect, and a voice so velvety he couldn't *think* of a word to describe it.

And then there was that kiss....

He caught himself grinning from ear to ear, like some girl-crazy schoolboy. Wade blocked the TV's flickering light with the crook of his arm, and shook his head. If he wasn't careful, this thing could take a nasty turn; if he didn't watch his step, he'd end up asking her out a second time, a third, even—and he couldn't let that happen. Anyone with eyes could see that she was an innocent, and he didn't have a clue how to behave with a woman like that!

Again he thought of their kiss. She'd felt so small, so vulnerable in his arms, that Wade had found himself wanting to shield her from all life's woes. He'd kissed quite a few women in his time, but he'd never felt *that*, not once, not even for an instant.

Weird, because he got the sense Patrice had earned the right to say, "I can take care of myself."

If he believed that, why did he want to protect her, *anyway?*

Because she was one of those people, he told himself, who shouldn't *have* to struggle, that's why. She deserved to have someone there, right beside her, to lean on at the end of a hard day, to fend off any trials and tribulations that dared force their way into her world.

Wade didn't know if he had what it took to be that someone, and the admission saddened him more than he cared to admit.

After tossing and turning for more than an hour, Patrice gave up trying to sleep and headed downstairs for some herbal tea. With her mug on the end table and a plate of chocolate chip cookies beside her on the sofa cushion, she cuddled under an afghan, scanning the morning paper. Unable to concentrate, she folded it neatly and laid it on the coffee table.

Maybe the plot of a good novel would take her mind off the evening with Wade…and that incredible, indescribable kiss….

Standing in front of the floor-to-ceiling bookshelves that flanked the fireplace, Patrice ran a fingertip along the spines of ancient volumes and settled on the family Bible. Maybe, printed on one of its crisp, gold-trimmed pages, she'd find the answer to the question that had kept her awake: *Do You want Wade to be a part of my life, Lord?*

As she slid the Good Book from its shelf, a photograph fluttered to the hearth. Even as she bent to pick it up, Patrice recognized her mother's familiar blue script, identifying the event and the date: *Timmy, first day of school.*

Nothing could have prepared her for the sudden, overwhelming sadness that brought her to her knees. Sitting back on her heels, Patrice clutched the Bible in one hand, Timmy's picture in the other. And holding her breath, she slowly turned it over, gasping softly at first sight of her little brother's pale yet cherubic cheeks, at his gap-toothed smile, at eyes too big...too filled with pain for a face so young.

She hadn't seen this snapshot in more than a decade, but she remembered the day well. It had begun like every other, with her fervent prayer for Timmy: "Make him well, Lord!" Even before breakfast, he had been sent to his room with a paternal admonishment never to put sugar in the saltshaker again.

Patrice couldn't help but smile at the bittersweet memory of the feisty child who, despite his diminutive size and infirmity, never once complained. Even as a girl, she'd suspected that Timmy knew, somehow, that his life would be short. Why else would he have worked so hard to squeeze so much living into every moment?

Back then, she hadn't understood why the Almighty didn't answer her plea. In truth, she didn't understand it any better now. Timmy had as much right as any boy to climb to the treetops, to chase fly balls in left field, to race two-wheelers with a mob of his pals, right?

The *why* of Timmy's death would remain a mystery, at least until she joined him in Heaven. She believed without question that the Lord had taken Timmy to Paradise for reasons of His own, believed just as strongly that she had no right to question those reasons.

Wasn't that the basis of faith?

Her mother's death, however, was another matter entirely.... Anger swirled in her heart, in her mind. *Dangerous territory,* Patrice reminded herself.

Standing, she tucked the photo back into the Bible and

returned to her corner of the couch. Resting her head against the back cushions, she closed her eyes.

"So, how'd it go?"

Patrice lurched and let out a tiny squeal. "Dad," she said, one hand pressed to her chest, "honestly!"

"Sorry," Gus said. "But you'll thank me later."

Grinning, she sat up. "Thank you? For scaring me out of the last ten years of my life?"

"Sure," he said emphatically. "Those are the years you'd spend in an overpriced nursing home, anyway."

Rolling her eyes, Patrice groaned. "Maybe this weekend I'll drive you down to Water Street, so you can audition at the Comedy Club."

He chuckled. "There's something else you have to thank me for—"

She waited for his punch line.

"—that rip-roarin' sense of humor of yours."

"Wow," came her dry reply. "And here I thought being thankful that I got your eyes was enough." She regarded him carefully. "You feeling okay?"

"Never better."

"Then, what're you doing up so late?"

"I could ask you the same question."

"And we could go back and forth like this till dawn...."

"Good point," Gus said. And winking, he added, "Couldn't sleep, that's all. Happens to the best of us, sometimes."

Patrice sipped her tea. "How 'bout I fix you a cup of—"

"No, thanks. I mostly just came in 'cause I thought I'd forgotten to turn out the lights." It was his turn to look suspicious. "You okay?"

The question surprised her. She could only hope it didn't show on her face. "Sure. Why wouldn't I be?"

"Well," he said, pointing with his chin, "there you sit, family Bible in hand, Timmy's picture poking out...."

Another sigh. "Well," she answered, forefinger following the contours of the Bible's gilded letters, "maybe I am feeling a bit wistful."

He rolled closer to the couch. "You're a good kid, Treecie. Have I told you that lately?"

Gus said it a dozen times a day. Oh, he substituted a number of words for *good*—terrific, fantastic, super, wonderful—but the meaning was always the same.

"So, how'd it go?" he repeated.

She flopped back against the couch cushions. "My date with Wade, you mean?"

Gus nodded, grabbed her mug and took a sip of the tea.

"I'd be happy to make you a cup, Dad."

"Nah. Not thirsty," he said, returning the mug to its coaster. Then he added, "You gonna keep me in suspense all night, or what?"

She met his dark, teasing gaze. Smiling, Patrice said, "It went well."

"Where'd he take you?"

"*Mi Casa.*"

He scratched his chin. "*Mi Casa, Mi Casa.* Doesn't sound familiar." He squinted. "Is it new?"

"Couple of years old." She sipped the tea. "It's at the corner of Route 40 and St. Johns Lane."

"Oh, yeah," he said, nodding. "That new building behind the bank."

They'd already discussed this, briefly, before Wade arrived. "Enough small talk, Dad. Out with it."

Palms upturned and brows raised, he feigned innocence. "Out with what?"

"May as well tell me what's on your mind, save us both a lot of hemming and hawing."

Gus opened his mouth to respond, then snapped it shut again. For a long, silent moment, he only stared at her, a pensive, faraway expression on his rugged face. "Do you have any idea how much you remind me of your mom sometimes?"

She'd never understood whether that was a good thing...or a bad thing. Patrice looked down, at the grain of the Bible's leather cover. If she thought for a minute opening it would provide him with comfort and peace, if it would give him the healing he so richly deserved—

"All I can say is, he'd better treat you with kid gloves," Gus said roughly. "You remember what I said when the last bum broke your heart...."

A sad smile lifted one corner of her mouth. "That you'd mow him down with your wheelchair, then back up and roll over him again."

"I would-a, too, if you hadn't begged me not to."

He didn't have it in him to squash an ant, let alone harm another human being. Still, he seemed to enjoy his little threat. Quiet laughter simmered in them, bubbled up and spilled softly out—proof of what they both knew.

For a minute or two, father and daughter sat in companionable silence. Then Gus reached out and patted her hand. "Better get to bed, Treecie. Didn't you say there's some kind of multiward party at Child Services tomorrow?"

She nodded. "Yep. Child Health Week starts this weekend."

"And let's not forget what tomorrow night is...."

Merriment twinkled in his eyes. She got up and

crouched beside him. "What're you dressing up as this year?"

"Molly helped me build a box for this baby." He slapped the armrests. "It's the spittin' image of an Indy 500 car!"

"Cool beans." She got to her feet. "But I think you ought to heed your own advice and get some shut-eye. Takes a lot of strength, setting up the stuff that'll scare the willickers outta unsuspecting trick-or-treaters."

He chuckled.

"Well, I'm off to Sandman Land. Need anything before I turn in?"

He shook his head. When she bent to get her mug, he grabbed her hand. "You sure you're all right, Treecie? This guy...this *doctor*...he was nice to you, right?"

The image of Wade—sparkling hazel eyes, patrician nose, boyish grin—flitted through her mind. "Yeah." She sighed. "He was nice." She remembered the kiss. "Very nice."

"Good," Gus said, popping a wheelie in his chair, "'cause I'd hate to—"

"—mow him down," they said in unison, laughing.

He rolled out of the room.

"G'night, Dad."

"Sweet dreams," he called before closing his door.

She licked her lips, remembering the cookie-sweetness of Wade's kiss.

Maybe, for a change, her dreams would be "sweet" too.

Patrice parked in the multistoried garage adjacent to Ellicott General and yawned. The night had been one gruesome nightmare after another about the tragedies that had befallen her family.

Thankfully, Molly had arrived a few minutes early, and Patrice had been able to sneak out of the house before her dad came down for breakfast. He'd know the instant he looked into her face that her dreams had been anything but sweet. *And you've already put him through enough,* she'd thought as she grabbed her briefcase and purse.

Patrice locked up her car and headed for the elevator. But thinking maybe the walk would clear her head, she took the stairs, instead. On the first landing, head down and deep in thought, she plowed into a white-haired man and nearly sent him headfirst into the iron railing.

"Oh, my goodness," she said, one hand on his arm, "I'm so sorry. Are you all right?"

He jerked free of her grasp. "No thanks to you!" he bellowed. "Are you crazy?"

Patrice hadn't expected a pat on the back for her blunder, but she hadn't expected this, either. "I—I—"

"Don't you watch where you're going, you stuttering idiot?"

Heart pounding and cheeks burning, she repeated, "I'm sorry, sir, really. I didn't see y—"

He eyed her warily. "Let me guess—you've done this before, haven't you. And one of your victims hauled off and clobbered you, right?"

She had no idea what he was talking about.

He pointed. "Is *that* where you got that ugly scar?"

She tried to escape his verbal abuse but couldn't seem to make her legs move.

"Young people today," he continued, forefinger inches from her nose. "You think you own the entire universe and everything in it, don't you? Well, I'm here to tell you—"

"What's going on here?"

Wade. She'd recognize that voice anywhere. *Great,* she thought, bowing her head, *all I need is for him to witness my humiliation.* "I'm fine," she told him. "I wasn't paying attention where I was going, and I ran into this—" it pained her to say it "—gentleman."

"I'm so-o-o-o glad to hear you're fine!" The old man adjusted the collar of his jacket. "I'm lucky you didn't send me smack into that iron bar, there, or worse, *over* it!"

Frowning, Wade looked from Patrice to the man and back again, then stepped between them. "Hey," he began in a friendly voice, "it was just an accident, so if you're not hurt, then I suggest we cut this short, because folks want to use—"

Until Wade brought it to his attention, the man didn't seem to notice that several people were staring. "Mind your own bee's wax," he growled at the lot of them, then stomped down the steps.

Wade slid an arm around Patrice's waist and guided her nearer the rail. "You okay?" he asked, searching her face as the small crowd passed by.

She took a deep breath, exhaled it. "Yes," she snapped. "I'm fine."

"What was that all about, anyway?"

"I already told you—I wasn't looking where I was going and I walked into him. I said I was sorry, but he didn't want an apology. The old grouch just wanted to argue."

She followed Wade's gaze to the entrance, one floor down, saw him watch the old man huffing his way toward the enormous revolving door. "Hard to tell what brought him here this early on a Saturday morning...."

As the fellow shuffled into the lobby, she realized that Wade was right. For all she knew, the poor man had come to Ellicott to visit a dying friend or relative, or to have an emergency consultation with a doctor for a serious condition of his own. A surge of guilt further reddened her cheeks. What an awful, mean-spirited person she was!

If she'd had a decent night's sleep, or had taken time to eat a proper breakfast, or hadn't run into a huge traffic snarl on the way to work… And if Wade wasn't looking at her with a "poor little thing" expression—as if she were a lost puppy and he the guy who'd found her—she might have dismissed the incident as an unpleasant experience for both her *and* the old man.

As things stood, she had more than a little trouble keeping the tears at bay.

"What're you doing here at this hour on a Saturday?" he asked.

She sighed. "There's this…this *thing*," she said, waving a hand beside her head. "Children's Health Week starts today, and three of the children's wards are having parties. I have to—"

"When do the parties start?" he asked, his voice calm and reassuring, his smile warm.

"Not till this afternoon, but—"

"But nothing," he interrupted, taking her elbow. "You have time for a cup of coffee." He led her toward the steps. "What did you have for breakfast?"

"Didn't."

"What?" He shook his head. "Surely you've heard that breakfast is the most important meal of the day."

She glanced at her watch.

"Cut it out," he scolded. "You have time for a bite to eat."

Patrice stopped on the next landing. "What're *you* doing here at this hour on a Saturday?"

"It's nearly nine-thirty, and I have rounds to—"

Slump-shouldered, she groaned. "Well, Wade, I feel bad enough already, getting into brawls with old men and all, without making you late for your hospital rounds."

He chuckled and started walking again. "It isn't a requirement. I do it because..."

When Wade stopped talking all of a sudden, she looked up into his face. "Because what?"

He wouldn't meet her eyes.

They'd reached the ground floor by now, and Wade held the door that led from the parking garage to the hospital's main entrance. "So what're you in the mood for?" he asked. "Scrambled eggs? Bacon? Bagel and cream cheese?"

Her own problems were quickly forgotten, replaced by concern for him. "Haven't said I'd eat breakfast...yet," she teased.

Wade slowed his pace. "You'd really let a hardworkin' doc eat alone?" A silent whistle passed his lips. "I gotta tell ya, Patrice, that's cold. Real cold."

Pleased at the smile that replaced his worried frown, she laughed softly. "You didn't by any chance sell used cars to pay your way through school, did you?"

"No...."

"Sell encyclopedias door to door?"

He looked puzzled.

"Work on the set of a Mafia movie?"

He shook his head. "Why?"

"'Cause you give a whole new meaning to the phrase 'make 'em an offer they can't refuse.'"

His laughter echoed in the marble-floored lobby, drawing the attention of the security guard and a taxi driver who waited for his fare to arrive. But Wade didn't seem to notice the curious stares following them as they entered the cafeteria.

Patrice slid into a booth, put her briefcase and purse on the bench beside her. "Maybe we ought to get in line."

"You stay here and guard our table. I'll be right back."

"Okay. I'll have an egg sandwich and coffee."

She watched him slide his red plastic tray along the polished chrome rails, pointing to toast and eggs and bacon as he passed the food stations. When he disappeared behind other cafeteria patrons, she craned her neck to find him in the crowd, and when at last she spotted him at the coffee urn, her heart pounded.

She couldn't very well let him catch her staring after him like some schoolgirl in the throes of a mad crush. Patrice rooted around in her purse and withdrew her compact to make sure the wind hadn't blown the hair from her face, exposing the scar. What she saw in the tiny, oval mirror surprised her; in place of the expected "you're sinking fast" symptoms, was a relaxed, friendly smile.

"You don't need that thing," Wade said, startling her. "You're gorgeous, exactly the way you are."

Snapping the compact shut, she dropped it back into her purse. He'd meant every word, as evidenced by the set of his jaw, the sincerity in his eyes. Pulse pounding, Patrice blinked. What was a girl supposed to say in response to a thing like that?

Three soft gongs pealed from the overhead speaker. *"Housekeeping to the cafeteria,"* said the practiced announcer's voice. *"Housekeeping to the cafeteria."*

Whew, she thought, grinning as he doled out the food, *saved by the bell.*

He bit the corner from a slice of toast. "So where's Mort?"

Pointing at her briefcase, Patrice sipped her coffee.

"Interesting animal," he said. "Where'd you buy him?"

"I made him."

His brows rose slightly and he stopped chewing. "You *made* him? But how?"

She shrugged. "Couple yards of fuzzy material, foam filling, couple of chopsticks, and—"

"Chopsticks?"

"For his arms and legs." She bent her own arm. "I connected them with some stainless steel swivel-y things I found at the hardware store."

"Fascinating."

And he meant it. She could tell by the admiring gleam in his eyes.

"How'd you learn to operate all those hairy limbs?"

Another shrug. "Trial and error, mostly. The good Lord was watching over those first few kids who met Mort."

His brows rose again. "Why?"

"Did your mother ever say to you 'You could poke an eye out with one of those!'?"

Wade nodded. "Yeah." He grinned.

"Well, let me tell you," she said, hiding a giggle behind one hand, "that warning echoed in my head those first few performances!"

He laughed.

Already, she loved the sound. Her father's warning leapt to her mind, and Patrice sat up straighter. Forefinger peeling back her cuff, she glanced at her watch. "Wow," she said, "I'd better get a move on."

He used a white plastic fork as a pointer. "But you haven't finished your egg sandwich."

The disappointment in his voice was evident. "I'll just take it with me," she said, wrapping it in a paper napkin. "There's a fridge in the hall, right outside my office door—"

"Patrice," he said softly, taking her hand, "relax."

Oh, right, she thought. Relax, with his big palm covering her fingers like a warm blanket.

"You keep up this pace, you're gonna end up in my waiting room."

Maybe his friendliness was just that. Maybe those "longing looks" he'd been giving her were just her imagination.

But what about that kiss?

Oh, grow up, Patrice, she scolded herself. *Look at him!* He was gorgeous, successful, intelligent, witty…and single. Everything, enjoyable as it was, could very well be part of an elaborate act. Practiced scenes he'd played out with dozens of women over the years.

Patrice eased her hand from beneath his and used it to snatch a napkin from the dispenser on the table. "Well," she said, standing, "thanks for breakfast. It was great."

He tucked in one corner of his mouth and regarded her through narrowed eyes. "Don't mention it," he said in cool, even tones.

"Better get going," she said, gathering up her purse and briefcase. "Have to make sure there are enough—"

"What?" he asked in response to her gasp.

"Cookies." She plopped onto a corner of the bench seat and rested her forehead on a palm. "I baked *dozens* of cookies for the kids. They're on the kitchen table!"

"Hmm." Wade pursed his lips. "Is there time to go home and get them?"

She shook her head. "I have to set up the tables, make sure the volunteers are in place, hang posters...."

He took her hand again. "Easy, kiddo. My mom always used to say, 'For every problem, there's a solution.'"

Oh, really? she asked silently. For the life of her, she didn't see a solution to this one.

"I've got an hour or so to kill. How 'bout if I pick 'em up for you?"

Slowly, she lifted her gaze. Surely she was hearing things.

No, the expression on his face told her that he'd fetch the treats if she asked him to. But *why,* when she was likely one in an endless parade of ladies in his life? "I couldn't ask you to do that."

"You didn't ask. I offered," he said matter-of-factly.

She opened her purse, riffled through her wallet. "Good," she said, snapping it shut. "I have more than enough cash to buy some junk food, right here."

He should have looked relieved to hear he wouldn't have to make the trip to her house and back. She didn't know him well, but if she had to guess, Patrice would say he looked...*disappointed* that she hadn't taken him up on his offer.

She held out her briefcase and her jacket. "Will you watch my stuff while I see what's on the menu?"

He took it, then gestured with a thumb over his shoulder. "I'll wait out there." And with a wink, he headed for the cafeteria's outdoor picnic area.

Ten minutes later, as she hurried from the cafeteria, Patrice caught sight of him, straddling the wide white wall that cordoned the grass from the concrete walkways. Her jacket, slung over one of his broad shoulders, flapped in the crisp autumn breeze like a cape. *My white knight?* she wondered, smiling despite herself.

When Wade saw her, he raised a hand. "Find everything you need?" he asked, heading her way.

She held out the brown bag, filled to overflowing with doughnuts and cookies and tiny fruit tarts. "This oughta hold 'em over."

Wade relieved her of the bag.

"But—"

He held up a hand to stanch her protest. "Humor me, will you?"

She returned his smile. "Okay, but it's quite a hike to my office, especially carrying that." She nodded toward her briefcase.

"If you can do it, I can do it." He paused. "But what've you got in this thing? Rocks?"

"Bricks, actually," she teased.

They walked a few minutes in silence before Wade said, "So what're your plans for tonight?"

"Candy."

"Candy?"

"It's Halloween, remember?"

"Now that you mention it, I do."

"I'll be helping my dad and Molly hand out candy to the trick-or-treaters."

"Who's Molly?"

"Dad's nurse." After a moment, she added, "What're *you* doing tonight?"

"Before or after I go trick-or-treating?"

Patrice laughed. "Before."

"Same thing I'm doing after—nothing."

"Then, why not come over? We could put you in charge of keeping the pumpkins lit."

"Would I have to wear a costume?"

"Depends."

"Uh-oh, I'm almost afraid to ask. Depends on what?"

"On what kind of mood Dad is in. He's a bigger kid than anybody who'll show up tonight. It's entirely possible he'll insist you wear a mask, at least."

They were standing outside her office door when he said, "Well, okay, but I get to choose the mask."

She unlocked the door. "I'd say that's fair."

Wade deposited her coat, briefcase and bag of treats on her desk. "So what time should I be there?"

"Five o'clock?"

He looked surprised.

"It's a family tradition to eat pizza before the doorbell starts ringing," she explained. "Keeps us from eating all the goodies."

"Sounds like fun. See you this evening, then."

"Thanks for everything, Wade."

"My pleasure."

She watched as he stepped into the hall and then rounded the corner. Just as she turned to hang up her coat, he peeked back around the door frame. "Anchovies?" he asked, wrinkling his nose.

"No anchovies," she assured him.

"You're the best."

The clock on her desk read a quarter-to-ten. "C'mon, five o'clock!" she said, grinning.

Chapter Four

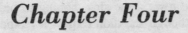

"Everything's ready," Gus called over his shoulder. "All we need now is a bunch of kids."

"It's only four-thirty, Dad. Give 'em time."

She closed the oven and set the timer. If all worked out as she had planned, Wade would arrive just as the pizzas finished baking.

Gus rolled into the kitchen and admired four loaves of fresh baked bread, cooling on the table. "Mmm," he said, closing his eyes to inhale the yeasty aroma. He punctuated the comment by popping a grape from the fruit bowl into his mouth.

Their "Pizza on Halloween Night" tradition had begun before Timmy's death. Back then, her mom bought frozen dough at the grocery story. It wasn't until Patrice turned fourteen—when she announced "I'm too old for trick-or-treating"—that she tried her hand at the home-made stuff.

"Looks like you outdid yourself this year, Treecie."

He said the same thing every year, whether the bread was edible or not. She might have given up that first

year, when the dough didn't rise at all, or the second
year when it rose too much, if not for Gus's loving en-
couragement. That, and the fact that he ate every scrap
of what she baked, tasty or not.

"We'll reserve judgment for the first slice," she said,
smiling.

He pointed at four more loaves on the counter. "Good
grief. It's just the two of us. How many did you bake?"

She turned toward the sink, hoping to hide her guilty
expression, though she didn't know *why* she should feel
guilty for baking extra bread. "Two for the pantry, two
for the freezer, two for Molly," she said, "same as always."

Peripheral vision told her his left brow had risen.
"Aha! So lemme guess. The other two are for your doctor friend."

Shrugging, she rubbed a terry dishcloth over the already gleaming chrome faucet. "I got a little carried
away with the dough this year."

"New recipe?"

Now she buffed the stovetop. "No. Same ol', same
ol'."

"Strange."

She rubbed the refrigerator door. "What?"

"Extra loaves from the usual recipe—that's what."

She heard the grin in his voice. Experience had taught
her that if she didn't distract him—soon—she was in for
a world of teasing. "The bread's still warm. How 'bout
I fix you a big buttery slice."

He rubbed his hands together. "Bribery will get you
everywhere."

Just as she was about to cut into a loaf, the doorbell
rang.

"Not dark enough to be the kids yet," Gus observed.

"And Molly isn't supposed to get here till six." He smirked and drummed fingertips on his chin. "So who could it be, who *could* it be?"

Patrice tossed the dish towel onto the counter and headed for the foyer. "You're such a card," she said, gently patting his head as she passed.

"Lemme guess...I'm the ace, right?"

"I was thinking more along the lines of the joker," she tossed over her shoulder, laughing.

In the hall, Patrice peeked into the hall mirror, smacking her lips and fluffing her hair before flinging open the door.

Ten silent seconds passed, fifteen, as she stared at the guest on their porch.

"Who is it?" Gus called.

The visitor stood, black boots shoulder-width apart and arms crossed over a broad chest, his masked face shadowed further by a wide-brimmed hat. The steady late-October breeze pressed the billowing folds of his shirt against muscular biceps, set the red-lined cape to fluttering around brawny legs. She'd more or less figured that under the baggy lab coats and sweaters she'd seen him in so far, Wade would be built like an athlete, but she hadn't expected this!

Gus rolled up beside her. "Well, pinch my nose and call me a jelly doughnut," he said, chuckling, "if it ain't Zorro, in the flesh."

Two fingers to his ball-fringed hat brim, Wade snapped off a smart salute, then bowed with an exaggerated flourish. "I hope you don't mind," he said, straightening to his full six-foot height, "I parked my ride out back."

"Well," Gus interrupted. "What're you standing out

there in the wind for? Bring your caped self on in here, man.''

The oven timer jangled as Patrice closed the door. ''Pizza's ready,'' she said, hurrying toward the kitchen.

''Wait till the kids get a load o' you,'' Gus told Wade as they moved toward the kitchen.

Wade removed his hat and mask, hung them on the back of a kitchen chair, then sat across from Gus at the table. For the next five minutes, as Patrice sliced the pizzas and set the table, the men swapped stock market gossip and sports scores.

Halloween had never been her favorite holiday, ever since her brother had been brought to the hospital for the last time on Halloween night, but she'd always gone along with the decorations and the costumes to humor her dad. If only she could adopt her dad's attitude and hand the whole burden over to Christ. Patrice sighed and said a silent prayer. Maybe this year, things would be different. Maybe this year, the memories wouldn't plague her....

Patrice poured iced tea into tall tumblers, while Wade unbuttoned his shirt cuffs and rolled each to the elbow. She watched from the corner of her eye as he slid a slice of pizza onto Gus's plate, then another onto hers before serving himself. Every bit the gentleman.

''Well, I guess they've had their fill.'' Gus shook his head. ''Kids didn't give up that easy when I was a boy.''

''You and Mom never let *me* stay out past ten o'clock on Halloween night,'' Patrice pointed out.

''Yeah, well....'' He chuckled and rolled himself into the foyer.

''Silenced in the face of logic,'' she teased, picking up an empty candy bowl.

Gus yawned and stretched. "Think I'll turn in."

"Without watching the eleven o'clock news?" She tucked the bowl under one arm and pressed her free hand to his forehead. "You're not coming down with something, are you?"

"Nah. All that squealing just gave me a bit of a headache." He rubbed both eyes. "Do we have any aspirin?"

It wasn't like him to ask for pain medication. Wasn't like him to turn in early, either. Especially on Halloween. Patrice bit her lower lip and frowned. "I'll fix you a cup of herbal tea, and bring something for your headache when it's ready." She kissed his forehead. "You do feel a tad warm...I'm going to bring the thermometer with me."

"Okay." He started rolling down the hall, then turned when he'd made it halfway there. "Thanks for helping out, Wade. Don't know what we would've done without you, seeing as how Molly cancelled on us."

Wade drew his sword, aimed it at the ceiling. "It was a job for Zorro!" he said, announcer style.

Gus gave a flimsy laugh. "Well, g'night. See you at dinner tomorrow?"

Wade resheathed the blade. "Wouldn't miss it for the world," he said, grinning at Patrice.

She looked at her father in surprise. This was the first she'd heard anything about Wade coming to Sunday dinner the following day!

As Gus disappeared into his room, she returned it with a halfhearted smile.

In the kitchen, Wade leaned back against the counter while Patrice loaded bowls, glasses and plates into the dishwasher. "You want me to give your dad a once-over before I leave?"

Her heart pounded. Why would Wade ask such a thing—he was a doctor, after all!—unless he suspected something was wrong? "Do you think that's necessary?"

He didn't answer right away. Instead, he studied her face. When finally he spoke, she detected a slight change from his friendly, upbeat tone. "I just thought you'd sleep better if I did a quick exam."

He wasn't fooling her. That was his "doctor voice." The one he had used on little Emily and her mother the other day at the hospital. She didn't even bother to dry her hands before grabbing his forearm. "What's wrong, Wade? And don't candy-coat it. I'm not—"

He chuckled softly. "If I hear that word again before morning, I might just have to punch something."

She gave his arm a slight shake. "What?"

The smile disappeared. So did the warm light in his eyes. "The word *candy*. It's Halloween, and we've been—"

"Okay, all right," she snapped. She let go of him and snatched the dish towel from the counter. "Ha-ha, I get it." For all she knew, Gus could be coming down with a virus, and there Wade stood, cracking jokes. Even the common cold could be deadly in his condition. *He's a doctor,* she thought, *so he should know that!*

With the toe of his boot, Wade closed the dishwasher door and stepped into its space. "I'm sorry," he said, sliding his arms around her, "I didn't mean to make light of it. I know how precarious a paraplegic's health is."

Pressing her cheek to the satiny fabric of his black shirt, she said, "Last time he caught a cold, he spent a month in the hospital—a week of it in Intensive Care."

"When was that?"

She shrugged and took a step back, but not so far that she broke the embrace. "Last year, around this time." She paused. "And tonight he sat out there for *hours* in that cold wind!"

"You brought him a parka, gloves." He touched the tip of her nose. "He didn't like it much, but he let you wrap a scarf around his neck, too."

Turning slightly, Patrice said, "I should've made him go inside. Should've turned out the porch light to signal 'Halloween is over at this house.' Should've—"

"I don't know Gus very well," Wade interrupted, "but something tells me nothing short of a hurricane would have sent him inside."

She sighed.

"Looked to me like he was having the time of his life."

Another sigh. "I suppose," she said. "Still..." Then she straightened her shoulders and took a deep breath. "Thanks, Wade, for understanding. You're a—"

He pressed a forefinger over her lips, silencing her. "Don't let the costume fool you," he said. "I'm no hero."

She forced a grin. "I wasn't going to call you a hero."

His brows rose slightly. "Oh, really. What, then?"

Truth was, she *had* intended to say exactly that! She searched her mind for another word that would fit into the sentence she'd constructed. "I was about to say you're a really sweet guy."

He stared into her face for what seemed like a full minute, brow furrowed, mouth taut, hazel eyes glittering with...

With *what*? Patrice wondered. She'd say...self-loathing, except, what reason would anyone as wonderful as Wade have to feel *that*?

"So where do you keep the thermometer?" he asked, breaking into her thoughts.

She swallowed. "In the bathroom across the hall. Top shelf of the medicine cabinet."

He'd already removed his hat, and as he headed for the hall, he took off the cape and scabbard, put them on a kitchen chair. "By the time his tea is ready," Wade said, turning on the flame under the copper kettle, "I'll have a preliminary diagnosis."

She watched him round the corner, then folded her hands. "Please," she prayed, bowing her head, "let Dad be all right."

She pictured Wade at her father's bedside—dispensing the same friendly compassion he'd shown little Emily Kirkpatrick and her mother…in a Zorro costume.

The image inspired a wan smile. Closing her eyes, she added, "And let Wade be 'the one.'"

Wade knocked softly on Gus's door.

"C'mon in."

He crossed the room in three long strides. "How goes it?" he asked, shaking down the thermometer.

"Aw, Treecie makes too much of everything." He gave a nonchalant wave. "I'm fine—just a little tired, is all."

"So look at it this way—when we're done here, you'll get to say 'I told you so.'"

That inspired a grin. "Well, now you're talkin' *my* language."

He opened his mouth, and Wade slid the instrument under his tongue. "I'll ask yes or no questions, so you won't have to talk."

Gus nodded.

"Feeling light-headed?"

He shook his head…then nodded.

"So you're not dizzy now, but you've experienced the sensations from time to time?"

"Mmm."

"More than once a week?"

"Mmm-hmm."

"Good. How many times a month?"

Gus held up three fingers, then two.

"Two or three times a month, then."

"Mmm-hmm."

"What about nausea?"

Another shake.

"Chills?"

This time, a one-shouldered shrug was the answer.

Wade gripped Gus's wrist, watched the second hand on the alarm clock and counted the beats of his pulse. "So the chills kinda come and go?"

"Mmm-hmm," he said through closed lips.

"I noticed you only ate one slice of pizza. Has your appetite been off for long?"

"Umm-mmm."

"Just today, then?"

He nodded.

"Could be you're just fighting off one of the viruses that's going around."

Gus shrugged. "Mmm."

"What about thirsty? You find yourself wanting to drink more than usual?"

He thought about that for a moment, then shook his head. He pointed at the thermometer.

Wade removed it and bent nearer the lamp to read what the mercury had registered.

"So what's the verdict?" Patrice asked, breezing into

the room. She placed a tray on Gus's nightstand, then stood back, arms folded over her chest, and waited.

"One-oh-one point four." He handed her the thermometer. To Gus he said, "Nothing to be concerned about…yet. Best thing for you is right here on this tray," he said, pointing at the mug of tea and tumbler of water that stood beside a tiny aspirin bottle.

Patrice shook two white pills into her palm, picked up the water glass and gave both to Gus. "Would you like a back rub, Dad?"

He downed the medicine, gasping once he'd drained the glass. "Nah. But thanks." He grabbed the remote, clicked on the small TV that sat across the room on his dresser. "I'll just watch the news and—"

"—and drink your tea," Patrice interjected, kissing his cheek.

"—then get some shut-eye," Wade finished.

Gus met Wade's steady gaze and harrumphed. "Two against one ain't fair."

Wade patted his shoulder. "Life ain't fair."

She led the way from the room, flicking out the overhead light as Wade stepped into the hall.

"But all's fair in love and war," Gus called through the door.

"Hey, that's a fair comeback!" Wade shot back.

"Fair-to-middlin', maybe," said the muffled voice.

"I'm *fair*ly close to screaming," Patrice teased.

After a short pause, Gus said, "G'night."

Back in the kitchen, Patrice poured Wade a cup of tea. "Obviously, the fever hasn't affected his sense of humor. I presume he's fine?"

"Well, *fair*ly fine."

She sat across from him and groaned.

"Sorry," Wade said, chuckling. "Couldn't resist."

Leaning forward, she wrapped both hands around her mug. "I heard you tell Dad there's no need for concern...*yet*. Why the qualifier?"

"Glad you brought that up."

Patrice took a sip of tea, hoping the action would hide the fear hammering inside her.

"How often does his temperature spike like that?"

Running the pad of her thumb along the mug handle, Patrice shrugged. "Once, maybe twice a year."

"When was the last time he had any blood work done?"

"Last year, in the hospital." She met his eyes. "Why?"

He shrugged. "He's probably slightly anemic, is all. Which could explain the dizziness and—"

"Dizziness? He's never said anything about dizziness."

Wade pursed his lips. "He didn't make a big deal about it. Said it happens, but only a couple times a month—"

She got to her feet so abruptly, the chair nearly overturned. Grabbing the phone, she hit the speed dial. "Molly? It's Patrice. Sorry to call so late, but—"

Nodding, she listened for a moment, hand to her forehead. "Good, good," she said rapidly, "glad to hear it." More silence, a few more nods, and then she said, "Yes, plumbers sure can be expensive. Thank the good Lord it wasn't a serious leak." When she hung up minutes later, Patrice flopped onto her chair. "Just as I suspected...he hasn't said a word about dizziness to Molly, either."

"It's probably nothing some extra iron won't cure. Happens sometimes with paraplegics."

Patrice swallowed, hard. She'd been hearing "paraplegic'' for what seemed like forever. Would she ever get used to the word?

"Limited amounts of cardiovascular exercise," Wade explained, "has all kinds of ill effects." He hesitated, as if uncertain whether to say more. "But I imagine you've heard that—and more—a couple hundred times over the years."

"Doesn't make it any easier to hear," she said softly, squeezing the cup for all she was worth. In a near whisper, she added, "Especially when it's your fault...."

He wrapped both big hands around hers. "You're not gonna start that nonsense again, are you? I thought you said Gus was hurt in a car accident?"

"He was, but—"

"What part of *accident* don't you understand?"

She took a deep breath, let it out slowly. "If it hadn't been for me, he never would have gone out that night."

"So let me get this straight. You, a mere sixteen-year-old kid at the time—and if you're this tiny now, you were probably just a slip of a thing back then—*forced* Gus to get behind the wheel."

"Dad was six foot two—or was, when he could stand—and over two hundred pounds." Wade heard the tremor in her voice when she added, "and a big ol' softie. He'd never learned how to say no to me, and I knew it. I used that to my advantage with regularity." She met his eyes. "I used it that night."

He saw her dark eyes begin to sparkle with unshed tears, felt her hands tense inside his own. Maybe pressing her to talk about it again wasn't such a good idea, after all. "Patrice..."

"As I mentioned the first time, it was raining and windy," she continued in a hollow, mechanical voice, "and the weatherman was predicting a drop in temperature. Marcy's party was my first invitation to an 'in crowd' function, and all the popular kids would be there. I was afraid if I didn't show up...

"It wasn't so bad—the weather, I mean—when Dad dropped me off. But by the time he came back for me at midnight, the rain had changed to sleet and the roads...the roads were—"

"Enough," Wade said. He walked around to her side of the table, pulled her to her feet and gathered her close. "No need to upset yourself rehashing—"

"We were a block from home," she said. Standing woodenly in his arms, she repeated it in a hoarse whisper: "A block from home!"

She was trembling from head to toe, and he didn't know what to do but hold her closer. "Shh," he said, smoothing her hair with one hand, rubbing soothing circles on her back with the other. "Your tea's getting cold."

Patrice took a step back, looked up into his face. "When you drove over here, do you remember passing a big brick wall that said Font Hill?"

She was gearing up to tell him it was the wall Gus had careened into that night. For the first time in decades, Wade wished he believed in God; if he did, he could ask for Divine intervention, because for the life of him, he didn't know how to comfort Patrice.

And he wanted that more than anything.

"When I came to, I looked over and there he was, smiling at me. 'You're gonna be all right, Treecie,' he said. 'I heard sirens, so help's on the way.'" She buried her face in the folds of Wade's shirt. "If I hadn't been so immature, so self-centered, Dad wouldn't be getting fevers, or dizzy...he'd be *walking* today!"

She'd walked away from the accident—with a scar on

her face. Wade could rattle off the names of half a dozen plastic surgeons who could've removed or repaired it. He understood, suddenly, that she wore it like sackcloth and ashes, as penance for what she considered her sins.

"I'm a horrible excuse for a daughter, a terrible person."

Oh, God, he prayed, face burrowing into her hair, *tell me what to say!*

It dawned on him then that Patrice didn't need him to say anything. What she needed was to know, without a doubt, that he believed she was wonderful, beautiful—inside and out—regardless of what *she* thought.

He lifted her chin on a bent forefinger, forcing her to meet his eyes, and with the pad of his thumb, brushed tears from her long lashes. "Y'know," he said, lips nearly touching hers, "if I heard anybody else sayin' stuff like that about you, I'd probably get arrested."

She blinked, sending a single silvery tear skittering down her cheek. "Arrested?" she said, brushing it away.

"Yeah." He doubled up a fist. "'Cause I'd punch 'em, right in the nose."

One corner of her mouth lifted in a sad smile. "So you'd fight for me, would you?"

"You bet," he said, kissing the tip of her nose. "In a heartbeat."

She stared into his eyes for the longest time, shaking her head and biting her lower lip. Wade couldn't help wondering what was going on in that pretty head of hers. And then she slid her arms around his waist and rested her cheek against his chest.

"And you say you're no hero."

The breath caught in his throat, because she really believed that. The proof was in her voice, in her touch, in her eyes.

"Your heart is beating a mile a minute," she whispered.

His palm cupped the back of her head. "That's quite an astute diagnosis. I think maybe you missed your calling. Care to suggest a treatment plan?" He hoped she'd pucker up and say something like "Take two of these and call me in the morning."

Instead, she said, "Stay away from weepy women?"

"Meaning you?"

She nodded.

"Sounds like bad medicine to me."

"Well, you're the heart doctor."

Fat lot of good his M.D. was doing him at the moment.

Patrice tilted her head and smoothed his collar, in that wifely way his sister so often tidied her husband's shirt. Grateful as he was that his sister had been blessed with a rock-solid marriage, Wade had always been slightly envious of it. Envious, because he couldn't convince himself he had a ghost of a chance at happiness like that.

Usually, he held such a tight rein on his emotions, it was a wonder he didn't squeak. And now, all wrapped up in her arms this way, he worried that maybe he was letting his heart do his thinking, instead of his head.

You're the doctor....

Trapped in the moment, his lips found hers. It started slow, and so soft it reminded him of feathers and satin and velvet, all at the same time. Gradually, it became more intense, more insistent. He could only hope she was getting as much solace from his kiss as he was finding in hers.

As if in answer to a prayer he hadn't yet prayed, a quiet moan bubbled up from deep inside her, and she combed her fingers through his hair. Wade answered with a groan of his own, bracketing her tiny face with his hands.

You're the doctor, she'd said.

Patrice...

Good medicine? asked his brain.

The best, answered his heart.

"Guess I'd better hit the road." Wade gawked at the kitchen clock as if unable to believe it read eleven-fifteen.

She felt as though everything stopped as he stood there near the door, looking at her.

"Don't worry about Gus, now, y'hear? If he isn't feeling a lot better by dinnertime tomorrow, we'll run him over to my office, do a couple tests."

"Okay," she said.

Side by side, they walked to the end of her drive, where he'd parked his car. "I had a great time. Don't think I'll ever think of Halloween in quite the same way again."

He gave her shoulder a gentle shove, reminding her of a boy with a crush, teasing a girl on the playground. She smiled.

"You're quite a woman, you know that?"

"Wade, stop. You're embarrassing me."

"The truth shouldn't embarrass you, Patrice."

His face loomed nearer hers, but when his lips made contact, it was with her forehead. Patrice pretended not to be disappointed.

She watched him climb into the front seat, realizing this tough-and-tender guy had touched a chord inside her. "Dinner's at two," she said, "but you can come earlier if you like."

He crooked his forefinger, beckoning her near. When

she took a step closer to the driver's door, he stuck his head through the opened window. "If you need me for anything tonight, I want you to call."

She hoped the darkness would hide her blush. "I don't think that'll be necessary. I shouldn't have asked you for free medical advice. It was—"

"Yes, you should have."

"I can take care of Dad." She said it with conviction and hoped he'd believe her. Because usually, she could.

He winked. "So, you have a character flaw, after all."

"I beg your pardon?"

"You're stubborn. I never would o' guessed it."

She grinned. "Perfection is boring."

He reached through the window and stroked her cheek. "I don't think you're the least bit boring." And with that, he backed out of the driveway.

She stood, heart thumping happily and fingertips resting on the spot he'd touched on her cheek, until his taillights were nothing but tiny red dots in the darkness.

After locking the door, Patrice leaned her forehead against the cool, dark wood. "If he isn't the one, Lord, I'm *really* in trouble this time...."

Chapter Five

The constantly changing numbers on the alarm clock beside his sofa bed told Wade he'd turned out the lights more than an hour ago. He'd booked an operating room for eight in the morning; after that, more back-to-back surgeries to perform. If he didn't get some sleep soon, he'd be dragging by noon.

None of the usual tricks were working—not visualizing a blank chalkboard, not forcing every muscle to go limp, and especially not counting sheep. As a kid, a quick bedtime prayer was all it took to guarantee a long, restful night.

Too bad he didn't still believe in God....

He'd left childlike faith with the rest of the nonsense adults dished out: "Brush and floss or the Tooth Fairy won't leave a dime under your pillow!" and "Be good or Santa won't bring that sled you want!" The year he found a fat potato amid chocolate rabbits and marshmallow chicks in his Easter basket, his mom had said, "Guess the Easter Bunny found out you never do your reading homework."

But Wade doubted he'd live long enough to hear a lie more malicious than the one his dad had told....

Punching his pillow, he rolled onto his side and squinted his eyes shut. It didn't keep him from picturing his father tucking him into bed. "Tomorrow," he'd said, "we'll go to the batting cages, and when we're finished, those Little League coaches will be fighting over you!" Wade had barely slept a wink that night, because his birthday party, a shiny new bike, and a trip to the batting cages would happen, all in one day!

He may have grown taller, heftier in the twenty-five years since that night, *but stupid things still keep you awake*, Wade thought bitterly. He tried concentrating on the upcoming week's hectic schedule, but not even back-to-back surgeries could keep him from remembering the morning after that childhood birthday.

He'd been the first one up, and thinking nobody would expect the birthday boy to fix the family's breakfast, he'd set the table. Pouring flakes into colorful plastic bowls, he noticed a note, propped against his mom's chicken-and-rooster napkin holder. He stood the cereal box on the edge of the table and grabbed the small sheet of paper.

"Dear Family," it said, "there's no easy way to say this, so I'll just say it. I'm leaving for..." As Wade struggled to sound out the next word, he remembered, he'd thought maybe his mom was right: he should've spent more time doing his reading homework. He remembered, too, how his heart thudded and his ears burned when he figured it out.

"...leaving for California," he read through the blur of tears, "to see if I can make it."

What did it *mean?* Wade didn't understand it any better tonight than he had all those years ago.

"When I get set up out there," the note went on, "I'll send money." And it was signed, simply, "Dad."

Dry-mouthed and breathing hard, he'd turned a slow circle, there in the middle of the sunny kitchen, to search out a good hiding place for the note, because if it hurt his mom half as much as it hurt him— His elbow had knocked the corn flakes box on the floor, instead.

Frustration. Another emotion Wade felt he'd never handled particularly well. But at the age of six...

He'd heard grown-ups say "I could kick myself!" But until that moment, he hadn't understood what they'd meant. He got the message loud and clear when his mom came into the kitchen and saw him in the middle of the room, bawling like a baby, hands over his ears...

The terrible message in one hand.

Moments later, it seemed, she was on the phone, biting back tears as she cancelled the birthday party. And later that day, as she muttered something about not having a clue how to put a boy's bike together, she returned it to the toy store. "Sorry, kiddo," she'd said, mussing his hair, "but I have a feeling we're gonna need that money for groceries."

That night, after a supper of beanies and wienies— Wade's favorite meal—she lit six candles on his cake and led Anna in a melancholy rendition of the birthday song. While they shoved blue frosting roses and chocolate filling around on their plates, his mom wondered aloud what kind of job she might be qualified to apply for in the morning...as if she knew, though he'd only been gone a few hours, that her husband wouldn't be back.

Of all his boyhood memories, that one was up there at the top of the list, because much as he'd wanted to comfort his mom, he didn't have a clue what to say, what to do. "Make Dad change his mind," he'd prayed that night. Hadn't his mother, his Sunday School teachers, Pastor O'Connor taught him "Ask, and ye shall receive; seek and ye shall find"? "Make him want to come back home."

After a few months, it was easier to hate God for not answering his prayer than to hate his dad for running away. So that's exactly what Wade had done.

And despite the fact that he'd taken enough psych classes in med school to recognize bitterness and resentment for what they were, he still hadn't let go of the anger. What would his professors have said? That diverting his attention when thoughts of his father invaded was evidence he hadn't reconciled with having been abandoned, that his hectic work and social schedules were still more proof that he'd never dealt with his "issues"?

It didn't take weekly analysis to figure out that a single event from twenty-five years ago had left indelible scars. It didn't take genius mentality, either, to know he couldn't afford to forget that event…lest he repeat his father's mistakes.

Wade knuckled his eyes and, feeling like a fool for continuing to give a moment's control to the man who had deserted him, his sister, his mom, he sat up. Throwing his legs over the side of the bed, he planted both feet on the tweedy brown rug.

Sometimes, a little knowledge could be a dangerous thing. Scientists had come a long way in DNA research. He need only review his own records for proof that grandfathers and fathers passed heart conditions to sons and grandsons. Health-related tendencies weren't the only factors passed from generation to generation; he'd read dozens of medical articles that proved behavior and habit could be linked among family members, too.

And his father's blood ran in his veins. Better—and safer—just to avoid the "relationship" thing.

Yes, knowledge could be a dangerous thing, for with age and wisdom came the mind-set that the fairy-Santa-bunny stories adults concocted for kids had but one purpose: control.

Wade sighed, scrubbed both palms over his face, then got to his feet and padded to the kitchen area of his tiny apartment. Standing at the sink, he downed two tall glasses of water, straight from the faucet.

It didn't wash the edginess or the gloom from his system. He knew full well what was at the heart of all this soul-searching. More accurately, *who*.

Patrice.

He'd need an abacus to count the women he'd known before her. So what made *her* stand out?

She was pretty enough, to be sure, but so were the others. Smart? Successful? Capable? She was all those things—and more—but then, so were the rest.

But their main goal, it seemed to him, was to mold him into their idea of what a man should be. From the first date, they started suggesting ways he could improve himself: stop listening to country and western music, start listening to opera; move out of the humble, one-room apartment and into something that said "class"; spend less time with patients and more with them. Truth be told, his father's DNA wasn't the only reason it had been easy to keep a safe emotional distance!

He refilled his glass, swallowed another gulp of tepid tap water, and pictured the way Patrice always looked at him—as if she were Cinderella and he Prince Charming. If he had to single out one thing that made her different, it was that, in her eyes, he seemed fine, exactly the way he was.

A mighty good feeling, he admitted.

No doubt about it…Patrice would be good for him.

Question was, would he be good for *her?*

The pastor's booming voice echoed from the high church ceilings. She'd been restless and edgy for days, now, so the first thing she'd done upon settling beside Gus in the pew was ask God to settle her unease.

All through the service her mind wandered, from the blustery wind that pummeled the church windows to what she'd prepare for Sunday dinner. Several times, shaking her head, she gave herself a good talking to. *Pay attention; how do you expect to hear God's message if your head is everywhere* but *in church!*

Patrice vaguely remembered the pastor's sermon topic…something about forgiving and forgetting. It had been her mother's favorite Biblical message. "The Father forgives us all our sins," she'd say when Patrice complained that a schoolmate had pulled her hair or there weren't as many Valentine's cards on her desk as on other kids', "and it's what He expects us to do, too."

Now, as the choir belted out a rousing rendition of "Just a Closer Walk with Thee," Patrice balanced the hymnal's spine on one palm, eyes closed and head bowed, and listened to what had been her mother's favorite holy song, the one she hummed while doing housework and cooking meals, and sang softly while puttering in her gardens. If pressed, Patrice would say she remembered hearing that tune while she was still in diapers.

The choir was on the third verse by the time Patrice opened her eyes. "'When my feeble life is o'er,'" they sang, "'time for me will be no more....'" Her mother had always sounded so...*sad*, Patrice thought, while singing those words. Could it be she'd wanted to die then, too? Or was the unhappiness merely in Patrice's imagination?

Were these signs and symbols the Lord's way of answering her prayer for peace of mind? Because surely He didn't expect she'd find it by forgetting that her mother had committed suicide. And since she'd long ago forgiven—

Or had she?

Using her thumb to mark the page in her hymnal, Patrice pressed the book to her chest. If she'd truly forgiven her mother, why did remembering that day still make her so angry?

"'...guide me gently, safely o'er,'" the choir continued, "'...to Thy kingdom shore, to Thy shore....'"

Though she'd found plenty of references to people killing themselves in the Bible, Patrice had never read the word *suicide*. So had her mother committed an unpardonable sin by taking her own life? Or was it an act God could forgive?

While still in high school, one of Patrice's classmates killed himself, inspiring a question-and-answer period in Sunday School on Sunday school. By the end of class, her teacher had filled the blackboard with proof that suicide was, indeed, a grave sin.

Suicide violates the Ten Commandments. The Bible does not condone ending one's life for any reason. Life is a gift from God. Suicide is an expression of self-hatred, and God directs us to love one another as ourselves. Suicide is proof of a lack of faith. Suicide is the ultimate act of selfishness.

New to the church, her teacher had no way of knowing how close to the bone the lesson had cut for Patrice. Patrice could only cling to the promise spelled out in Romans 8:1. ''...there is therefore now no condemnation to those who are in Christ Jesus.'' Her mother had invited the Lord into her heart at an early age, a fact that would have comforted Patrice...if it wasn't in direct opposition to the message in I Corinthians 6:19–20. ''Do you not know that your body is the temple of the Holy Spirit who is in you, whom you have from God, and you are not your own? For you were bought at a price; therefore glorify God in your body.''

It was a battle she'd fought from the age of fourteen, when she found her mother there on the living room couch...and one she'd likely fight till she drew her last breath. Then, as now, Patrice needed to believe that even though her mother's act was in direct rebellion against the Father, He had promised to remain faithful to His word. Because if that were true, she'd meet up with her mother someday in Paradise—

''Earth to Patrice, Earth to Patrice...''

Her father's gravelly whisper brought her back to the here and now. She met his eyes, saw the teasing glint there, and smiled.

''Well, *you* were about a billion miles away,'' he said, as fellow parishioners filed out around them. ''In Paradise, I take it?''

In place of an answer, she stepped into the aisle behind his chair, and, grabbing its handles, headed for the side door, where the men of the parish had installed a wide wooden ramp to accommodate the elderly and the handicapped. ''So what are you in the mood for today? Roast beef? Spaghetti and meatballs? Stuffed pork chops?''

"I have a new nickname for you," he said over his shoulder.

"Oh, really. And what would that be?"

She predicted he'd say Betty Crocker or Suzie Home-maker. Maybe even Master Chef. Patrice wasn't the least bit prepared to hear "Mistress of Evasion."

Stunned into silence, she maneuvered the chair along-side his minivan.

"You want to talk about it?" her dad asked as she rolled him onto the ramp.

"Talk about what?" she asked, though she knew per-fectly well what he meant.

"Whatever has you in such a dither this morning."

"Dither?" She forced a laugh. "Such talk, and on church property yet!"

Gus buckled himself into the passenger seat. "The Mistress of Evasion strikes again!" he teased. Then he reached out, wrapped a hand around her wrist. "Seri-ously, Treecie, you know you can come to me with any-thing, right?"

Well, Patrice thought, *almost* anything. Talk of her mother, of the suicide, had always been off limits, be-cause long ago she'd decided that in his shoes, *she* wouldn't want to discuss it. For the same reason, she rarely spoke of Timmy. "'Course I know that," she said, patting his hand. "Really, Dad, I'm fine."

He gave her an "if you say so" look.

She walked around to her side of the van and slid in behind the steering wheel.

"Pork chops," Gus said.

Cranking the motor, Patrice met his eyes.

"For Sunday dinner?"

"That sounds good. It's been a while since I've made—"

"Not just *any* pork chops," he said good-naturedly, "you said *stuffed*."

It took so little to please him that even if she'd been in the mood for something else, Patrice gladly would have shelved it in favor of his choice. "Okeydoke. You want to come with me to the grocery store to pick up what we need? Or would you rather I drop you off at home first?"

Chin out and lips pursed, he considered her question. "Maybe I'll just tag along, see if I can talk you into some junk food." He reached over the console, gave her shoulder an affectionate shove.

"Junk food, huh?"

"Well, sure. You can't invite an eligible bachelor to dinner and not serve a decent dessert."

Eligible bachelor.

"He doesn't seem like the fussy type to me."

"Bachelor of the Year, two years running?" Gus chuckled. "Ri-i-ight."

"Bachelor of the Year?"

"I figured news like that was all over the hospital. I looked him up on the Internet. Seems Mr. Footloose and Fancy Free really gets around."

"Gets around?"

"Y'know, like those auctions where rich gals bid on a guy and the money goes to charity? One article I read said that all by himself, Wade brought in something like ten grand." He whistled through his teeth. "Think of it…some broad paid ten thousand bucks for *one date* with the guy!"

She ignored the admiring tone in his voice. "Dad," Patrice said, "it's not polite to say 'broad' these days."

"Why not?"

"It's not politically correct, that's why."

"Politically correct, my foot," he said, harrumphing. "Why should any woman be offended? Don't they know it's a term of endearment?"

Grinning, she merely looked at him.

"No, really," he said, and as if to prove his point, added, "In my day, the term was a compliment! Guys used it to describe a gal they *liked,* someone down-to-earth, who wasn't all froufrou, who wasn't into playin' games."

"Froufrou?"

"Y'know, a nose-in-the-air, I-know-what's-best-for-you snob. Your mother was a broad, I'll have you know, and proud of it, too."

"Really."

"Really. The woman was a saint, I tell you. She wasn't afraid of hard work, wasn't above getting dirty doin' it, either. Sweetest, most loving, humblest human being I ever met, present company excluded. Person couldn't help but love her."

Patrice heard the sadness in Gus's voice and prayed that God would steer the conversation to a happier subject.

Gus shrugged. "I give up. The feminists have ruined all the great words, if you ask me."

Thank you, Lord, she thought.

The conversation had definitely taken a turn, but experience had taught her it wasn't necessarily for the better. "Nice weather we're having, don't you think?"

"Yeah, if you like cold wind and rain." He gave her a sidelong glance. "Okay, I give up. Why the change of subject?"

"I just think we ought to talk about something else."

"Why?"

"Well, you just left church for one thing—it'd be a shame for all those blessings to go down the drain just because the subject of feminism came up."

"You make a good point," he agreed. "And my hat's off to you, by the way."

"Whatever for?"

He raised his hands in a gesture of helpless supplication.

"Okay, all right, I get it. The Mistress of Evasion, right?"

A chuckle was his only answer.

"How's this for evasive. Why'd you look Wade up on the Internet?"

"You're my only kid, let's not forget. What kind of dad would I be if I *didn't* check him out?"

"He's a well-respected surgeon," she pointed out. And giggling, she added, "What did you think you'd find—that he's an ax murderer in his spare time?"

He shrugged yet again, than wagged a forefinger at her. "You can never be—"

"—too careful these days," she finished with him.

"Yeah, well, that smile on your face tells me you agree." He grinned.

"Maybe it means I think you're a lovable old kook."

He narrowed his eyes. "Hey, who you callin' *old?*"

Laughing, she wheeled the van into a handicapped space in front of the grocery store. "Well, here we are."

He peered through the windshield and feigned surprise. "That we are, Miss E, that we are." He unbuckled his seat belt and reached into the back seat. "Tell you what," he said, grabbing the Sunday paper. "Think I'll wait here while you shop."

She opened the driver's door. "What about the junk food?"

He slid the comics from the rest of the stack. "Guess I'll just have to trust you to do the right thing."

"Oh? And what would that be?"

He peeked out from behind the funnies. "Chocolate cake or apple pie, your decision." Wiggling his eyebrows, he added with a smirk, "Just don't forget the vanilla ice cream."

Once dinner was ready for the oven, Patrice tidied the house, and herself. She'd worn an old favorite to church, and probably wouldn't have changed it…if Wade wasn't coming for dinner. Swapping the gray corduroy jumper and white blouse for blue jeans and a white turtleneck sent just the right message, she thought. Patrice McKenzie could be as casual and relaxed as anyone! Of course, she'd never admit—not even to Gus—that it had taken nearly an hour of frenzied searching to come up with the easygoing look.

When the doorbell rang at precisely one o'clock, she'd just looped a pair of stylish silver earrings through her earlobes. One last peek in the foyer mirror, one last pat to ensure her curls covered the scar. "Ready or not," she whispered, a hand on the knob, "here he comes."

He smiled when she opened the door. "Hi. Hope I'm not too early."

His loose-fitting tan sweater brought out the gold in his hazel eyes—eyes that bored into hers with such an intensity it made her heart beat double time. Patrice hid her agitation by checking her wristwatch. "You're right on time. C'mon in."

Wade pointed at the bakery box balanced on his right

palm. "Cherry cobbler," he announced, his grin broadening.

Another dessert...when she'd bought all the ingredients for home-baked chocolate cake at the grocery store earlier. Looked like Gus would be able to fill his junk food quota today! "Thanks," she said, closing the door, then led him down the hall toward the kitchen. "Can I pour you a glass of iced tea or lemonade? There's a pot of hot water on the stove, for tea or cocoa."

"What're you having?" he asked, putting the dessert box on the countertop.

She nodded toward the mug on the counter. "Tea."

"Yep, that's my girl," her dad said, grinning as he rolled into the room, "predictable as sunrise and sunset."

She felt like saying, *Thanks, Dad, that's sure to charm the man!* Instead, Patrice went back to slicing vegetables for the salad and hoped that by the time Wade and Gus finished shaking hands, her blush would have faded.

"Good to see you again, sir," Wade said. "I appreciate the invite to Sunday dinner."

"Thank Patrice, not me." He waved the thanks away. "She's the chef in the family." He patted his belt buckle. "And as you can see, she's a little too good at it!"

"I get the impression there isn't much your daughter *can't* do, Mr. McKenzie."

"You got that right." He winked at Patrice. Then to Wade, he said, "But I thought we agreed you'd call me Gus. Mr. McKenzie was my dad's name." Facing his daughter once more, he added, "I'll be in the family room, hunting up a good John Wayne movie on cable. When y'get a minute, I wouldn't mind a cup of tea."

She put down the paring knife and reached for the tea canister.

Wade grabbed it before she could pry off its lid. "Let me do it for him," he said, nodding toward the salad fixings. "You've already got your hands full."

Patrice hesitated for a second before saying, "The mugs are in the cabinet above the coffeemaker, and the spoons are there." She indicated the drawer directly behind him.

Wade reminded himself that he'd spent most of the previous night tossing and turning, trying to make a list of reasons why he should stay away from this woman. He couldn't explain what made him gently tuck a wayward curl behind her ear...but the action exposed her scar, and she quickly fluffed her hair back into place.

"Call me stubborn," he said, pressing a hand to her cheek, "but it seems a cryin' shame to hide a face this gorgeous." He punctuated the comment by finger-combing her hair back. "There, much better."

She was visibly uncomfortable, as evidenced by her tense stance, the taut set of her jaw. Her gaze darted around his face, as if searching out the sincerity of his words.

Words.

Not long before her death, he'd given his mother one of those blank-inside greeting cards. After reading what he'd written inside, she said, "Wade, I've never understood why you haven't tried your hand at writing, because you've always been so good with words!" A few months after the funeral, he enrolled in a writing class, and quickly discovered he didn't have what it took to draft the Great American Novel, but the cardinal rule of fiction stayed with him: Show, don't tell.

Why not apply the lesson now?

The canister clunked against the countertop as he pulled her close. "I gotta tell you," he whispered, gently tracing the scar, "I'm kinda glad you have this thing."

She met his eyes, blinking, as if unable—or unwilling—to let herself believe him.

Fingertip following the permanent reminder of the car wreck, he added, "What other proof do I have that you're human?"

She laughed at that and turned slightly, hiding the scar from view. "Oh, believe me, I'm human, all right."

He raised his brows, shook his head. "I dunno... 'cause you sure have cast a spell over me."

When she looked up at him with those *eyes* of hers and smiled, Wade felt as though the sun had burst through the gray skies. He wanted to kiss every inch of that delicate face, from the freckles sprinkled across her pert nose, to the cheeks that still glowed rosy red, to the full, slightly parted lips.

And so he did just that.

And to his delight, Patrice relaxed against him, returning his kisses with equal emotion. She felt so good, so *right* in his arms that he couldn't for the life of him remember why he'd tried to talk himself out of this in the first place.

Then it came to him, as quickly as lightning slices through a stormy sky. But knowing everything he'd just said would seem phony if he admitted it now, he broke the warm, wonderful connection, gradually, all the while remembering his mother's tired old line: *This hurts me more than it hurts you.*

"I—I'd better take a peek at the pork chops," she said, fingertips pressed to her lips.

Wade was barely aware that his arms were still wrapped around her as he responded with a flimsy

"Yeah, and your dad's probably wondering what gives with his tea."

One side of her mouth lifted in an adorable grin that started his pulse to pounding...again. Patrice probably had no idea what she was doing to him—what she'd already done to him. Her innocence, her sweetness, had wrapped around him like a warm blanket on a cold night, making him feel comfortable and cared for, making him think maybe the DNA stuff was just nonsense. Maybe he could risk getting involved...with *this* woman.

He pretended to busy himself, stuffing tea bags into mugs, adding boiling water. From the corner of his eye, he saw that Patrice's hand shook slightly as she picked up the paring knife, trembled even more as it hovered over a slice of red bell pepper. Wade stirred sugar into the hot brew, the spoon clanking against the sides of the mug as he wondered what he could possibly say or do to calm her...and knowing at the same time that he was solely responsible for her jitters.

Her knife came down then, a little harder than she'd intended. "Oops," she said, stuffing the finger into her mouth. "That one was too close for comfort."

"Lemme see."

"It's nothing," she mumbled around the fingertip, "just a teeny nick."

"I'll be the judge of that." He grabbed her hand and inspected the injury.

"So what's the diagnosis, Doc?"

She'd been right—just a small cut. So why was his heart hammering? Why was he breathing as if he'd just run a four-minute mile?

"I think I'll live." And smiling, Patrice reclaimed her hand. "But just to be safe, I'll go put something on it."

"Good idea."

"Y'better take the tea bag out of the mug," she advised, "or you're never gonna get that spoon out of the sludge."

"Oh, right," he said, remembering Gus's teacup. "Right."

Tearing a paper towel from the roll, she wrapped it around her finger, then patted his arm. "Right," she echoed.

Even before she left to fetch a bandage, Wade knew the kitchen would feel cold and empty without her. Fact was, his *life* would seem cold and empty without her. *Should o' thought of that before you went and got yourself all involved,* he told himself. He'd promised to keep a safe distance to protect *her;* if he'd realized his own heart would be so much on the line, too, maybe he would've demanded a little more self-control of himself.

Not much chance of getting a good night's sleep tonight, either, he knew, with all this to mull over.

"Be right back," she said from the hall.

He felt himself nodding dumbly, but couldn't seem to muster a response. "Okay," he muttered into the empty room. Suddenly, he was aware what he must have looked like—standing in the middle of the kitchen, arms hanging limp at his sides, staring at the doorway like a pup waiting for his mistress to return home, doggy treat in hand. No woman had ever made him feel more like a mindless clod—not starlets or fashion models or female politicians.

Not that they hadn't tried.

And therein was the rub, he thought, dismissing how he'd messed up Shakespeare's line. Patrice had accomplished what the others couldn't, without even trying, which made her all the more desirable.

He sighed heavily and grabbed Gus's mug. *Since*

you're behaving like a mindless idiot, anyway, he told himself, heading for the family room, *you may as well perform a mindless chore.*

When Wade rounded the corner, Gus looked quickly away from the door. Did that guilty look mean he'd been spying on them? Or that he'd put two and two together and realized something was developing between his daughter and Wade?

One thing was sure: Gus had no objection to Wade's involvement in Patrice's life, and the proof was written all over his smiling face.

"Thanks," Gus said when Wade handed him the mug. "Where's Patrice?"

"Putting a bandage on her finger. She had a little run-in with a carving knife."

"Like the farmer's wife, eh?"

Chuckling, Wade said, "Something like that." He had to admit, Gus would score fairly well in the father-in-law department.

Patrice walked into the room just then, smiling that smile of hers, big brown eyes twinkling.

"See?" she said, bandaged finger aimed at the ceiling, "all better."

You'll make some guy a dynamite wife was his silent comment.

Some guy? Why not him?

He pocketed both hands, stood a little taller. *Why* not *me?* he wondered.

Chapter Six

He'd never been much good at small talk. Still, Wade felt he owed it to Patrice to have a go at it. With any luck, it would take her mind off Gus's pallid complexion—at least while they ate. "So I hear you're up for another award at the hospital," he told her.

Gus looked from his dinner guest to his daughter and back again. "Where'd you hear that?"

"Now that you mention it, I'm not sure." Wade gave it a moment's thought. "Personnel circulates a newsletter, I could've read it there. Either that, or it was tacked to one of the bulletin boards."

Gus aimed a suspicious glance at Patrice. "Well, it's news to me."

Wade couldn't help but notice that she quickly looked down and busied herself, tidying the napkin on the biscuit basket, rearranging the silverware beside her plate—making sure her hair covered her scar.

"Will there be a presentation?" Gus asked.

Uncertain if the question was intended for him or Patrice, Wade filled the uncomfortable pause with "I'm not sure." He leaned forward slightly, dipped his head to catch her eye. "Patrice, do you know if the hospital is planning an awards ceremony?"

In place of an answer, she held a finger in the air and sipped her water. Replacing the goblet on the table, she said, "Who wants more salad?" She started to stand. "There's plenty more in the kitchen—"

"Relax, Treecie," Gus said, "we have plenty of rabbit food right here." He put down his fork and turned to Wade. "So what's this award for?"

Obviously, there had been other awards Patrice hadn't told Gus about. Strange, because these two seemed so close.

His attention was quickly diverted by Patrice's uneasiness at the turn the conversation had taken. If he'd known the simple question would do this to her—though for the life of him, he didn't understand why it had—Wade never would have asked it. "I'd rather have another pork chop," he said, grinning as he reached for the meat platter. "How 'bout you, Gus? Care for seconds?"

A look of silent understanding passed between the men, as their eyes met briefly.

Gus harrumphed. "Nah. I'm stuffed."

"But Dad, you've barely had a bite to eat," she said, nodding toward his still-full plate. "You're still not feeling well?"

He shoved away from the table. "I'm fine. Just… I didn't sleep very well last night, is all." And turning the chair, he headed for the hall. "Think maybe I'll catch a few winks," he said, smiling weakly. "Wake me in half an hour or so. Maybe I'll feel like having a slice of cake with you guys."

She got to her feet as if to help Gus, but Wade shook

his head and gave the "okay" sign. He'd noticed when he arrived that her dad looked pale and tired. There had seemed to be no sense worrying them over what might be nothing; more than likely, a full belly would put the pink back into Gus's cheeks.

It had not.

"So what do you think?" she asked, once Gus had left the room.

Wade glanced toward the hall, where shadows crisscrossed through the spokes of Gus's chair, telling Wade that her father wanted to hear his answer, too. "I think you ought to let me help you get these dishes into the kitchen."

Patrice followed his gaze. "Okay," she said, nodding, "but I warn you, it's a—"

"—dirty job, but somebody's gotta do it," he finished.

Mouthing a silent *thank you,* she began stacking plates, chattering as she worked from her side of the table. "I can't believe how much I have to do tomorrow. I have to escort some corporate types around in the hopes of getting a donation to the Child Services Center, then there's a party in the Harriet Lane Clinic—all before ten." Looking up, she met his eyes. "How 'bout you?"

She looked afraid, troubled, sad, all at the same time. He remembered what she'd told him about Gus's accident. If she still felt responsible for his being in a wheelchair, she probably also blamed herself for every cough and sneeze and minuscule rise in temperature the man suffered. Wade wanted to take her in his arms, say something reassuring, something comforting. But he didn't, because if he hadn't learned anything else, his years as a cardiologist had taught him that even the most well-intended, carefully chosen words could be woefully in-adequate.

"I have back-to-back surgeries in the morning," he said, grabbing the silverware, "then rounds in the after-noon." He picked up the napkins. "Why? You thinking of inviting me to lunch?" When all else fails, he thought, resort to absurdity.

She met his eyes. "Do I look like the type of girl who makes a habit of asking men out on dates?"

"No," he said, returning her smile, "but there's a first time for everything."

In the instant of silence that followed, the unmistak-able *tick-a-tick-a-tick* of Gus's wheelchair told them he'd moved farther down the hall.

Patrice released an audible sigh of relief, then carried her load into the kitchen. Wade followed close behind. "I don't want you to worry," he said softly. "Remember what I said last night."

Plunking the dishes onto the counter, she turned on the hot water. "That it's probably nothing a little extra iron in his diet won't cure." Staring out the window above the sink, she added, "I hope and pray you're right."

Wade put the forks and knives next to the plates and stood close beside her. "We'll get to the bottom of it, whatever it is. I promise."

She looked up at him and smiled sadly. And when she leaned her head on his shoulder, his arm automati-cally went around her waist. Just a simple, unromantic gesture, really, one shared countless times by friends and family around the globe, probably since the dawn of Man.

If it was so unassuming, he wondered, why had his heart started beating faster? Stranger still, where were the usual warning bells that sounded when he got too close to a woman, too soon?

She sighed, a musical sound that, despite its whisper-softness, filtered into his head and reverberated there, like the strains of a sonata. And he realized that with Patrice, there was no such thing as "too close."

The admission spooked him. "I'm gonna check on your dad, okay?"

"Okay, Slick."

He faced her. "Slick?"

"I never figured you for one of those guys who'd resort to trickery to get out of doing the dishes."

Chuckling, he said, "One of the perks of my profession." Hands on her shoulders, he kissed her forehead. "Seriously, I won't be long. If you can wait a couple minutes—"

Patrice grabbed his hand and led him to the wide, arched doorway. "Don't be silly. I'll have this mess cleaned up before you can say 'open wide.'"

A sudden urge to bundle her in his arms and kiss her came over him. This time, he didn't resist. Several seconds into it, he opened one eye a slit.

Cheeks pink and eyes closed that way, she reminded him of the angel that had once topped his boyhood Christmas tree—sweet, innocent...and trusting. Every fiber in him yearned to protect her from heartache.

Without warning or reason, that night at the railroad tracks burst into his mind: flashing lights, sirens, the *whap-whap-whap* of helicopter blades as it airlifted a dying family man to University Hospital because of that reckless, ridiculous prank.

Once again he couldn't help but wonder who would protect her from *him?*

Straightening, Wade drove a hand through his hair and

gave a sideways nod. "I, uh, guess I'd better get in there, see how ol' Gus is doing."

It seemed she felt the chill, too, when they parted, for Patrice shivered slightly. "Well," she said, crossing both arms over her chest, "you know where to find me when you're finished."

He licked his lips...still tingling from their kiss, and watched her walk back to the sink. *So much for staying an arm's length away,* he chided himself. Wade knew where to find her, all right; she'd permeated his being, and he doubted he'd ever draw a breath again without thinking of her.

"You think maybe you can take his temperature and talk him into seeing his doctor tomorrow?" she said, then peeked over one shoulder.

He met her wide, hopeful eyes. "I'll give it all I've got," he promised.

"Thanks," she said, "'cause he's all *I've* got."

Her simple statement sliced through him like a knife, because he'd give anything to be able to say *That's where you're wrong, Patrice—you've got me.*

"I know the signs," Gus said, one hand in the air. "Every year about this time, I get bronchitis or pneumonia." He gave a noncommittal nod. "SOP in my condition, or so they tell me."

"Standard Operating Procedure?" Wade echoed. "Who fed you that line of bunk?"

A one-shouldered shrug this time. "My doctor, for one."

Wade hated to disagree with a peer, even one he'd never met. But it had always made him angry when medical professionals spouted inaccurate diagnoses and prognoses. "Lemme put it to you this way, Gus. That's malarkey. There's absolutely no reason to believe lung ailments should be part and parcel of being wheelchair-bound.''

Gus's dark brows rose slightly. "Really?"

Wade dismissed the suspicion in the man's voice; it wasn't at all unexpected for Gus to defend his doctor. Most patients were loyal to their physicians—sometimes to the death…. "You eat healthy meals, you live in a wholesome environment.'' He dragged the desk chair closer to Gus's bed. "Tell me, what kind of exercise do you get?''

Chuckling, Gus flexed his biceps. "How's a hundred chin-ups in a row sound?"

"Sounds great. Anything else?"

"Molly does stuff to my legs and feet every day.''

"'Stuff'?''

"Yeah, y'know…lifts 'em and flexes 'em—stuff like that.''

"Molly's a physical therapist?''

"Nah, but she's read up on all the latest, as it relates to paraplegia, that is.''

There was a note of personal pride in Gus's voice when he described his nurse. "How long have you two been together?''

Gus planted both palms on the mattress, shoved himself into a seated position. "Years and years. She was a friend of the family before—'' He cleared his throat, ran his tongue over his top teeth. "Her husband walked out on her, oh, about twenty years ago, when she lived across the street. Molly and my wife…''

His voice trailed off, and this time, a frown creased his brow before he continued. "They were like this,'' he said, forefinger crossing index finger. "Molly had to move away, sell the house after that bum ran off and left her.''

The words hit hard, right in the pit of Wade's stomach. Men who left their families were hard to like. What would jovial, accepting Gus McKenzie say if he knew Wade's father had done the same thing?

"She got herself an apartment," Gus was saying, "went to night school, got her nursing degree. She didn't come around as much, what with having to work two jobs to support herself, but we stayed in touch."

Gus grabbed the tumbler from his nightstand, took a long swallow of water. "Good thing, too, 'cause when this happened," he said, slapping his thigh, "we sure did need her." He met Wade's eyes to add, "Did you know she stays with me all day, then works the second shift at Howard County General?"

Wade shook his head. "No. I didn't. Sounds like a great gal and a good friend."

A look came over Gus's face just then, one that made Wade suspect Molly was more than a friend. Much more. Almost immediately, he dismissed the idea. They'd been together for years; if Gus and Molly had feelings for one another that were more than nurse–patient, why hadn't they—?

"So, you gonna take my temperature? Do an exam? Draw blood?"

Gus's question put Wade on his feet. "I told Patrice I'd check things out. I can do a more thorough job if you'd agree to come to my office tomorrow."

"What for? I already have a doctor."

"When was the last time your doctor did an EKG?"

He leaned against the pillows. "Can't say that I recall." His head popped up again and he asked, "Why?"

Skepticism rang loud in his question—not that Wade

blamed him. Wade was, after all, a virtual stranger...
with a hunch that Gus's recurring illnesses were connected, somehow, to a malfunctioning heart. But to
know anything for sure, Wade would have to run tests,
do a thorough exam. "Let's just say I'm nosy."

Seeing his answer hadn't satisfied Gus, Wade scooted
the chair forward another few inches, leaned elbows on
his knees. "I have this theory, see, that the heart's ven-
tricles and auricles can be compressed by sitting in a
wheelchair, causing obstruction of blood flow."

Gus grinned and pointed to the copy of *Gray's Anat-
omy* on his bookshelf. "You'd be amazed what a guy
will do to pass the time once he loses the use of his
legs."

Patrice hadn't said exactly what Gus had done for a
living before the accident, but since they used to live on
a farm Wade assumed that hard manual labor had probably been Gus's way of life. He admired the man for
having fought off self-pity and depression any way he
knew how when his physical activities had been seri-
ously curtailed after the accident.

"If I had to guess, I'd say I've read that book, oh,
fifteen, twenty times," Gus continued as he met Wade's
eyes. "So believe me when I tell you that I know a
ventricle from an auricle." He softened slightly to add,
"Nice try, Doc, but humor me, why don't you, and tell
me what you *really* think."

He took a deep breath and said, "I don't know. But
I promised Patrice I'd try to find out. That's why I'd like
you to come down to the office."

Gus settled back into the pillows again and gave an
approving nod. "That's more like it." Then he added,
"So what *are* your intentions toward my daughter, anyway?"

Gus's directness caught him off guard. If asked, he would have said questions like that went out with the horse and buggy. But then, he'd never dated any woman long enough to arouse her father's parental curiosity.

Wade pressed his back against the chair's slats and crossed both arms over his chest. "She's concerned about you, and I'm a doctor." Makes perfect sense, he told himself, *right?*

"Oh, I get it." Gus nodded sagely. "So all these visits, and lunches, dinners—they were for the purpose of interviewing her about my health."

Nothing could be further from the truth, but Wade held his tongue. He'd spent those hours with her because he enjoyed her company, because he respected her, because—

Because you're falling in love with her.

"Uncle," Wade said, both hands in the air. "I give up."

Gus wiggled his forefinger, and when Wade leaned closer, he whispered, "She's got a generous heart, that girl of mine, and it's put her in the corner more times than I care to count."

Wade sat back to ask "In the corner?"

"You run in the fast lane. Surely you've met girls like Patrice before, who fall head over heels almost from the first eye blink." Gus gave him a long, hard stare. "She's over twenty-one and all that—so she has no one to blame but herself for all the heartaches...." He narrowed his eyes and stared harder still. "But I'm her father, and wheelchair or not, I'll do what I can to protect her."

The image flashed in Wade's head of him, holding a dimple-kneed, rosy-cheeked baby girl who said around a toothless smile, "Da-da!" Unlikely as that prospect seemed, if Wade ever had a daughter, he'd likely feel exactly as Gus felt. "I haven't known your daughter long," he said, "but I can promise you this—I'll do what I can to protect her."

Gus studied his face for what seemed a long time before his stern expression softened slightly. "From herself? Or from you?"

It was a fair question, one that deserved an honest answer. "Both."

Nodding, Gus took another drink of water. "You seem like a good egg, Doc," he said, putting the glass back on the nightstand. "So okay, I'll come to your office tomorrow, let you run some tests…if it'll calm Patrice's fears." His hand formed a flesh-and-bone pistol. Aiming it at Wade, he said, "But you have to promise me something first."

"What?"

Gus was dead serious when he said, "If you find anything, you keep it to yourself, you hear? *I'll* be the one to decide what to tell Patrice about my health. Got it?"

He didn't bother to repeat the doctor–patient confidentiality part of his oath; he had a feeling Gus already knew, anyway. "Got it."

"So what time should I be there?"

"The afternoon is wide open. How's two o'clock?"

"I'll have Molly call your office first thing in the morning, get directions. She'll drop me off."

"Sounds good." Wade got to his feet. "Now tell me, where will I find a thermometer?"

"In the nightstand drawer over there. Why?"

Shaking the instrument down, Wade shrugged. "Told Patrice I'd do it, that's why."

Gus rolled his eyes. "I might've known." Then he added, "Word to the wise, Doc. Watch what you say to that girl. She has a memory like a steel trap, and she'll hold you to every word that comes out of your mouth.''

Sliding the thermometer between Gus's lips, Wade said, ''Thanks for the tip.'' He could hardly believe his own ears when he added, ''So does that mean you approve? You don't mind if I keep seeing your daughter?''

With a wink and a sly grin, Gus answered his question.

Wade stared at his watch's face, pretending to follow the second hand as it counted the minutes. *So this is how it feels,* he thought, *to make a commitment.*

He held his breath, half expecting that, at any second, a bolt of lightning and a crash of thunder would sound to let him know he'd made a dreadful, life-altering mistake.

But all he heard were Gus's soft breaths and the soft *chik-chik-chik* of the wristwatch.

And the rib-racking throbbing of his heart.

Patrice couldn't help noticing that Wade looked tired and drawn when he came into the kitchen. She could only hope it didn't mean something awful was wrong with Gus. ''I just poured myself some tea. Want me to fix you a cup?''

He slumped into a ladder-back chair. ''That's be great.''

''And how about some dessert?''

''Sure. Why not?''

''Cherry pie or chocolate cake?''

''Surprise me.''

He sounded even more exhausted than he looked. Which worried her, because he'd seemed fine when he went into Gus's room....

Patrice slid a knife from the countertop block. ''So,''

she said, cutting a wedge from the chocolate cake, "you going to tell me what's on your mind, or do I have to 'feed' it out of you?"

He looked at the huge wedge and grinned. "You don't really expect me to eat the whole thing, do you?"

At least smiling, he looked a little less weary. She grabbed a fork from the silverware drawer. "Waste not, want not," she said, handing it to him.

"He's got a low-grade fever."

"How low?"

"Almost one hundred," he said. "Not too bad, considering temperatures naturally rise at night."

"I thought that was an old wives' tale."

"Maybe," he said around a bite of cake, "but nobody has been able to explain why so many old wives were right about so many things."

The slight twinkle in his hazel eyes made him look more handsome, if that was possible. "You think he picked up a bug somewhere? Or is the fever caused by something else?"

He met her eyes, and for a moment only stared at her. Without thinking, she finger-combed her hair over the scar.

"Don't do that," he said, his voice gravelly and quiet.

"Don't do what?"

"Hide behind your hair that way. No need to hide that gorgeous face. Especially not from me."

She felt the heat of a blush color her cheeks.

"This is terrific, by the way." He used his fork as a pointer.

No one had ever looked at her quite that way—with such admiration, such caring. Not even Gus. *Lord,* she prayed, *show me a sign of some sort...if this is the man*

You've chosen for me, tell me now, before I get in any deeper.

But who was she kidding? The only way she'd get in any deeper was if Wade said he loved her, too.

Too?

So there it was, out in the open. Knowing how stupid it would be to dive feetfirst into another relationship, she'd been trying to deny it for days, now, pretending the pleasant conversations were part of every budding friendship and nothing more.

He poked out his tongue just then, to catch a crumb of cake that had stuck to his upper lip...and reminding her of the sweet kisses they'd shared. Kisses that had warmed her heart and soul, making her wonder if they'd inspired "forever" thoughts in Wade's mind, too.

"Gus agreed to come to my office tomorrow."

Blinking, she looked up. "He did?"

Wade grinned. "You sound surprised." Chopping off another forkful of cake, he said, "I can be mighty persuasive when I put my mind to it."

"Really." *Then, persuade me to be your one and only* was the silent message she sent him.

She swallowed, feeling silly and irrational and a whole lot foolish.

Wade met her eyes, and for an instant, as she probed the glittering, golden eyes and gentle smile, she wondered if maybe he'd read her mind.

Would he start trying to persuade her?

She sipped her tea. "So what time is his appointment?"

"Two o'clock. Gus said Molly would drop him off. Then you can pick him up after he's finished."

"Sounds good. What tests will you run?" she asked.

He took a drink of his own tea. "I want to do the

whole nine yards—EKG, EEG, CAT scan, MRI, blood work...."

She bit her lower lip. "What will you be looking for?"

"Nothing, everything," he said, shrugging. "This is routine, to rule out anything serious that might be causing the fevers and—"

She wrapped her hands around her mug and squeezed it tight. "But, you must suspect something. Why else would you run a battery of tests?"

He pressed his hands atop hers. "You've been around doctors and hospitals enough to know that most of the time, our so-called detective work doesn't turn up a thing."

"And sometimes, it turns up something horrible."

"Then, it's good to catch it early, isn't it?"

Pulse racing, she stared at their hands. "I suppose."

"Except for his occasional bouts with bronchitis and pneumonia, he tells me he's been healthy as a horse."

That much was true, but still...

"Then, you have nothing to worry about." He gave her hands a gentle squeeze. "Where's your faith? I thought all you Christians believe it's a sin to worry."

The way he'd said "all you Christians" told her he wasn't a believer. On the other hand, he'd known the Christian attitude toward worry. Could it mean that maybe, once upon a time, he had been a follower? Because if he had, it wouldn't be such a long walk back...with a little help from his friends....

Show me the way, Lord, she prayed, *show me the way.*

Still holding her hands, he added, "And if I haven't worn Gus out too badly, maybe the three of us can go to Little Italy for dinner."

"Be careful what you ask for," she warned, smiling.

"Gus *loves* Italian food. He'll say yes even if he's down to one ounce of energy left."

"Good, because I'm looking forward to getting to know him better."

He was looking forward to getting to know her father better? What could that mean, except—

"Well, guess I'd better be makin' tracks," Wade said, getting to his feet. "My first surgery starts at eight."

"Let me pack up some dessert for you first." She rummaged in a cabinet for a plastic container. Not the throw-away kind, but one that would have to be returned.

"But it's just me at home—"

"It'll keep a week in the fridge." And as she slid a thick slab of each dessert into the bowl, Patrice added, "Just microwave a slice at a time when you're in the mood...unless you like cold cake or pie."

"Guess I've learned to live with 'cold.'"

She heard more in his grating tone than a simple response to her question; there was a certain sadness, and loneliness, too. Patrice snapped the lid in place. "What do you mean?"

"Don't have a microwave."

He'd recovered nicely...or so he thought. Patrice wondered who he thought he was fooling with that stand-up-tall demeanor and practiced smile.

Patrice flashed her best imitation of a smile. "No microwave? You're kidding, right?"

"Even if I had one, I doubt my landlady's electrical system could power it. Besides, there's barely room in my kitchen for *me*."

"Must be one small apartment...."

"It's a studio. Bet the whole thing could fit into your living room."

"You're a big-shot doc," she teased. "Surely you can afford a house."

His smile vanished more quickly than a candle's flame can be doused, making her regret her little joke.

"Guess I just never saw the point. I mean, what's a single guy need with a whole big house?"

"Don't you ever entertain?"

"Never saw much point in that, either."

Patrice got a picture of a cramped, dimly lit place, furnished with relatives' dull castoffs, and had to bite her lower lip to keep the tears at bay. Wade deserved better. He was the kind of man who made women want to do more than send him home with leftover sweets; surely they were lined up for blocks, waiting to cook a meal, do his laundry, make sure he started every day with a healthy breakfast.

Patrice got a picture of the snaking string of females, each looking longingly at handsome, intelligent and thoughtful Dr. Wade Cameron. She quickly blinked the image away, because she wanted to be the only woman in that line!

"See you tomorrow, then." He picked up the blue-lidded plastic bowl and grinned. "And thanks for breakfast."

Walking beside him into the foyer, she waved his gratitude away. "I'll say a prayer for you tonight."

He chuckled. "Whatever for?"

"So you'll get a good night's sleep," she said, opening the front door. "You'll need to be well rested. For surgery tomorrow."

One side of his mouth lifted in a boyish grin. "That's downright sweet, Patrice. Thanks."

But she didn't want his thanks; she wanted his heart.

"You have a good night's sleep, too." He put the

bowl on the table beside the door and took a step closer, slid his arms around her.

He didn't say he'd pray for her, she noted.

His brows furrowed slightly as he inspected her face. "You gonna be okay?"

She nodded.

"'Cause chances are real good that Gus will be fine, y'know."

Another nod.

"Dinner was great. Did I tell you that already?"

He hadn't, but she nodded again.

For a moment, he stood there, simply staring at her, wearing a flirty half smile on his face that confused and exhilarated her at the same time.

Patrice had always prided herself at being able to read people's expressions; it was but one of the reasons she interacted so successfully with hospitalized kids. But if someone asked her to define Wade's emotions right now, she'd be at a total loss.

Strong and rock-solid, he had all the qualities of the right man...of a *husband*. But he wasn't interested in her. Not in a permanent kind of way.

Or was he?

He had flirted, blatantly, right from the get-go. It had been Wade who'd sought out her company, not the other way around. And he'd hinted that since they were friends, she should feel free to talk about her childhood, the recent past, the present.

But he hadn't told her a single thing about himself.

Sometimes, he wore the weathered look of a man who'd slung more than his share of burdens across his shoulders. What sort of suffering had created those burdens? Patrice could only hope that one day he'd tell her, and that when he did, she'd have the grit to behave like a true friend.

Something told her she'd need more than strength, though, if he unfolded his past for her to see, because nothing short of "horrible" could have put that haunted look in his beautiful eyes.

His face moved ever so slowly closer, making her wonder what this latest mysterious expression meant. That he was falling in love with her, too? Or did he simply intend to kiss her good-night?

He didn't leave her wondering for long.

His lips pressed against hers, gently at first, then more firmly. It felt so good, so *right* to be in his arms. She read it as a sign that God approved of this relationship; would it feel this wonderful if He *didn't* approve?

Yes, Wade was tall and well muscled, more than capable of taking care of himself. But how was she to explain the way he melted against her, trembling slightly, murmuring softly as his warm breath puffed against her cheek?

She sensed his vulnerability, and it made her feel strong. Strong enough to risk loving him so completely, so thoroughly that the pain of the past would soon become a distant memory. It didn't seem quite so scary this time, taking that leap of faith....

Tenderly, she wove her fingers through his shining waves and gathered him near, inviting him into her heart, into her soul, into her *life*.

Chapter Seven

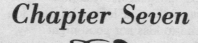

Gus stared out the window behind Wade's desk, while beside him, Patrice fidgeted with her purse strap. "What's taking him so long?" she wondered aloud. "How long could it possibly take to read a few—"

"Easy, kiddo," Gus said, laying a hand on her arm. "He put a rush on the test results—something he'll pay for till this time next year, probably."

She met his eyes. "What do you mean, he'll pay for?"

He shrugged nonchalantly. "I heard him on the phone, barking orders at some li'l gal down in the lab. He didn't go too easy on the fella in radiology, either." He shook his head. "You've worked in this place long enough to understand the pecking order isn't something to mess with."

True enough. For all its medical miracles, Ellicott General had its share of bureaucratic red tape; she'd learned long ago that if she wanted something done, correctly and quickly, a honeyed attitude beat a sour one any day of the week. "Oh, great," she complained. "I can just see us a month from now, cobwebs hanging from our noses, still sitting here waiting to get your test results.''

''Sorry, kiddo, I know how you hate to wait.'' Gus patted her hand. ''And who can blame you. I guess you've done more than your fair share of waiting in your lifetime, haven't you.''

Patrice hadn't meant it to sound as though she held Gus responsible for the delay, and started to say so.

Using a bent forefinger, Gus closed her mouth. ''If you had a dollar for every hour you sat alone in cold waiting rooms while your mom and I waited for your brother, you'd be a rich young woman.''

''I never minded. I was too worried about Timmy to pay much attention to anything else.''

''I know,'' Gus said, smiling. ''Which is just one of the thousands of reasons I love you to pieces.''

''I love you, too.'' Which was the *only* reason she'd spent a good part of the night on her knees, begging God to make sure there'd be nothing serious wrong with her dad. This morning, though achy and drowsy, she'd faced the day with a smile. And why wouldn't she? God had promised that with faith the size of a mustard seed, she could move mountains, hadn't He?

''Okay, out with it,'' Gus said.

She looked up quickly. ''Out with what?''

''What's eatin' you?''

''Nothing.''

''Don't give me that. You've been acting…*weird* ever since you sat down there.'' He grabbed her hand, gave it an affectionate squeeze. ''I'm gonna be fine, just fine.'' He leaned forward, forcing her to meet his eyes. ''You know that, right?''

Patrice nodded. ''Sure, I do.'' She smiled. ''You've

been at the top of my prayer list for...forever. Why *wouldn't* you be all right!''

He raised one eyebrow, tucked in one corner of his mouth. ''Now, why do I get the feeling my leg's being pulled?''

She was uncomfortable when he made any reference to ''feeling'' in his lower body. Shifting position in the chair, she fiddled with her purse strap some more.

''Did I ever tell you the story about the carrot, the egg and the coffee bean?''

Patrice grinned. ''Only about a thousand times.''

He sat back, pretended to be offended. ''Okay, then, smarty-pants. Since you know it so well, you tell it to *me*.''

Smiling gently, Patrice sighed and told the tale she knew so well. ''A teary-eyed young woman went to her father and said, 'Life is horrible! Everything is always going wrong. It seems the harder I try, the worse things get. What's the point of even trying!'''

Gus nodded approvingly. So far, so good, she thought.

''So her father, a chef, took her by the hand and led her into the kitchen,'' Patrice continued, ''where he put three pots of water on the stove and started them boiling. After a while, he put raw carrots in one pot, raw eggs into another and coffee beans in the—''

''Don't forget,'' Gus injected, ''how he turned on the gas under each pot....''

Patrice put a finger over her lips to silence him, and, laughing, proceeded with the fable.

''Soon, the father took the pots from the stove, cooled them under running water, and asked his daughter to feel the carrots.

'''They're all squishy,' she said.

Gus took the part of the father. '''And the eggs?'''

Humoring him, Patrice played the daughter. "'Hard!'"

"'What about the coffee beans?'"

"The daughter peeked into that pot and said, 'They've turned the water a rich, dark brown, and it smells delicious.'"

"'So which are you?'"

"'I don't know, Father.'"

"'If the boiling water represents life's hardships,'" Gus said in a voice two octaves deeper than his own, "'something in one of the pots represents you. Are you the carrot, who goes into adversity hard...and comes out weak and soft? Or arc you like the egg, starting out with a fluid center that turns brittle and rigid when tested by trouble?'"

Sandwiching her hand between his own, Gus said, "I'll tell you which you are, Treecie...."

Patrice knew what he'd say, because he'd said it every time she helped him through a physical trial.

"You're the coffee bean, who takes disaster and makes something useful of it."

In her mind, there had been no nobility in what she'd done for him. If not for her own immaturity and self centeredness, he'd bc the hale and hearty man he had been before the accident. A sob ached in her throat at the memory of that night....

"Softie," Gus said, thinking his words had caused her tears.

Patrice shook her forefinger at him. "Dad, you know what that story does to me." Not the truth, exactly, but not a lie, either.

He gave her a playful shove as she poked around in her purse for a tissue. She laughed. "I'm depending on you to explain to Wade why I'm blubbering like a baby."

Pacing just outside the door, Wade tried to screw up the courage to face them. After all these years, shouldn't it be easier to deliver bad news to patients and their families? he wondered. If not easier, then less awkward, at least. Overhearing that fable and being witness to the closeness of this father and daughter sure hadn't helped matters.

He took a deep breath and, tucking Gus's file under his arm, walked into the room. "Sorry it took so long," he said, settling into the high-backed black chair. He laid the folder on his desk, patted it with the palm of his hand.

Gus shrugged. "Hey, you can't expect miracles from mere mortals."

Almost from the moment he'd finished Gus's exam, Wade had been doing verbal battle with four hospital departments. But neither calm pleas nor irate shouts had inspired their cooperation, and he knew little more about Gus's condition now than before he'd arrived. "Maybe not," he blurted, "but we should be able to expect—" Wade cut himself off mid-sentence. It was important for patients to believe their medical professionals were always operating at the top of their game; to show anger and frustration only proved the opposite.

"So how soon till we hear something?" Gus asked.

Stifling a sigh of frustration, Wade ran a hand through his hair. "Two days, three at most, I expect." He tried a smile.

"What do we do in the meantime," Patrice interjected, "about Dad's fever, his loss of appetite, his insomnia...?"

"Lots of liquids and NSAIDs," Wade said. He extended his hands in a gesture of helplessness. "Afraid that's the best I can do until I have a little more concrete evidence."

"Evidence of what?" she asked. "Surely you have some idea what's causing Dad's problems."

Yeah. He did. But to admit it now would only worry them. He tried a wider smile. "It's really too early to speculate."

She held his gaze, her eyes boring hotly into his, as if she expected to find answers to all her questions imprinted on his pupils. Wade looked away—feigned busyness by tidying a stack of papers on his blotter, adjusting the cord, paging through his calendar—because he wasn't at all sure he could hide his concern from her.

From his very first patient ever to the one sitting before him, he'd had to work harder than his contemporaries to keep a safe, professional distance. Being driven by emotions instead of cold, hard facts, Wade feared, would cost him the "edge" that allowed him to make choices, state hard facts, do the right thing by those under his care.

Like it or not, he'd crossed that invisible line on this one, big time. And if he didn't do something about it, fast, who knew how things would turn out?

He'd invited them to dinner. He could only hope they'd forgotten, or that Gus would rather head home to catch that TV show he'd been raving about during the examination.

Gus furrowed his brow. "You said I should take NSAIDs…?"

Grateful for even the slight change of subject, Wade said, "Aspirin, ibuprofen—anti-inflammatory and fever-reducing products."

"Doctors," Gus said on a laugh. "You guys could save us all a lot of time, y'know, if you'd just speak English to start with."

The man had a point, and Wade admitted it.

"So what's this I hear about dinner in Little Italy?"

Patrice's response was to wrap both hands around the strap of her purse, flexing her fingers on its buckle. "You sure you're up for it, Dad?"

"Yeah, Gus," Wade said, "it's been a long, hard day. We can take a rain check if you're—"

"You guys are kiddin', right?" He looked from his daughter to Wade and back again.

Patrice and Wade exchanged an uncomfortable glance.

"Who knows when I'll get another chance to wolf down some of Chiaparelli's gnocchi?"

"What does *that* mean?" Patrice said, laughing. "It isn't like this is our last chance to have dinner in Little Italy. It's only a twenty-minute drive from our house, so—"

"Yeah, well, there's a lot riding on those test results."

She stood abruptly and raised her hands, like someone being held up at gunpoint. "I won't listen to that kind of talk. You're going to be fine. You *have* to be fine—" she sat again, looking embarrassed at her outburst "—because I am *not* training another chess partner!"

Nice save, Wade told her mentally.

Sort of. She might have fooled Gus with that whole giggle-and-tease routine of hers, *but you're not foolin' me.* Wade had heard the tremor in her voice, had seen the way her hands trembled, too. The rapid rise and fall of her chest told him her pulse and heart rates had increased at the mere thought of losing her dad.

If he had it in his power, Wade would snap his fingers

and fix everything that was wrong in her life, starting with Gus. But since he didn't, the least he could do was try to steer the conversation in a more positive direction. "So, how do you guys want to work this?"

"Work what?" she asked him.

"The trip to Chiaparelli's—who's driving?"

Wade wondered how much longer the purse strap would hold up under all that nervous fidgeting; he knew why *he* didn't want to go to dinner, but what was Patrice's reason?

"Need the van—" Gus slapped the arms of his chair "—for Ol' Bessie, so I guess you'd better ride with us."

"That'd be great if I didn't have surgery first thing in the morning. How 'bout I just follow you over there?"

"Sounds good to me," Patrice said, smiling stiffly.

She'd been so relaxed, completely at ease with him during dinner at her house. Could Gus's uncertain condition be the cause of her jitters? Or had she been thinking what *he'd* been thinking—that this…whatever it was, developing between them, wasn't such a good idea?

He hoped not. And that made no sense. No sense at all.

Wade stood, hung his lab coat on the tree behind his desk and shrugged into his sports jacket. "Ready?" he said, holding the door.

Gus rolled toward the door. "I was born ready, so let's blow this pop stand!"

As Patrice walked beside her father to the elevator, Wade followed close behind, telling himself this had to be the last time he saw her on a personal basis. *Had* to be. Once he had his—what had he called it?—nyaw-kee, Patrice would drive him home. And that would be it. Period. End of story. Because it wouldn't be fair to string out this…this *whatever* it was, any longer than necessary.

Wouldn't be fair?

Fair to whom?

Gus grumbled about the weather, asked Patrice about her day; she told him about a kid who'd nearly pulled Mort's leg off, then said something about a puppet show for the kids. Before Wade knew it, he heard Gus say, "Well, this is our floor."

Wade had been so deep in thought, he barely noticed they'd entered the parking garage, let alone that they were standing at the first-floor elevator. "I'm on three," he said, hitting the up button. "I'll meet you over there, okay?"

Gus nodded. "Park out front. I'll spring for valet parking."

"You don't have to—"

"Hey, it's only fair, since you're paying for dinner." He wiggled his eyebrows. "Besides," he added, straight-faced, "I have a favor to ask you."

Wade waited to hear what it was.

"You up for hoistin' an old cripple into the restaurant?"

Patrice gasped. "Dad, really!"

"What," he said, laughing, "you think maybe the Politically Correct Police will slap cuffs on me for saying 'cripple'?" He spread his arms as if to say *look at me!* "If I don't have a problem with the word, why should anybody else?"

"Chiaparelli's doesn't have wheelchair access," Patrice explained to Wade.

He squeezed Gus's shoulder as half a dozen clichés flitted through his mind: When life gives you lemons, make lemonade; make the best of a bad situation; don't cry over spilt milk…. He had to give the guy credit, because self-pity was the last thing Gus wanted.

"Okay," Wade said, "but I think it's only fair to warn you…I had Caesar salad for lunch."

Smirking mischievously, Gus made a rolling motion with his hands. "And that's relevant because…?"

"Well," he said, looking around conspiratorially, "you might not get arrested for saying 'cripple,' but I'll bet my garlic breath violates *some* kind of law." He fanned a hand in front of his face.

Gus rolled himself over to his van. "I like this guy, Treecie," he said over his shoulder.

Wade found himself following, then, without so much as a second thought, he helped Gus into the passenger seat.

Funny thing, but *Wade* liked Wade in the presence of these people. It made no sense, really, feeling so comfortable with this middle-aged, wheelchair-bound guy and his pretty daughter, considering he'd spent so few hours in their company. But there it was, easy to read as the graffiti on the garage's concrete.

"I like him, too," she said, "even if he is a doctor."

Wade waited until Patrice walked around to the driver's side of the van to ask Gus, "What's that supposed to mean?"

Putting a hand beside his mouth, he whispered, "Last guy who broke her heart was a doctor." After a quick check to make sure Patrice couldn't hear, he quickly added, "Matter of fact, so was the one before that."

Wade wasn't too proud that members of his profession had hurt her. Worse still, she'd fallen hard enough for the bozos that they could hurt her in the first place.

But what did it matter if he was her first love or not,

when after tonight, they'd only be together professionally...if at all?

"See you in a few minutes," Patrice said, sliding in behind the steering wheel.

As Gus slammed the passenger door, Wade winked and saluted, then headed for his car.

Winked and saluted! Confused by his own spontaneous behavior, he shook his head. The longer he was around her, the more he behaved like a knobby-kneed youngster, and frankly, Wade didn't know if he liked the feeling; if this "kid stuff" was a sign he'd started backsliding to boyhood, was there a chance his acne would come back? Grinning at the thought, he headed back to the elevator.

During the drive from Elliott General to High Street, Wade pondered his peculiar actions. On the one hand, he couldn't deny that Patrice's optimism and enthusiasm were contagious; being around her made him feel energetic, younger than he had in years. Amazing in itself, he'd felt a hundred years old, emotionally, since before he could vote. And the way she looked at him, as if he'd invented the airplane and earned a hero's medal and won a Pulitzer, well, what man wouldn't like being around a woman like that!

On the other hand, she scared him witless, because though he'd dated several women over the years, not one had managed to get him thinking the *C* word, let alone thinking about saying it out loud. Commitment wasn't his style. Or so he'd told himself since before he could vote....

When he pulled up behind the van in front of the restaurant and watched her climb out of the driver's seat with a peppy little hop, his ears went hot and his hands got cold. If he didn't know better, he'd say he was coming down with something.

Something like love?

Scrubbing both hands over his face, he groaned. *Get a grip, man, before—*

Patrice knocked gently on the hood of his car. He looked up, saw her wave as she passed in front of him. And while she was busy helping Gus out of the van, an image flashed in his mind: Patrice, in a rocking chair, humming nursery rhymes to their baby girl. *Their* baby girl!

He shook his head. *If you know what's good for you—and her—you'll cut it out, and pronto!*

Handing his car keys to the valet, Wade joined Patrice and Gus on the sidewalk. They both looked slightly self-conscious, as if the prospect of getting Gus inside might be more traumatic for him than for Gus. After giving the situation a quick once-over, Wade decided the door was plenty wide enough to accommodate the wheelchair. Grabbing its handles, he rolled Gus nearer the porch. Patrice held the door open as Wade backed the chair up the steps.

The hostess guided them to their table, sliding a chair aside to make room for Gus. They were barely settled when a resonant baritone called, "Patrice? Patrice McKenzie, is that you?"

Her blush told Wade she'd recognized the man's voice; the fact that she didn't turn around told him the guy was probably one of the doctors Gus had mentioned.

A tall, swarthy man in his early thirties stepped up to the table. "Patrice," he said, "it really *is* you."

She pressed her fingertips to her temples for a moment before looking into his face. "John. What a surprise."

If *John* noticed that her voice had lost every bit of its

beautiful musicality, it didn't show. The way he stood, ramrod straight and hair slicked back, reminded Wade of a silent movie actor.

Crouching beside her chair, John shook Gus's hand. "Good to see you, too, sir."

Patrice's dad grunted and pumped John's arm up and down. If he kept that up, Wade thought, water might just start to trickle from John's fingertips!

"This place is a little, uh, *unposh* for the likes of you, isn't it, *John?*"

As if he hadn't heard Gus's sarcasm, John nodded toward a table near the back wall. "Birthday party."

Gus peered around him at the merrymakers. "You with the blonde or the brunette?" Then he turned to Wade. "See," he whispered loudly, pointing with his thumb, "this guy left Treecie for a blonde." He said it matter-of-factly, as if ordering an iced tea from the waitress.

It was almost imperceptible the way John's lips thinned and his eyes narrowed. Almost.

Smiling, Patrice turned slightly in her chair. "Whose birthday?"

Said a bit too brightly, Wade thought.

John smiled.

More like a sneer, Wade decided.

"You remember Jenna?"

"Of course" was her snappy retort. "Your youngest sister."

Who could blame her for sounding piqued, Wade thought; the guy's tone made it clear he didn't think Patrice was smart enough to remember.

"Jenna's the brunette," John said to Gus.

Patrice tilted her head. "My. I haven't seen her in... How long has it been?"

Her eyes were glittering, as if she was getting ready to let it fly with both barrels. A decent person would've warned John to back off. But Wade wasn't feeling particularly charitable toward a guy who had hurt Patrice.

"So how is Jenna?" Patrice asked.

Said like any woman scorned, Wade mused...with just the right amount of icy bitterness in her voice.

"It's been nearly five years," John said, feigning hurt that she hadn't remembered. "Say, here's an idea. Why don't you join us, and ask her yourself."

"We were just about to order," she said.

John looked at Wade then, as if seeing him for the first time. "Who's your...friend?"

Laughing, Gus said, "Sorry, seems we clean forgot our manners." He slapped Wade's forearm. "This good-lookin' young fella here is Dr. Wade Cameron." He slid a disapproving glance to John. "Wade, meet John Travers. He's a doctor, too."

John's hand shot across the table. "Good to meet you," he said as Wade shook it.

"Same here." *Liar,* he told himself.

John adjusted the knot of his navy silk tie. "What's your specialty?" He tugged at his French cuffs, revealing diamond-studded cuff links.

Who wore those things anymore? Wade wondered. "Cardiology," he said. "Yours?"

"Plastic surgery."

Wonder how much work he's done on himself? "I see."

"Well, John," Gus put in, "we don't want to keep you from your little party. You have a good time, y'hear? And *do* wish the birthday girl many happy returns." With that, he picked up his menu and motioned for Wade and Patrice to do the same.

But John wasn't so easily dismissed. He pulled out Patrice's chair and took her hand. "Seriously, you have to come say hello. Mom would love to see you again, and you know Jenna always thought the world of you...."

She did it with grace and ladylike charm, but there was no mistaking her mood: "I think not," she said, sliding her hand from his grasp.

If they hadn't been in a crowded restaurant, Wade would have hugged her for that!

"Well, then. Yes." John cleared his throat. "See you later."

Or not, Wade thought as the man walked stiffly away.

"Jerk," Gus muttered.

"Da-a-ad," Patrice whispered. "It was a long, long time ago. Let bygones be bygones, okay? I have."

"That's because you're a better person than I am."

"No...it's because I prayed about it. You know...'what would Jesus do'?"

"I think even Jesus would o' had a hard time bein' nice to that guy." He put down his menu. "'Cause for one thing, he's a jerk."

Wade didn't quite agree with Gus. If John passed up a chance at having Patrice in his life, he wasn't a jerk. He was a *fool*.

"I need to use the ladies' room," she said, rising. And grabbing her purse, she looked at Wade. "If the waitress asks what we'd like to drink while I'm gone, will you order me a glass of water with a lemon wedge, please?"

What was it with this woman? If she put her mind to it, she could probably brand a man with those big brown peepers of hers. She blinked once, twice, luscious lashes dusting her freckled cheeks.

On second thought, Wade decided, she could brand a

man with those eyes even if she *didn't* have a mind to. "Uh, sure," he stammered, "glad to."

"Don't be too long," Gus cautioned.

Patrice clutched her purse to her chest and pouted prettily. "Only long enough for you to tell Wade how John Jerk broke my poor widdo heart." She punctuated her comment with a giggle and left them alone.

If he were a praying man, Wade would have prayed Gus wouldn't do that. He didn't want to hear the details involving Patrice's feelings for some other guy.

Unfortunately, the Green-eyed Monster seemed to have taken a nasty bite out of him; picturing her with another man made Wade want to punch the nearest wall. He'd never been jealous over a woman. The fact that he had the feeling now unnerved him, scared him.

But the bigger problem, as he saw it, wasn't *how* he felt, but *why,* because only one thing could explain it.

He'd gone and fallen in love with the Monkey Lady.

Alone in the ladies' room, Patrice stood at the mirror, applying lipstick, fussing with her hair and hoping she wouldn't run into John again before leaving the restaurant. It hadn't been a messy breakup—because she'd chosen to walk away with her dignity intact. Which might have been easier, if he hadn't been so *honest* about his reasons for dumping her.

He believed her never-ending devotion to Gus was unnatural, unhealthy and, quoting an issue of *Psychology Today,* called her an "enabler." "Gus will never be able to live on his own if you don't quit babying him," he'd said. To this day, she hadn't figured out why he'd felt it necessary to add, "Besides, I'm seeing someone new." She'd asked him to please keep the particulars to himself, yet John felt duty-bound to "'fess up": "She's the most beautiful woman I've ever seen, perfect in every way.'' Patrice hadn't needed a Mensa membership to figure out what *that* meant.

Staring into the mirror at the scar, Patrice slid her comb back into the outer pocket of her purse and remembered how, when they'd first met, he'd said the scar didn't matter. That's what they'd all said…at first. *And you believed them, you little ninny.* Like the rest, Wade had said it, too. Would there come a time when being seen in public with her would be a burden for him, as well?

"Say it ain't so, Lord," she prayed, looking at the sad-eyed woman in the mirror. "Let him be *the one*…."

Rolling her eyes, she sucked in a deep breath, let it out slowly. *Get back out there,* she told herself, *before you drown in self-pity!* Raising her chin a notch, she slung her purse over one shoulder and made her way back to the table, determined to make the best of this evening, of every evening she might have with Wade— because who knew when he'd want to put a stop to things?

You silly twit, she chided. *There's nothing to put a stop to!* He'd been the perfect gentleman; hadn't made a single promise, hadn't so much as hinted at a future with her. He was a good guy, so his sweet gestures, his kind words, had merely been a result of his basic decency.

If she'd conduct herself like a grown-up for once, instead of a teenybopper in the throes of a knee-weakening crush, maybe she could avoid looking like a colossal fool a week, a month, six months from now; maybe she could sidestep another shattered heart.

She caught sight of his profile as she neared the table. There wasn't an actor in Hollywood who wouldn't give up a major role to have a smile, a chin, a *face* like that. And there wasn't an actress in the world who wouldn't do the same for a chance to star opposite him on the big screen.

Her acting skills were so bad, she considered herself lucky to have played trees and cereal boxes and clouds in school plays, but tonight, she'd have to put on the performance of her life…and *act* as though she hadn't fallen noggin over knees for him.

As promised, Wade had ordered her a tall glass of water, complete with a slice of lemon. "Thanks," she said, taking her seat. And in a voice much brighter than her mood, she added, "So, what's everybody having for dinner?"

Gus shot an "Are you kidding?" look in her direction. "You get three guesses, and the first two don't count."

She glanced at Wade. "You're both having gnocchi?"

Nodding, he shrugged. "I like to try new things. Spices life up, dontcha think?"

Patrice sent him a smile that she didn't mean, because she read that to mean *she* was that "Spice": *Give the girl with the scar a test run, Wade old boy; you've never done anything like* that *before, have you!*

"How 'bout you?" Gus asked her. "You gonna order the same ol', same ol'? Or something different for a change?"

She tucked her hair behind her ears. *How's that for different?* was her defiant question.

Gus grinned. "I'll take that as a no." And turning to Wade, he said, "Well, there's one thing to be said for predictability."

Grinning, Wade put in, "I've always hated surprises."

And how predictable of him to come to her defense,

Patrice thought. "Then, you must love me like crazy!" she blurted.

Instantly, she slapped both hands over her mouth, prayed the raucous laughter of the salesmen at a nearby table had drowned out her words. But Wade had heard her, all right, and the proof was written all over his red-cheeked, wide-eyed face.

Their waitress stepped up to the table just then. Bella, her name tag read. "Have you folks decided what you'd like to order?"

Saved by the Bella, Patrice thought, grinning sardonically.

"I'll have the gnocchi," Gus said.

"Same here," Wade echoed.

Pen poised above her pad, Bella looked at Patrice. "And you, ma'am?"

"Um, sure. Okay...." She looked at the menu, but it was no use. She couldn't focus on anything except her dopey declaration. Patrice looked up at Bella. "I, uh... Me, too."

The waitress tucked the tablet into her apron pocket and picked up their menus. "Gnocchi times three," she said. "I'll be back in a jiffy with your salads."

While Patrice took tiny sips of her water and Wade picked at a loose thread on his napkin, Gus polished his spoon with a corner of the tablecloth. "Just wait till you taste this salad, Doc," he said, breaking the clumsy silence. And touching all four fingertips to his thumb, he smacked his lips. *"Bellissima!"*

Wade held Patrice's gaze for a spellbinding moment. "You can say that again" was his grating reply. "Then you can say it *again.*"

Heart beating like a parade drum, she swallowed.

Whether he meant it or not didn't much matter, because she was a goner.

Give me strength, Lord, she prayed, looking into Wade's mesmerizing eyes, *But it sure would be nice if I didn't need it.*

Chapter Eight

It wasn't like Gus to fall asleep in the car. If he hadn't endured endless hours of medical tests, Patrice knew, he'd be wide awake now, saying "Watch out for that truck!" or "There's a red light up ahead!" Much as she appreciated the quiet, it unnerved her.

Would the tests Wade had performed uncover the reasons for Gus's lethargy, his lack of appetite? Would they explain his occasional dizzy spells and insomnia? She prayed they would. Prayed, too, that Wade wouldn't have to disqualify himself as Gus's doctor, because the men were slowly becoming pals—as evidenced by their joviality during dinner—and wasn't it a violation of some medical rule for a doctor to treat a friend?

Thanks to Wade, tonight her dad had seemed more animated, more like his old self than he had in weeks.

And so had *she*....

Patrice smiled, remembering those last minutes at Chiaparelli's, as they waited for the valets to bring the cars around. Gus had rolled himself to the end of the block in an attempt to see if he could figure out "Where do those kids *put* our cars, anyway!'' leaving Wade and Patrice alone on the sidewalk.

It had started to drizzle, and Wade insisted she join him under the big green awning at the restaurant's entrance. ''It's Dad who ought to be under here,'' she'd said, frowning.

He'd given her a little sideways hug, kissed her temple. ''You worry too much. He's a smart guy—I think he knows enough to come in out of the rain.''

Patrice now turned the windshield wipers a notch faster and licked her lips, remembering that just as she'd opened her mouth to agree, Wade had given her a long, sweet kiss that she could taste still. When it ended— much too soon, she thought—he'd looked deep into her eyes and smiled. ''Okay to call you later?''

''Sure,'' she'd said, grinning and nodding dumbly.

She hadn't asked why he wanted to call, because what if he said in that oh-so-serious doctor tone of his that it was a subject better discussed in private? And what if that subject was their relationship...such as it was?

The dashboard clock glowed a bright blue 9:55. Another fifteen minutes and they'd be home; ten minutes later, Gus would've downed his aspirin with a big glass of water, and God willing, he'd be sleeping—peacefully for a change—before the grandfather clock struck ten thirty. How long till Wade called?

''Whatcha thinkin' about?'' Gus asked, his voice sleep-foggy and quiet.

''Oh, this and that.''

''Any of 'this' have to do with Wade?''

She only sighed.

''He's a good guy. I think you picked a winner this time.''

A winner, indeed. What proof did she have that Wade

wanted more than a friendship? Still, a girl could hope…. She glanced at Gus, and seeing that he'd meant it, smiled. "You really think so?"

"Well, nothing in this world is absolute. But something tells me you'll be safe with him."

Safe. How would she recognize something so elusive? Another sigh. "I dunno."

"Yes, you do." He reached out, laid his hand atop hers on the gearshift knob. "You're the coffee bean, remember?"

She shot him a feeble grin. "Sometimes no coffee at all is better than a weak brew."

He chuckled. "What a horrible metaphor! Besides, you don't really expect me to swallow that. You're strong as they come. Why, you wouldn't know 'weak' if it bit you on the big toe."

Patrice wheeled the van into the driveway and killed the headlights. Turning slightly, she looked him in the eye. "You're a piece of work."

"Why d'you say that?"

"Because you always know just the right thing to say to make me feel better."

He shrugged. "Apple doesn't fall far from the tree."

"And an apple a day keeps the doctor away."

"You are the apple of my eye," he sang.

"Apple polisher," she teased.

"Now, now, don't upset the applecart."

She'd given it her best, but Patrice just wasn't in the mood for their traditional "Top that Pun" game. Hands high in mock surrender, she said, "You win. I give up!"

She hurried around to the back of the van to get his wheelchair, then standing beside the passenger door, the note of concern that had been ringing in her head became a chord as she watched him climb into it. Gus had lost the use of his legs, but constant exercise had made his arms strong and steady as oak trees...so why were they trembling so badly now?

As she locked the van, Patrice saw him run a hand over his face. It was what he always did when exhausted or frustrated...or in pain....

She pushed his chair up the wide wooden ramp, parked it near the front door. "You okay, Dad?" she asked, digging in her purse for the house key.

"'Course I'm okay," he barked. "Why wouldn't I be?"

She ignored the brusqueness of his tone and unlocked the front door. "Well, I'm sure beat. It's been a long, grueling day and I can't wait to get into my robe and slippers."

He nodded as she pushed the chair toward his bedroom. "Yeah, that pillow is gonna look mighty inviting tonight."

"Think I'll have a cup of tea before I turn in. How 'bout I fix you one while I'm at it?"

"No thanks. I'm just gonna hit the hay." He grabbed her hand. "But thanks, Treecie," Gus said, smiling wearily. "You're a peach."

She pretended not to notice the slight hitch in his voice, tried not to question what might have put it there.

She got onto her knees beside the wheelchair and began unbuttoning his shirtsleeves.

Gus stopped her by grabbing her wrist. "I can do it myself."

She straightened, regarded his haggard face, his worried eyes. "Well, of course you can," she said, forcing a brightness into her tone that she didn't feel. Then, looking right and left, she whispered, "I'm just looking for excuses not to sit alone in this storm."

A house-shaking roll of thunder was followed by a sizzling bolt of lightning, as if to remind him how much she'd always hated storms. *Thank You, Lord,* she prayed silently.

"Good thing you're a counselor," he said, giving her hand a gentle squeeze.

"Why?"

"'Cause you'd make a terrible salesperson."

Brow furrowed, Patrice said, "I don't get it."

He touched the tip of her nose. "I ain't buyin' your 'I'm scared of storms' malarkey." And with a light kiss to her forehead, he added, "Now, go fix your tea and let your old man catch some Zs, will ya?"

She got to her feet. "You sure you don't want a cup?"

"Positive." He waved her toward the door. "Now shoo. Skedaddle. Make tracks."

From the hall, she said, "G'night, Dad. Love you."

"Love you, too."

And as she pulled the door to, she heard his gentle postscript: "Till the day I die...."

Heart hammering, Patrice paced the family room, left forearm pressed to her waist, chewing on her right knuckle. She'd never been any good at waiting, and yet, it seemed to be the thing she was forced to do most. Wait for the coffee to perk, wait in Beltway traffic, wait for donations to trickle in on behalf of the hospitalized kids.

Wait for test results....

Something was wrong, terribly wrong with Gus. And it was more than Gus's pale complexion, his sluggish voice, his shaking hands that frightened her—he'd experienced all that before, and had come back stronger than ever—it was the look in his eyes that worried her.

No, she corrected, it was more what she *didn't* see—that old spark, the mischievous glint, the teasing twinkle....

She'd been around the hospital long enough to know that when a doctor said "two or three days," it could very well take a week to get test results. She prayed Gus's health wouldn't get worse in the meantime. "And, Lord," she whispered, "please give me the fortitude to be strong for Dad."

Her pacing set the crisp, thin pages of her Bible to fluttering slightly. It sat on the coffee table, right where she'd left it after morning devotions. Patrice bent to retrieve it, pressed it to her chest. "You said 'Ask and ye shall receive,' so I'm asking." She closed her eyes. "No, I'm begging. Whatever it is, let it be minor, something easy to fix, because he's already been through more than anyone should have to bear."

The muted, hollow gongs of the grandfather clock announced the quarter hour. Ten-fifteen. Is that all? she wondered. It seemed like hours had passed since she'd left Gus's room to check on him and take his temperature.

After putting the Bible back where she'd found it, Patrice walked into the kitchen and turned on the teakettle. She started for the stairs, thinking that by the time she'd changed into her pajamas, the water would be hot enough to brew a mug of herbal tea. Then she'd sip it in the family room, with the Good Book in her lap.

Another clap of thunder shook the glass in their panes, making her freeze halfway up the steps. The unrelenting rain pummeled the roof as the wind moaned around the house. It was the kind of night that would have her up, walking from window to window, checking to see that every tree was still upright in the yard, every flowerpot secure on the porch.

Smiling a bit as she stepped out of her shoes, Patrice marveled at how well the Father knew her.

The only cure for a heart burdened with worries and distress was time with Him, so He'd given her a storm to provide her with that time.

There was one chair in the cramped apartment, and Wade sat in it now, ankle propped on knee, fingers steepled under his chin, wondering how it had happened. Because it *shouldn't* have happened, not after his vow to remain a bachelor, forever. He remembered the precise moment when he'd taken the oath.

Just shy of his twelfth birthday, he'd started hanging around with Buddy Mauvais and his bunch. The five boys had a lot in common, from being fatherless to the mediocre grades they earned in school. Individually, they were outcasts; together, a strange family. One night, he'd come in nearly two hours past his curfew; his mother, tired after a long workday, had waited up for him. Tugging him by the ear, she'd plopped him onto the seat of a kitchen chair.

After several tense minutes of silent pacing, she sat across from him. "I'm trying my hardest to be both mother and father to you, Wade, but you have to help me out, here." He'd tried *his* hardest to look older, wiser, badder than he was—a "Buddy lesson" mastered in the principal's office—and found out real fast that what worked on Mr. Gardner *didn't* work on his mom. "Keep this kind of behavior up," she'd steamed, "and you'll become the kind of man who leaves a trail of broken hearts everywhere you go. Is that what you want!"

"The kind of man" meant "like your father," though she'd never uttered those exact words.

If he hadn't paid attention in biology class the week before, he wouldn't have known a whit about genetics. But the subject had fascinated him; he'd even taken notes! So he understood that his hazel eyes and sandy-brown hair were his mom's doing, while his dad's input had been a ruddy complexion and a burly build. He hated the fact that he got teary-eyed at sad movies—that, he could blame on his mom. What horrible characteristic could he charge his dad with? The inability to follow through on a promise?

Staring at the phone now, Wade remembered the delicious, soul-stirring kiss under the awning at Chiaparelli's. Every time he'd taken her in his arms, she'd melted against him like butter on a hot griddle. If he closed his eyes, he could see her uptilted face, eyes aglow with a light that could only be love.

The thought sat him upright. What had he ever done in his life to earn the love of a woman like that!

It didn't seem enough that Wade had cleaned up his act after that night in the kitchen with his mom—working harder in school, getting a part-time job, helping out more around the house. God in Heaven knew his mom deserved his best. And after a while, it became second nature, got easier still when he saw his name on the honor roll, or got appointed the youngest assistant manager, at sixteen, in Burger Stall history, or saw the pride in his mom's eyes when he was awarded a full scholarship. He'd gotten downright *good* at presenting himself as "good." But in truth, the performance got tougher with each passing year.

He hadn't worked for stellar grades, or a promotion at the burger place, or the four-year scholarship because he'd *wanted* those things. He'd done it to keep peace, because *peace,* it seemed—even at twelve, at fourteen, at thirty-one!—was the dream state that seemed to elude him.

Except when he was with Patrice, that is.

With her, he hadn't felt the need to perform, because everything about her made it clear she liked him best when he was being himself. And Gus echoed that attitude.

Was it any wonder he felt drawn to the simple, cozy Victorian they called home?

Sitting forward, he grabbed the telephone, started to dial her number. But the clock read 10:35. Too late to call? he wondered, punching in the last digits.

She answered on the second ring.

"Hey," he said, unaware of the width of his smile. "Glad you made it home okay. There was a big wreck on Route 40. I heard about it on the radio."

After a slight pause, she said, "Who is this?"

Wade recognized that teasing tone, could almost picture her, smiling as she said it. "Officer Stoneface, from the Wisecracks Police. Are you aware that you're in danger of violating the Serious Code?"

Her merry laughter filtered through the phone lines, caressing his ear and soothing his soul. "You're a nut," she said on a giggle. "So, how're you?"

Chuckling, he said, "Same as I was half an hour ago—fine."

Another lull, and then she said, "It was more like an hour ago. Lots can happen in an hour, you know."

Don't I know it, Wade thought. *A guy can realize he's completely dazzled by a li'l gal and—*

"Could I ask you a favor?"

He acknowledged a trace of worry in her voice. "Sure, anything," Wade said, meaning it.

"Is there any way you could hurry up the results of those tests? I don't know if it's such a good idea to—"

She sighed, and the sound surrounded him like a chill wind. "What's wrong? Is Gus worse?"

"Not really. Sort of." An exasperated sigh this time. "He's always steady as a rock, but when he was getting out of the van tonight, his arms were shaking so badly, I thought he'd never make it to the house."

"Did you take his temperature?"

"Yeah. It's still ninety-nine point eight. He took the aspirins but didn't want any tea."

"Is he sleeping now?"

"If you can call it that. He reminds me of a fish out of water, the way he tosses and turns."

"I'll get on it first thing in the morning. Maybe I can get 'em to speed things up a mite."

"Thanks, Wade. You're the best."

If only that were true, maybe he could admit some of what he was feeling. Maybe he could tell her he couldn't remember feeling more comfortable with anyone in his life. And maybe he could say "I love you" to a woman—and mean it—for the first time in his life.

"Wade? You still there?"

He cleared his throat. "Yeah."

"Oh. I thought maybe the storm had cut us off. It's terrible over here. What's it doing there?"

Truthfully, Wade hadn't noticed. But now that she mentioned it, there did seem to be one doozy of a storm going on outside. "Raining like gangbusters," he said. "And the wind's howling like a tornado." He pictured her, huddled under an afghan in the family room, chewing her lip the way she did when something upset her, cringing at every thunderbolt. "You okay? Still have electricity and all that?"

"All's well on the western front…or however the saying goes."

Again, he heard the smile in her voice. It made him want to jump back into the car, speed over to her house and wrap her in a bear hug. Instead, he just gripped the phone a little more tightly and said, "Good."

"So, do you have surgery tomorrow?"

"As a matter of fact, I do. Some patients to see at the office, hospital rounds, that's about it." He hesitated, then said, "How 'bout you?"

"Couple meetings in the morning, then I'll visit the kids on the oncology ward in the afternoon."

"Maybe we could meet in the cafeteria for lunch."

"Well, I, uh, sure. That'd be nice."

"Hopefully by then I'll have something to report— about Gus's tests, that is." No sooner were the words out of his mouth than Wade remembered that Gus had made him promise not to tell Patrice anything about his condition until he gave the go-ahead. *Another fine mess you've gotten yourself into,* he thought, mimicking Oliver Hardy.

"If I ask you a question," she said, slowly, softly, "will you tell me the truth?"

He could only presume she intended to ask about Gus's tests. "Depends on the question." Surely not the answer she'd hoped for, but under the circumstances, it was the best he could do.

"What do *you* think is wrong with Dad?"

He exhaled a sigh of relief; *that* he could tell her without violating doctor–patient confidentiality. "Honestly, I don't have a clue, Patrice."

A hush fell between them suddenly, and Wade knew she was waiting to hear him add, *If I knew, I'd tell you.*

"Well, then, do you think it's going to be serious?"

As in life threatening was her silent follow-up. ''Not from what I've seen so far.'' *Careful,* he warned himself, *you're treadin' on thin ice here.*

''So it's probably nothing, then. Just some weird strain of a virus or something.''

''Hopefully, we'll know soon.'' Then he asked, ''So what kind of tea are you drinking?'' hoping to change the subject.

''How'd you know I was drinking tea?''

''Because every time I've been over there, you've offered me a cup of tea.'' He chuckled. ''Besides, didn't you say while we were waiting for the valets to bring our cars around that you were going to fix yourself a big mug soon as you got home?'' It was certainly something she might've said, but Wade didn't know for sure. He was grasping at straws. Steering the conversation from Gus's condition wasn't going to be easy.

''It's chamomile,'' she said.

''With sugar?''

''Yes.''

''Seems a waste.''

''Why?''

''You're sweet enough already.''

A line like that would've come easily to him…with another woman. But saying it to Patrice, well, it was true, so did that make it a ''line'' or didn't it?

''You're making me blush.''

''The truth shouldn't make you blush, Patrice.''

She cleared her throat, then said, ''So, what're *you* doing?''

He grabbed the remote, selected channel thirteen and hit the mute button. ''Watching the news,'' he said. ''What about you? Waiting for the weather report?''

''No,'' she said softly. ''I'm reading the Bible.''

What for? he wanted to ask. She wouldn't find answers in there. Experience had taught him the only thing the Bible was good for was raising *more* questions. Like why did a man leave his wife and kids without a dime, and never look back? And why did a kid hang around with a bunch of juvies who only got him into trouble? And why did his mother, the sweetest most loving woman in the world, have to die of cancer?

"I was thinking maybe it would give me some peace," Patrice added. "I'm not sure if it's the storm or what, but it isn't working tonight."

"Meaning, it usually does?" he asked.

"Sometimes, when I'm troubled, I read something that's so pertinent, well, it brings me such peace, I tingle all the way to my fingertips!"

He'd tingled, too, the night his mother died. But as he recalled, it hadn't been a good feeling. In fact, it had been the worst experience of his life.

"I take it you're not a regular churchgoer," she said.

"That's putting it mildly." He hadn't meant it to come out so harsh, but he'd been down this road before. Every time he talked to his sister, it seemed, she was after him to come to Sunday services. "You need the Lord in your life," Anna would say. "Besides, what sort of example are you setting for your niece and nephew?" Seemed to Wade it was up to Anna and Frank to set a proper example for their kids—not him. But he'd never said so. After all, she was all the family he had left.

"There have been a few episodes in my life when I've turned from the Lord," Patrice said. "But He never lets me get too far away. Somehow, He always knows just what to do...and when, to bring me home."

Home? He would've asked what she meant by that if

she hadn't said, "Well, it's getting late. I suppose I should let you go."

"Yeah, I suppose."

"What time do you want me to meet you?"

"Uh…meet me?"

"Tomorrow, for lunch. In the cafeteria?"

"Oh. Yeah." He blew a stream of air through his lips. *Idiot,* he chastised. It had been his idea, after all. So much for his vow never to see her again on a personal basis. "Twelve, twelve-thirty, whichever is best for you."

"Noon it is, then."

He didn't want to let her go. Or didn't want her to let *him* go…. "You sure you're okay over there?"

"Sure. This is an old house, but it's built like a fortress."

Wade only half heard what she'd said, because he was too busy inserting what he wished she'd say instead: *No, I'm not okay. Would you come over and check things out?* or *I'd feel so much better if you were here, holding me….*

"Wade?"

"Yeah?"

She giggled softly. "Thought I'd lost you there for a minute."

If he could make all his problems disappear, they'd be together, forever.

As in married?

The question made his heart lurch. "See you tomorrow, then."

That image of her, sitting in a gigantic rocking chair, suckling their baby girl, flashed in his mind again. Thumb and forefinger pressing into his eyes, Wade shook his head. *You're losin' it, old man.* And chuckling to himself, he added, *Losin' it, my foot...you've already lost it!*

"Okay. Well, sweet dreams."

"G'night, Patrice." He replaced the telephone receiver in the cradle, flopped back against the chair cushions and groaned aloud.

It was risky, Patrice knew, turning on the computer during a raging thunderstorm. But she simply had to find out more about him; the Internet had never let her down before.

She pulled up her favorite search engine, fingers drumming on the desktop as it loaded onto the screen. At last, she was able to type "Dr. Wade Cameron" into the "search for" field. Seconds later, a listing of articles appeared, each bearing some reference to him. Scrolling down, she found one that said "Cameron in Camelot" and clicked on the pale blue letters.

Careful what you ask for, she thought, frowning as she gaped at the photograph of Wade, arm in arm with a tall, beautiful blonde. "Spring wedding planned for heart doc and his heart throb," the caption said.

Why hadn't he told her he'd been engaged? she wondered, scrolling down to the next article. "Why should he?" she said aloud. "It's no business of mine...."

Half an hour later, after reading a dozen articles about Wade being crowned Bachelor of the Year, Wade pulling in more money than any man in the history of the Heart Association's Bachelor Auction, Wade attending one charitable function or another with a gorgeous glamour queen on his arm, she shut down the computer, wishing the stormy weather had prevented her from taking this little tour through cyberspace. *What ya don't know won't hurt you,* she thought, clicking off the desk lamp.

The things she'd learned online shouldn't hurt so much, but it did! She'd begun to think maybe she *did* have half a chance with Wade, but now she knew better. He'd grown accustomed to fascinating, striking women with thrilling careers and exciting lifestyles; even if she had a mind to, Patrice felt she couldn't begin to compete with that.

So back in the family room, trusty Bible in her lap, Patrice searched the Word for comfort. Since childhood, she'd relied on God to lead her to relevant passages. Now, teary-eyed and feeling sorry for herself, she snugged into the double-wide easy chair, let the Good Book fall open and read the first verse that came into view: Revelation 21:4.

"...for the Lamb which is in the midst of the throne shall feed them, and shall lead them unto living fountains of waters, and God shall wipe all the tears from their eyes...."

If she needed proof that her Father in heaven had seen her tears, there it was, in black and white. It made her smile a bit, knowing He was so involved, even in the silly minutia of her daily life!

She flipped through the pages and read from the book of Job: "My soul is weary...I will speak in the bitterness of my soul...." Then, Hebrews 2:10 said, "...in bringing many sons to glory, to make the captain of their salvation perfect...through sufferings."

Patrice sighed. Sometimes, she didn't think she *wanted* to grow stronger, physically or faithfully—not if she had to suffer to acquire that strength!

One more verse opened unto her: "...God is faithful," read I Corinthians 10:13, "and will not suffer you to be tempted above that ye are able; but will with the temptation also make a way to escape, that ye may be able to bear it...." God's personal guarantee that no matter what life forced her to endure, He'd always see to it she had the strength to get through it.

So her feelings for Wade would wane. She'd get over her schoolgirl crush—what more could it be, after such a short time?—and get on with the life she'd been leading before he came back into her world.

Closing the Bible, Patrice held it against her chest, remembering that night in the emergency room. She'd probably spent a couple hundred nights, all told, waiting for her parents to see her little brother through yet another crisis. But that night was different, from the glaring pain in Timmy's eyes to the terror in her mother's.

Then a shaggy-haired boy had strolled into the waiting room, hiding his concern behind an "I'm so *bad*" stride and a tough-guy expression—an expression that softened and warmed the instant his eyes met hers. His gentle smile, the genuineness of his smile, the careful questions he'd asked about Timmy, well, was it any wonder she'd thought of him hundreds of nights since then?

She had to learn to be satisfied with things, just as they were. "Folks only get hurt when they wish for the impossible," Gus had always said. "Remember, 'it is what it is,' so satisfy yourself with that instead of wishing your life away."

Quietly, privately, she'd been wishing something deeper would develop between her and Wade; what she'd read on the computer screen had shown her that was impossible. Patrice reminded herself that God had promised to provide a means of escape, so she'd be able to bear it when things didn't turn out as she hoped. The promise did little to ease the pain of realization, but it was a comfort nonetheless.

Although her heart was breaking, as she drifted off to sleep, she couldn't help remembering how it felt when he held her in his arms and gave her a kiss so soft and gentle it made her think of angel's wings.

Chapter Nine

The minute she'd finished hanging her coat on the hook behind her office door, Patrice looked up Wade's extension in the hospital phone directory. Tucking her purse into a deep drawer in her desk with one hand, she dialed his number with the other, hoping he wouldn't be in yet.

Thank You, Lord, she prayed when his voice mail picked up the call. The rich robust voice sent a shudder up her back: *"You've reached Dr. Wade Cameron…"*

"Hi, Wade," she said after the beep, "it's Patrice." She cleared her throat and, in an attempt to sound upbeat and pleasant, she smiled, as if smiling would blot his dating history from her mind. As if it made no difference that his Little Black Book was likely the size of the Baltimore phone book. "I'm afraid I can't make lunch today," she said, biting back the jealousy. "Something has come up." It was true, after all: his *past* had come up. Admittedly, it wouldn't have been so bad, if what she'd learned hadn't made it so clear she was anything *but* his type. "You'll let me know the minute you hear anything about Dad's tests, won't you? I'll be in and out all day, so feel free to leave a message...."

She could wrangle deals with corporate heads, finesse donations from the grumpiest tightwad, balance the Child Services books to the penny, and convince even the whiniest child to eat brussels sprouts. Co-workers, friends and fellow parishioners often commented on her levelheadedness, her good sense. But where men were concerned, Patrice considered herself dumb as a post.

Much as she cared about Wade, what choice did she have but to avoid him? "My extension is 410, by the way, to save you having to page through that horrible directory."

Stop rambling, she told herself, *and just say goodbye!* "Bye-bye!"

Bye-bye? Now there's a mix of maturity and professionalism that's sure to set him on his heels! Patrice gripped the receiver to tightly she nearly dropped the phone. Maybe she hadn't sounded as ridiculous to Wade as she had to herself...?

As she hung up, a Bible passage sprang to mind. "Be ye not unequally yoked together with unbelievers." It had popped into her head last night, too, following Wade's gruff response to her mention of the Bible. Try as she might, Patrice hadn't been able to ignore II Corinthians 6:14, because the last half of the verse made it clear she had a decision to make: "...for what fellowship hath righteousness with unrighteousness, and what communion hath light with darkness?"

Nothing could make her see Wade as "darkness."

Not even the articles she'd read, highlighting his fast-lane life?

She sat back in her chair and gave it a moment's thought. His behavior hadn't exactly been wholesome, but then, there was no reason to believe it had been sinful, either. The photograph of him with the voluptuous clinging blonde entered her mind. Squinting didn't block the mental picture, nor did rubbing her eyes.

Funny, but they hadn't *looked* like a couple in love. In fact, neither Wade nor his fiancée seemed the least bit happy. And shouldn't the announcement that they planned to spend the rest of their lives together have produced *some* sign of joy on their faces?

The question made her recall an incident from her own past, when a young man she'd been seeing proposed marriage. Patrice had said yes, not because she'd loved Jerry, but because the timing seemed suitable; she'd been twenty-three, the right age, she'd thought, to start a family. Fortunately, Jerry backed out even before an announcement could be made. Had it been that way for Wade and his beautiful blonde? If that was the case, which of them had called off the engagement?

Not that it mattered. She'd decided to stop seeing Wade before things got out of hand, anyway. It would be best that way, for both of them.

Without warning, the photograph of Wade flared in her mind. Only this time, *she* sat beside him, one hand resting lightly on his bicep, and this time, the smiles on their faces were proof how much they looked forward to sharing a lifetime.

"Oh, cut it out," she scolded herself. "You're only making it harder to do what needs to be done."

Sighing, Patrice grabbed the phone again, dialed her home number.

"Hello?"

"Molly," Patrice said, "I'm so glad you answered and not Dad. Where is he?"

"Napping," Gus's nurse answered. "I checked on him not ten minutes ago."

"How's his fever?"

"One hundred point eight."

Up a degree from last night, she realized. "Did he take anything for it?"

"You know Gus," Molly said on a sigh. "He doesn't make anything easy." Molly deepened her voice. "'One of these days,'" she quoted him, "'I'm gonna turn *into* a pill!'" Laughing, his nurse added, "I said, 'Too late…that happened the day you were born!'" She laughed softly, then sighed. "I finally convinced him to take two aspirins and get into bed just before you called."

Well, Patrice thought, at least he'd agreed to that much. "Thanks, Molly. You're a peach. I'll try to get off a little early today."

"Good idea. You usually have better luck getting him to behave than I do." The nurse clucked her tongue. "If I didn't know better, I'd say the man has a crush on me, because sometimes, he reminds me of the boys in the playground."

Patrice had always suspected Gus had feelings for Molly that had more to do with her spunk and adorable personality than her nursing skills. Smiling, Patrice said, "Just say the word, and we'll cancel recess for that naughty boy."

"I might just tell him you said that!"

Patrice hung up slowly, remembering how years ago she'd jokingly speculated that Gus's feelings for Molly were more personal than professional. Stern as a fire-and-brimstone preacher, he'd said, "Molly is a good person, and she deserves only the best." Patrice read that to mean he didn't consider himself "the best," and knew he wouldn't feel that way—if not for the condition that kept him confined to a wheelchair.

And if it hadn't been for your self-centeredness, Patrice thought, *he wouldn't be in that chair in the first place.*

Covering her face with both hands, Patrice sighed heavily.

The phone rang, startling her so badly she nearly knocked the pencil cup from her desk. One hand over her chest, she pressed the intercom button. "Yes, Lisa?"

"You asked me to let you know when it was eleven o'clock," said her secretary. "Need me to call ahead, let 'em know you're on your way over to Pediatric ICU?"

"No, that's okay, but thanks just the same."

"Have fun," Lisa said. Another click and the intercom went silent.

She had to get into a better frame of mind, for the kids' sake. Standing, Patrice squared her shoulders and took a deep breath. "He only gives you what He knows you can handle," she reminded herself, grabbing Mort McMonkey from his special spot on the bookshelf. Exhaling, she forced a big smile and started for the elevator. She'd make the rounds in the children's wards, then head back to her office, where, with any luck, she'd find that Wade had called with news about Gus's condition.

She punched the up button, then stepped back and watched the pale yellow numbers above the double doors light up. "Let it be good news, Lord," she prayed, as one by one, tiny *pings* announced each floor.

Because if it wasn't, that Bible verse was going to be tested to its limits this time.

* * *

As he stepped out of the elevator, Wade pulled back his sleeve. Eleven twenty-five, read his watch. He'd examine Emily Kirkpatrick, then use the phone at the nurses' station to call Patrice—make sure she hadn't forgotten about their lunch date.

He'd been in a rotten mood till that thought, what with one emergency room procedure ending badly and post-surgical complications arising for another patient. The thought of sitting across from Patrice in one of the cafeteria's padded booths raised his spirits. He could almost hear her delightful laughter, her lilting voice. If he closed his eyes, he could see her smiling face and dancing brown eyes, and that adorable way she had of tilting her head whenever he spoke, as if every word out of his mouth was truly important to her.

She made a man feel good, he decided. Made him feel like the center of her universe. Well, not exactly the *center;* she'd made it abundantly clear that spot was reserved for God.

Lost in thought, Wade rounded the corner and nearly crashed headlong into his partner.

Adam laughed. "Where are you headed in such a hurry?"

Red-faced, Wade grinned. "Hey, how goes it?"

"Never better."

And it appeared to be true. Wade had practically grown up with Adam Thorne, and couldn't remember seeing him look more fit...or happier. "Seems marriage agrees with you, ol' buddy," he said, slapping his bicep. "Maybe you oughta go away on a honeymoon every couple o' months."

Adam laughed. "I'd say 'practice what you preach,' but God hasn't created the woman who could pass your Miss Perfect test."

That might've been true…once. But not anymore. Not since he'd met Patrice.

As if on cue, he heard her voice. *"You take a nice, long nap now,"* she said on behalf of Mort McMonkey. *"I'll be back tomorrow to make sure you ate all your supper tonight, so you'd better clean up your plate, y'hear!"* Waving, she stepped into the hallway and hurried into Emily Kirkpatrick's room, oblivious to the two lab-coated men standing several yards behind her.

Wade sensed rather than saw Adam follow his gaze. Arms crossed over his chest, his friend nodded.

"Ho ho," Adam said, smirking, "what's this?" He leaned in for a closer look at Wade's face, then straightened and chuckled. "Has the Bachelor of the Year hung up his certificate?"

The heat of a blush crept up his neck. "Get real," Wade said. "She's cute, but—"

"Don't gimme that, pal. I've seen you gawk at 'cute' before, and you never looked like *that*."

Like what? he wondered as the heat moved to his cheeks. Running a hand through his hair, he grinned. "Maybe you should have stayed in Cancún another couple of days, cuz you're seeing things." But he knew Adam. Once that guy got on a topic…

"So how's Kasey?" he asked, hoping to change the subject. "All tan and rosy from hours on the beach?"

"She's great, just great."

Adam hadn't needed to say it; what the man felt for his bride was written all over his face.

"Glad to hear it, because she promised to make a home-cooked dinner for me when you guys got back from the Yucatán." Wade tapped a forefinger to his temple. "Some things, a guy doesn't forget."

"Yeah, well I'll remind her, just in case." Adam

glanced toward the room where Patrice was doing her monkey voice, then met Wade's eyes again. "You want to invite somebody? I'm sure it'll be fine with Kasey...."

The last blush had barely faded when he felt another tint his cheeks. "So, have you been to the office yet?"

Grinning, Adam shook his head. "Subtle, Cameron. Real subtle." He chuckled, then added, "Matter of fact, I just came from the office. Man, y'wouldn't believe the stack of paperwork on my desk!"

Wade and Adam had been partners in their cardiac practice for several years now, sharing office space, a secretary, a receptionist and one another's caseload. "You should've seen it before I sorted out the junk mail for you."

"Thanks, pal. I was just telling Kasey this morning that you're a handy guy to have around." He laughed, playfully punched Wade's shoulder. "Well, got me a patient to check on. Catch you at the office in the morning...or do you have surgery?"

"Nah, easy day tomorrow, for a change."

"Catch you there, then."

Adam headed for the elevator, and Wade caught up to him as he hit the down button. "Set aside half an hour or so for me, will you? I have this new patient, see, and I'd like a consult."

"Sure thing." The elevator doors opened, and Adam stepped inside. Smirking, he leaned forward and whispered, "If you get the lead out, you can probably catch the Monkey Lady before she moves to the next floor."

The doors hissed closed before Wade had a chance to make a comeback. *Just as well,* he thought, smiling despite himself. What sort of retort could he have made, considering Adam had practically read his mind?

He started for Emily's room, mentally thanking Patrice. By showing up when she did, she'd spared him the ordeal of groveling with the head nurse for use of her phone. Judging from the scowl on the nurse's face, she'd have put him through his paces.

Frowning, the head nurse looked up from her clipboard as he passed her in the hall. "What's that, Doctor?"

"Nothing," he said, topping off his plastic smile with an equally half-hearted salute. "Just thinking out loud...."

The soothing softness of Patrice's voice stopped him just outside the door to Emily's hospital room. "Aw, don't cry, sweetie," she was saying. "Dr. Cameron is a friend of mine, and I happen to know that he'd never let a thing like that happen!"

A thing like what? he wondered. He was about to enter the room, when Emily's small, weak voice said, "My roommate Julie says I'm going to die...."

Wade heard the little girl sniff before continuing. "Julie says she heard the nurses talking about it when I was downstairs, having X rays this morning."

Patrice clucked her tongue. "She actually heard them say your name?"

"Well, no-o-o-o, but Julie says they were sayin' stuff 'bout my heart condition."

"My goodness, I'm very impressed with Julie!"

Wade listened to an instant of silence, then heard Emily's timid "Why?"

"Well," Patrice explained, "she's awfully young to be a doctor, don't you think?"

Emily didn't answer right away, but when she did, Wade heard the smile in her voice: "Julie's only nine. Ever'body knows nine's too young to be a doctor!"

"Hmm, then tell me, Emily Kirkpatrick, how would she know it was you the nurses were talking about? Do you have any idea how many patients there are on this floor of the hospital?"

"I dunno. Lots, I guess."

"Yes, lots. And I know, because Mort and I visit them, almost every day."

"So how many kids are here?"

"Today, there are eighteen."

Silence.

"So you think the nurses were talking about one of the other kids?" Another sigh. "I'll say a prayer for whoever it is, 'cause it's sad if they're gonna die...."

Despite her empathy, there was no mistaking the note of hopefulness in Emily's voice. Wade made a mental note to thank Patrice for that later, over lunch.

"Oh, you know how those nurses are," Patrice said, laughing. "I'll just bet they were talking about a character on one of their TV shows!"

"Yeah. I never thought of that."

Emily's weak giggle made Wade sad, wishing he could do something to help her. It didn't matter that he'd already done everything medically possible; he wanted to send her home, healthy and happy, with a long bright future ahead of her. The helplessness reminded him how he'd felt when his mother was dying of cancer.

One thing was certain: First chance he got, he intended to have a word or two with those nurses, make sure they paid a lot closer attention to anyone who might be listening when they swapped confidential patient information as if it were yesterday's gossip.

But first things first....

"Hey, there, Miss Emily Kirkpatrick," he said with all the cheerfulness he could muster. "How're you today?'' After grabbing her chart, he stood beside her bed. ''Uh-oh, it says here that you didn't eat your lunch again.''

Emily wrinkled her tiny nose. ''Soupy mashed potatoes and some kind of gray meat. Oh, and green Jell-O.'' She grimaced and shook her narrow shoulders. ''Bloooey.''

He glanced at her food-laden tray. What did it matter whether or not she cleaned up her plate, when he knew full well that her poor little heart wasn't going to heal, even if she ate every morsel? ''Green Jell-O, eh?'' He gave a sympathetic wince. ''Yuck.'' Glancing around the room, he added, ''Where's your mom?''

''In the chapel.'' Emily rolled her eyes and sighed heavily. ''She's there *all* the time!''

It had been Wade's experience that certain family members sensed the truth about their sick relatives long before he reeled off a prognosis. ''Goodness,'' he said, ruffling Emily's hair, ''then, maybe we'd better get her some knee pads!''

Patrice sent him an apologetic half grin, telling him she understood his predicament. She didn't know it, but that expression told him that *she* was one of those sensitive few whose loving, nurturing ways made them aware of things that bypassed most folks.

He smiled feebly. ''So how 'bout we have a look at that incision?'' he said, bending over Emily.

''Can Mort stay?'' she asked, clutching the covers to her chest.

He glanced at Patrice, who nodded her assent.

Finger-combing Emily's bangs from her forehead, Wade smiled. '''Course he can stay.'' He leaned closer and whispered, ''But don't tell the other kids. Then they'd *all* want Mort around when their doctors examine them.''

While Emily giggled, Wade decided that Mort could take up permanent residence right there in her bed, could take her on a sight-seeing tour of the toy store jungle where he was born, if that's what she wanted. Even if her family had been rich or important enough to get her name moved from the bottom to the top of the list of patients waiting for compatible transplant donors, her condition had weakened too many of her other vital organs. The horrible fact was, little Emily Kirkpatrick had, at best, a month to live.

Carefully, he pressed the stethoscope to her tiny chest. So many "ifs," Wade thought, listening to the meager beats of her debilitated heart. *If* he'd met her a couple of years ago...*if* she'd been stronger...*if* God had seen fit to spare her in the first place....

"What's wrong, Doc?"

He looked into Emily's sweet blue-eyed face and straightened. "Nothing. Why?"

"Well, you look so...so *mad*...."

Truth? He *was* mad. Furious, even. Because this so-called merciful God that Patrice thought so highly of had allowed his mother to die a long, agonizing death, and He hadn't lifted an Almighty finger to protect little Emily from—

Wade had blocked out a lot of what he'd learned in Sunday School, but he remembered this: "Ask and ye shall receive." Well, he'd asked on behalf of his mom— *pleaded* was more like it—but like everything else he'd prayed for in his life, God had turned a deaf ear.

The child continued to look up at him with enormous, trusting eyes, waiting for an answer to her simple question.

To admit what he'd been thinking was a surefire way to take away the one thing she had left: Hope.

"Dr. Cameron is just concentrating, sweetie," Patrice said, rescuing him. "Do it again," she pressed, smiling and wiggling her eyebrows. "Show us your 'I'm concentrating' face."

If they'd been alone, he'd have hugged her for that. But the child in the bed beside Emily's, her parents and siblings, and Emily, too, watched and waited.

And so Wade summoned the most serious frown he could, inspiring peals of laughter from every corner of the room. "Well, it wasn't *that* funny," he said, feigning hurt feelings. The laughter continued even as he added, "Keep it up, and you guys are gonna give me a complex."

"A complex, eh? Quite a feat," Patrice said, "considering you're the most *un*complicated man I've ever met."

She blushed as if she hadn't expected the compliment to pop from her gorgeous, curvy pink lips any more than he'd expected to hear it.

He might've reddened, too, if not for the thoughts jumping in his head. For one thing, if anyone had asked him to describe himself in a word, *uncomplicated* wouldn't have come to mind; for another, it was about the last word he would've hoped Patrice might use to characterize him.

"Well," she said, breaking the uncomfortable silence, "guess I'd better go." Putting Mort into action, she added in the monkey's voice, *"So many children, so little time!"*

"Bye, Mort," Emily said, waving.

"G'bye, you li'l sweetie!" Patrice stepped up close and kissed the girl's forehead, made Mort mimic her

actions. And pressing a palm to Emily's cheek, she said, "See you later, okay?"

Wade doubted anyone else heard her voice waver, didn't think the others had seen the flicker of uncertainty in her eyes. He couldn't say *how* she knew Emily didn't have much time left, but Patrice knew....

As if reading his mind, she met his eyes. What message was she trying to send him on the invisible current that connected them? he wondered. She seemed trapped in the sadness of the moment. She'd rescued him earlier, now he'd return the favor.

"So, you ready for lunch?"

She frowned slightly, then blinked. "You didn't get my message?"

"What message?"

"I, um..." Shrugging, she sighed. "Just...well, it's no big deal."

Wade offered her his elbow, and she took it.

"I'll be back later today," he told Emily over his shoulder.

"Me, too," Patrice said as they stepped into the hall.

She continued to hold on to his arm as they moved silently toward the elevator. He rather liked the warm weight of her hand pressed into the crook of his elbow. How much nicer it'd be, he thought, if she leaned her head on his shoulder, too.

Get a hold of yourself! he told himself. Daydreams were for fools. Especially *romantic* dreams.... "So," he began again, "what're you in the mood for today? Pizza? Hot dogs? Hamburger?"

She hit the down button, both hands now clutching Mort to her chest. The spot where her hand had rested on him was noticeably cold. He was wondering about that when she said, "Oh, soup and a salad probably. I try to eat light at lunch, since I fix a big supper every night.''

Wade nodded, trying to imagine what it would be like, having balanced meals, prepared lovingly for him every night. ''Just the opposite with me. My fridge is too small for real food, so I eat most of my meals here.''

She looked up at him, then. ''You're welcome to join us. Gus probably won't eat much, anyway, considering he's still under the weather.''

I'd love to, he wanted to say. ''Hate to wear out my welcome'' is what he said, instead.

Patrice's soft laugh filtered into his ears. ''Impossible.''

The elevator arrived, and as several staff members stepped into the hall, he held out a hand, inviting her to enter the car ahead of him. She grinned. ''So chivalry isn't dead, after all.''

''Easy to be gentlemanly around a true lady.''

While Patrice's blush intensified, two nurses, leaning against the back of the elevator, exchanged knowing looks. One of them, Wade recognized as working Emily's floor. Eyes narrowed, he almost read her the riot act for talking about the child's case in front of the patients. That'd wipe that smirk from her face. But there was a time and a place for everything.

Besides, he didn't know if he wanted Patrice to see what he could be like when riled. ''You ladies heading for the cafeteria?'' he asked.

''Nope,'' said Emily's nurse. ''Just getting back.'' She smiled sheepishly and patted her purse. ''Forgot my kid's birthday, so I'm headed to the gift shop for a card.''

Wade nodded.

"Friendly warning," she added, "stay away from the chili. Looks like it's been in the pan for a decade."

He answered with only the hint of a smile. "Thanks. I'll keep that in mind."

The nurses exited, leaving Wade and Patrice alone in the car. "What was *that* all about?" she asked.

He pretended not to understand the question. "What was what about?"

She giggled. "Let's just say I wouldn't want you aiming that glare in my direction."

"Glare? I didn't—"

She pointed at two holes in the elevator wall, where formerly, drawings colored by kids had hung. "You drilled those babies with your *eyes*, Dr. Cameron," she teased.

The elevator stopped at their floor, and Wade held the door. "That ain't nothin' compared to what she's gonna get when I finish lunch."

"Why?"

He noticed that Patrice had to walk quickly to keep pace with his stride. Wade slowed down. "She blabbed some confidential stuff in the presence of that young pediatric patient Julie, and you know what Julie did with the information." He grunted. "Of all the unprofessional—"

"I'm sure she wasn't aware Julie was in earshot."

He stared. "After seeing what the news did to Emily, you're defending her? I can't believe my ears."

She held Mort up as a shield. "Ouch," Patrice said.

"Sorry," he said. "Didn't mean to take out my annoyance on you."

She slid onto the seat of a nearby booth, and propped Mort up against the wall. "Apology accepted." Once he'd settled in across from her, she added, "You want me to save the booth while you stand in line, or the other way around?''

It was common knowledge around the Ellicott General cafeteria that between staff, ambulatory patients, and visitors tables were in short supply. Wade slid his wallet from his pocket, peeled off a twenty. ''I'll stand guard,'' he said, handing it to her, ''if you'll get me a burger and fries and a medium soda.''

She started to protest, but he held up a hand to forestall it. ''Let me do this, Patrice. After all the terrific meals you've fed me, the least I can do is buy you a bowl of lousy soup and a plate of wilted salad.''

For a moment, it looked like she might refuse the offer. Then she dumped her purse on the seat beside Mort. ''Okay, but this means you owe me one....''

Chuckling, he said, ''Good thing you're not keeping score, 'cause I'd owe you more than one.''

She made a move to get into line when he grabbed her wrist. ''Just out of curiosity,'' he began, meeting her eyes, ''what do I owe you?''

One corner of her mouth lifted in a smile as she arched one brow. Tilting her head, she winked. Oh, what he'd give to be alone with her, so he could wrap her in his arms and kiss those beautiful, shapely lips!

''Supper is at six, sharp,'' she said, waving the twenty under his nose.

She slid her gaze to where his fingers wrapped around her wrist...her silent signal that he should release her. Much as he hated to, he let go. And watching her step into line behind an orderly, Wade licked his lips.

''Hey, Cameron!'' a voice to his left called.

Turning, he saw Adam on the other side of the cafeteria. Wade returned his wave.

"C'mere," his partner said. "I have something to show you."

Forgetting about Patrice's purse and puppet on the bench seat across from him, Wade rose and headed across the room. "What's so important it couldn't wait until after lunch?" he asked, standing beside Adam's table.

"Feast your eyes." Adam handed him a stack of photographs. Kasey, in sunglasses and a wide-brimmed hat; Adam posing beside an enormous, gnarled tree; the newlyweds on the seat of a gilded carriage.

"Nice," Wade said. "Real nice." He looked up, to where he'd last seen Patrice, amazed at the depth of his disappointment that she wasn't in sight.

"Gimme those," Adam said, grabbing the pictures, "and get back to your li'l honey." Shaking his head, he grinned. "Looks to me like you're next, pal."

That got Wade's attention. "Next? Next for what?"

Smirking, Adam pointed to the photo of himself and Kasey, fully attired as bride and groom. "Need I say more?" he said, wiggling his eyebrows.

"You're delusional, pal." As an afterthought, Wade dug around in his lab coat pocket for the business card a patient's wife had given him earlier, and handed it to Adam.

"'JoEllen Smith,'" Adam read, "'Clinical Psychologist.'" His brows drew together in confusion.

"Need I say more?" Wade echoed.

"Funny," his partner said as he headed back to the table. "Very funny."

Laughing to himself, Wade spotted Patrice at the cashier's stand. He stopped walking so he could watch, unbeknownst to her.

Of all the women in line, she was by far the prettiest,

with eyes almost too big for her delicate face and a smile that would put the sun's glow to shame. Though petite, she had a certain strength to her bearing. The harsh overhead lights illuminated her face. As if she sensed someone looking at the scar, she fluffed her hair to hide it.

Most women would have seen a plastic surgeon by now to have the thing removed. The fact that Patrice *hadn't* reminded Wade just how responsible she felt for Gus's condition.

He made a mental note to do a better job of convincing her that the accident hadn't been her fault, that the scar didn't matter a whit to him—because in every way imaginable, she outshone every other woman he'd known.

Patrice looked up just then, and when her eyes locked on his, he smiled. Maybe Adam was right, he thought as his heart hammered against his rib cage; maybe Patrice was "the one."

The fact that he'd never so much as entertained the thought before had to mean *something*.

Didn't it?

Chapter Ten

She could only hope the cashier was an honest woman. How was she supposed to double-check the correct change with Wade standing there, looking at her like *that?* Sighing, Patrice thanked the lady at the register and tucked the money under her salad plate.

If only he wasn't so all-fired good-looking, maybe it would be easier to stick to her decision. As it was, she had this lunch—and one more dinner—to get through, thanks to her limited willpower…and his irresistible smile.

"Who was that man?" she asked, sliding the tray onto their table.

"My partner," Wade said, sitting across from her. "Adam Thorne. Amazing, isn't it, that people can work at the same complex for years, and never meet?"

Shrugging, she took their food from the tray. "Well, it's like you said, this place is like a small city." The amazing thing to her was, long before that so-called "first day" in Emily's room, she'd noticed *Wade…*brow furrowed in concentration as he studied patient charts, looking sympathetic and understanding as he discussed diagnoses and prognoses with relatives, explaining treatment to the nurses.

She'd seen him in the elevator, looking harried and hurried as he frowned at the numbers above the door, and in the halls, lab coat flapping behind him like a superhero cape as he rushed from room to room completing his rounds.

Patrice grinned as she handed him his silverware, because Wade didn't know it, but she'd stood behind him right here in the cafeteria line once…and ended up chiding herself for staring in open admiration of his tall, muscular body.

The smile vanished, though, when she pictured the ravishing blonde from the newspaper's engagement announcement. Patrice supposed if she, herself, had been model-gorgeous, he might've noticed her, maybe only once, but since she wasn't…

He squirted catsup on his burger. "I said that?"

His question brought her back to the moment. "Uh-huh. The day we met—or rather, met again—in Emily's room, you said something about Ellicott General being the size of a small city."

Topping off the catsup with a dollop of mustard, he nodded. "Oh, yeah. When you were giving me directions to your office." He smiled. "How could I have forgotten one of the best days of my life?"

She'd just speared a slice of cucumber, and his comment halted its trip to her mouth. In a feeble attempt to hide her surprise, Patrice reached for her bottle of springwater. "Don't forget your change," she said, pointing at the coins and bills still lying on the tray. "Thanks for lunch, by the way. I forgot to pack mine and—"

He looked up, brows drawn together in confusion.

"Why would you bring your lunch when I said I'd treat you today?"

She remembered the message she'd left him earlier. How would she weasel out of this one? she wondered.

"So what came up?" he asked.

Blinking, Patrice said, "Came up?"

"You said earlier you'd left me a message. To say you had to cancel?"

"Oh, that..." She dipped the cucumber slice in blue cheese dressing. "I, um, managed to rearrange things." At least she hadn't needed to resort to dishonesty.

"You were great with Emily before. Thanks for calming her down."

"I was glad to do it." She put down her fork and, elbows on the table, linked her fingers together. "If I'm not out of line, do you mind telling me how long she has?"

He shook his head slowly. "Couple weeks, a month at best."

Patrice groaned softly. "I hate this part of the job."

"Losing patients, you mean?"

Nodding, she said, "I wish we could send them *all* home happy and healthy and—"

"Then, why do you do it?" He dabbed a paper napkin to the corners of his mouth. "You could walk away from this any time...do something less depressing for a living."

"It isn't *all* depressing. There are plenty of joyful moments. But even if there wasn't even one, anyone who works here could walk away, find a line of work that's easier on the heartstrings."

He thought for a moment. "Good point." Picking up the hamburger again, he continued. "I know why I stay—why do *you?*"

Patrice sighed. "There's no simple answer to that question. I know it'd be a lot easier," she admitted, "working in a traditional clinic setting, counseling schoolyard bullies and kids with Attention Deficit Hyperactivity Disorder, or helping children deal with divorce.... But there are plenty of well-trained professionals willing to do that kind of work. *This*," she said, hands out to indicate the hospital, "this is a *calling*."

"Like the ministry?"

She told herself that note of sarcasm in his voice lived only in her imagination. "Exactly." Then she said, "So why do *you* stay? Your job is a lot harder on you than mine could ever be on me."

He shrugged one shoulder. "Like you said, there's no easy answer." He met her eyes to add, "I guess if I had to sum it up in a sentence, I'd have to say I'm here because I don't have any choice."

"What do you mean? 'Course you have a choice!"

His hazel eyes glittered darkly, reminding her of the ring Gus used to wear, the one with the tigereye stone set in sterling.

"Don't presume to know what makes me tick, Patrice."

His voice, the set of his jaw, even his posture had changed in the brief instant it took to make the blunt statement. "I'm sorry," she said, meaning it. "I never meant to pry, or imply that—"

Wade's eyes never left hers, not as he put down his burger, not as he wiped his hands, not even as he reached out and grabbed her fingertips. "No, I'm the one who's sorry. I never should've barked at you. That was totally uncalled for." Brow furrowed and lips taut, he stared at his plate and shook his head. "Maybe someday, I'll tell you the story of why I became a doctor in the first place." And meeting her eyes, he added, his voice softer, his expression gentler, "For now, trust me when I say I don't have a choice in the matter. Okay?"

Patrice looked at their hands, linked companionably. "Okay," she whispered. "It won't happen again, I promise."

His brows rose. "What won't?"

Sliding her fingers from his grasp, she said, "I resent presumptuous people. Resent it even more when I become one of them."

He caught one hand, and this time held it between his own. "Patrice, you're one of the finest human beings I've ever met, bar none. I've never said that to a woman in my life, and that's the God's honest truth."

She didn't know how to respond to his straightforward praise, and so Patrice stared silently at the class ring on his left hand. Maybe someday, he'd replace it with a wedding band…one she'd slide onto his finger as he said—

"And you're beautiful, to boot."

Her dreamy girlish thoughts were dangerous, and she knew it. After giving his hand a gentle squeeze, she wriggled free of his grip. "I don't suppose you've seen any of Dad's test results yet?"

Chuckling, Wade said, "Nice save, kiddo." Then, "No, I haven't heard a word yet, but I lit a fire under 'em down in the lab." A corner of his mouth lifted in a mischievous grin, and he narrowed an eye. "One of the technicians owes me a favor, and promised me he'd put Gus at the top of the list." He downed a gulp of soda. "We oughta know something by end of business today."

"I don't know why I'm in such a hurry to know," Patrice admitted.

"What do you mean?"

"Well," she began haltingly, "I have this horrible sinking feeling that it won't be good news."

Leaning forward, he chucked her chin. "Aw, now, where's my positive-thinking Patrice?"

Your Patrice?

"Whatever it is," Wade said, patting her hand, "we've probably caught it early."

"If you had to guess, what would you say is causing his fevers?"

His expression went immediately from friendly to professional. "I'd rather not guess," he said, his tone all business.

Nodding, Patrice said, "I understand."

"Good grief," interrupted a deep voice, "why do you two look so glum?"

Wade sat back and gave the man an uncomfortable smile. "Adam, hey."

Plopping a hand on Wade's shoulder, he gave it a brotherly shake. "Where do you find all these good-lookin' ladies!"

Shaking his head, Wade grinned. "Patrice McKenzie, this is Adam Thorne, my business partner and all-round pain in the neck."

Adam shook Patrice's hand. "Don't let him pull the wool over your eyes," he told her, winking. "He needs me like a baby needs his mama—my main purpose in his life is to keep him humble—"

"Yeah, well," Wade interrupted, chuckling, "you do a stellar job at that!"

"So," Adam said, glancing at Mort, "at long last, I meet the Monkey Lady, face to face."

Patrice looked from Adam to Wade, then back again. "You've heard about me?"

"Everybody around here has heard of you."

"Good things, I hope."

"Nothin' but! I once heard a nurse say that watching you work is like seeing a rainbow after a thunderstorm. Now, I've never had the pleasure of watching you do your magic, but your reputation precedes you." He glanced at Wade. "And since you somehow managed to tame *this* monster, I'm inclined to agree."

She said a quiet prayer of thanks when Adam and Wade discussed some sort of office business. While they talked, her mind replayed Adam's last comment. *Tame* Wade? To do that, wouldn't she first have to capture him?

Patrice's heart beat faster as she watched them. It was plain they'd been friends, close friends, for a long time. Had Wade maybe said something to his partner about her—something to indicate his feelings went deeper than "relative of a patient"?

She recalled their last kiss, and even now, the memory warmed her right down to her toes. *That* certainly hadn't been evidence of a professional relationship!

"...do you say, Monkey Lady?"

She hadn't heard a word Adam said to her. "I—I'm sorry. You...were saying?"

Chuckling, Adam began again. "I was just wondering if maybe I could borrow you sometime. I have a feeling you and your li'l pal there could do as much good for some of my adult patients as you've done at the Child Services Center."

She looked at Mort, too, slumped in the corner of the booth, smiling his ever-pleasant monkey smile. "I—I don't know. I'm not trained to—"

"Sleep on it, why don't you, and get back to me. I

have a feeling you'd be very good therapy for patients of any age.''

She'd never considered using Mort with grown-ups. But maybe she should have…especially the terminally ill—

"You look surprised," Adam said.

"I am, a little."

"Well, it's no wonder, if you've been hanging around with this old grouch." He jabbed a thumb in Wade's direction. "Way he feels about hospital volunteers, it's a wonder he hasn't scared 'em all away!"

Her gaze slid to Wade. "You don't approve of volunteers?"

Adam laughed. "Uh-oh, I think I've opened a can of worms. That's my cue to leave. See you in the a.m., Wade. And you," he said, pointing at Patrice, "stop by the office sometime soon, so we can discuss which patients I think you oughta pay a visit to."

She gave Adam a noncommittal smile. "Nice meeting you."

"Ditto." And with that, he was gone.

"He seems like a very nice man," she told Wade.

He nodded. "He is. The best."

"Known him long?"

"We practically grew up together." He laughed. "Seems we spent our teenage years at his house or mine."

"So you met in school?"

Another nod. "Yeah. In school."

Why would he say "school" with that ominous note in his voice?

"So, let's get back to this volunteer thing. I had no idea you didn't approve of the hospital volunteer program."

He frowned slightly. "It isn't that I don't approve, exactly...."

"What, exactly?" she pressed.

He shoved his plate away and folded his hands on the table. "Well, sometimes volunteers—" He shook his head. "I don't know if I can explain it."

"Aw, go ahead and try," she coaxed, grinning.

He gave her a "you asked for it" look, then said, "They're overzealous, for starters." Brows knitted, he added, "And I can't help but wonder about their motives. I mean, why would they spend their free time *here*, of all places? Do they do it so they can go home and brag to friends and family about their altruistic deeds? Do they come because when compared to the patients' lives, their own seem better? What do they get out of it?"

She sat quietly for a few seconds, taking it all in. "For someone who didn't think he could explain himself, you did a pretty good job!"

Chuckling, Wade shrugged. "Sorry if I didn't say what you wanted to hear."

"Oh, I don't think you're sorry at all." She hesitated, then blurted, "But you have a right to your opinion—" she grinned "—even if it's one hundred percent wrong."

His brows rose again.

"You heard me right. Even the almighty doctors among us can be wrong."

She stacked their plates and silverware on the blue plastic tray, then leaned forward. "I'll have you know that volunteers are almost as necessary to patient care as the equipment and the meds and the personnel around here. I've seen children go from vulnerable, physically, to being on the mend, just because a volunteer took the time to make them laugh or smile.

"I've seen kids who, one minute don't seem to care if they live or die, start looking forward to getting well and going home the next. And it wasn't *medicine* that made the difference—it was a volunteer."

She punctuated her speech by jabbing her fingertip at the tabletop.

For a moment, Wade only looked at her. "And I've seen them come in here," he began, "with head colds and stomach viruses, infecting my patients. I've seen them get people who oughta be resting quietly all riled up, sending their blood pressure skyrocketing and their pulse racing."

Patrice sat back, crossed her arms and said quietly, "I wonder how you'd feel if I maligned your profession the way you've just maligned mine?"

He winced. "If that's how I sounded, then I apologize." Shaking his head, Wade fiddled with a corner of his napkin. "I'll admit, I had a lot of negative opinions about volunteers before…before I met you." He met her eyes to add, "But I saw what you did for Emily Kirkpatrick. A guy doesn't need much more convincing than that."

Patrice clucked her tongue. "Shame on you."

"What?"

"Girl gets up a good head of steam, and you fizzle it with a sincere apology," she said, grinning.

Wade chuckled. "Sorry."

She checked her watch. "Well, guess it's true what they say."

"What do they say?"

"That time flies when you're having fun?"

He laughed out loud at that. "I'd call that speech of

yours a lot of things, but 'fun' wouldn't be one of them!"

Patrice got to her feet and reached into the booth to gather her purse and her puppet. "I'll make it up to you tonight at supper."

He stood beside her. "What's on the menu?"

"Spaghetti and meatballs. I started the sauce before I left for work this morning. Molly promised to stir it every couple of hours."

Sliding an arm around her waist, he led her from the cafeteria. It felt good, felt right being this close to him, and Patrice found herself second-guessing her decision to end it with Wade. Later, she'd pray on it, find out if the Almighty agreed she'd been too hasty.

"Homemade spaghetti sauce, eh?" he asked, licking his lips. "Where have you been all my life, Patrice McKenzie?"

Right here, she thought, smiling happily, *I've been right here....*

He sat back in his chair, too stunned to do anything but stare at the test results on his desk. When his buddy in the lab called to deliver the news, Wade insisted he run the tests again, *Stat,* because surely there had been an error.

Moments ago, his friend in the lab had hand-delivered the file, had spent the past ten minutes explaining how his staff put everything else on hold to give Gus's tests priority one...*three times in a row.* "The only other possibility," he'd said, "is that your patient's blood work got mixed up with somebody else's."

Impossible, since Wade had taken Gus's blood and labeled those vials himself.

He glanced at the clock on his desk and realized that,

in an hour and a half, he was supposed to have dinner with Gus and Patrice. Suddenly, homemade spaghetti sauce didn't hold quite the appeal it had earlier in the day.

Adam knocked on his open office door. "I'm through for the day, so I have time to go over that—" He stepped into the room and closed the door behind him. "Good grief, Wade," he said, sitting in one of the chairs in front of the desk, "you look awful."

"Thanks," Wade said, shoving Gus's file closer to Adam. "Take a gander at that, and you'll know why…."

He sat back, fingers steepled under his chin, watching his friend and colleague flip through the paperwork. The more he read, the deeper the frown on Adam's forehead grew. After several moments, he looked up. "You've gotta be kidding. Chagas' disease?"

Nodding, Wade leaned on the edge of his desk. "They ran the tests to Sunday and back for me, so there's no mistake."

"Wish I could be more help, pal, but I'm afraid I don't know much about this one."

"I spent a couple hours in the hospital library, after the first results came back, just in case." Wade pointed to the stack of computer readouts topping the stack of papers in his In box. "Only question left to answer is how Gus got exposed."

"You want me to take over?"

"Why?"

"Well, you're mighty sweet on the Monkey Lady. Might make things harder still if—"

"Don't call her that, okay?"

Adam tucked in one corner of his mouth. "Sorry, pal. You know I didn't mean anything by—"

He waved the apology away. "I know, I know. It's just…" *It's just I'm in love with the girl,* he told himself, *and I don't have a clue how I'm gonna break this to her.*

Chagas' disease could be deadly for a healthy man. For a guy in Gus's condition—

"What's the next logical step?" Adam asked.

Sighing, Wade ran both hands through his hair. "Find out how he came into contact with the parasite in the first place, I guess. Maybe that'll give me a clue what to do next."

Adam tapped Gus's file. "Says in here it's progressed to cardiomyopathy." He shook his head. "Not much you can do but monitor him, now."

Wade nodded sadly.

Rising, Adam dropped the file onto the desktop. "If there's anything I can do…"

"I know." He met his friend's eyes. "Thanks."

The phone rang, startling them both.

"You headed home?" Adam asked.

"Yeah."

Wade reached for the receiver. "Tell Kasey I said 'hi.'"

"Will do. And Wade?"

The bell sounded again. "What?"

"Kasey and I will say a prayer for you, so you'll know what to say and how to say it."

God, Wade thought. *Fat lot of good* He'd *be. Why didn't the Good Lord intervene* before *this happened?* But Adam was a devout Christian; questioning the man's faith certainly wouldn't solve Gus's problem. "Thanks," Wade said, lifting the receiver.

"Dr. Cameron?"

Adam waved, then headed out the door. "Call me if you need me."

Nodding, Wade said into the phone, "Speaking."

"Thank God, you're still here. I'm Myra Jenkins, Emily Kirkpatrick's nurse and—"

"I'll be right there," he said, slamming down the receiver.

He'd scheduled an appointment to talk to Emily's mom, first thing in the morning. That's when he'd planned to tell the poor woman that her only child wasn't going to make it. Looked like he'd have to tell her sooner rather than later, Wade thought. Unless of course the worst had already happened....

He ran out of the office without even bothering to close the door behind him, darting around hospital staff and visitors who peopled the hallway as he raced for the elevator. With any luck, the car wouldn't take an eternity to arrive, as usual; he couldn't afford to waste a single second.

His cell phone didn't work in here, or he would've used it to reserve an operating room. So Wade did the next best thing.

"Call Pediatric ICU," he said, slapping both palms on the nurses' station counter. "Get 'em to line up an OR, *Stat.*"

"Patient's name?" the nurse asked, pen poised above a scratch pad.

He heard the unmistakable *ping,* announcing the arrival of the elevator. "Emily Kirkpatrick, age six," he shouted as its doors opened. The nurse was on the phone even before they hissed shut again. When this crisis passed, he'd apologize for his brusqueness and thank her for her quick thinking. Right now, he couldn't focus on much more than the slow-moving car.

"Dr. Cameron," Emily's mom cried when he rounded the corner. "Thank God, you're here!"

He took a second to lay a hand on her shoulder. "Margie," he said to a passing nurse, "get the lady a cup of coffee and take her to the waiting room."

"Sure thing, Doc," Margie said with an understanding smile, and guided Mrs. Kirkpatrick from the bustling room.

"I'll keep you updated," Wade told the teary-eyed mother. "I promise."

Immediately, he grabbed a pair of surgical gloves from the cart at the foot of Emily's bed. "See if that OR is ready yet," he barked to the nearest orderly. With a curt nod, the young man hustled to the nurses' station.

"Fill me in," he ordered, popping the gloves against his wrists as he studied the monitors.

In an attempt to bring him up to date, two nurses started talking at the same time. Wade pointed at one. "You, talk to me."

She rattled off the facts as she knew them: Emily had been complaining of dizziness, followed by a period of nausea, followed by a bout of coughing. An electrophysiologist had been on the floor, evaluating another patient; he'd been called in to evaluate Emily's situation...and immediately insisted the child's cardiologist be contacted.

"So where is he?"

"His beeper went off a few minutes ago," she said. "He said it was an emergency."

Wade sighed in frustration as the orderly returned. "Operating room's ready for you, Doc."

"Then, let's get her prepped," he demanded.

The team bundled up the wires and electrodes attached to little Emily and released the brakes on her hospital bed. In seconds, the bunch of them were running down the hall with Wade in the lead. "Hold that elevator!" he shouted.

Minutes later he was scrubbing up, when a surgical nurse stepped up beside him and pulled off her mask. Laying a hand on his forearm, she said quietly, "No need for that, Doctor."

Wade froze, hot water running over his fingers, suds running down the drain. Then, leaning on the edge of the sink, he hung his head. "Has anyone told her mother?"

"Not yet."

He nodded as a breath of grief escaped his lungs. "She's probably still in the waiting room in Pediatric ICU."

"I'll have someone go and—"

"No." Wade shook his head. "I'll find her."

He dried his hands, and in a fit of rage, threw the towel into the semicircular bin with such force, the bin began to rock. Stomping into the hall, he blasted through the swinging doors and stood, hands at his sides. The doors' creaks and squeaks slowed and quieted, then stopped.

Like little Emily's heart.

He spotted an orange plastic chair against the wall, its chromed legs and armrests gleaming in the harsh overhead light. Wade trudged over to it and slumped onto its seat. Elbows resting on his knees, he held his head in his hands. If only he had been with her at the end.

He could almost hear her frail little voice, calling his name....

Emily Kirkpatrick's life had ended before it had a chance to begin. And now he had to find her mother and break the horrifying news—just one of many reasons he avoided caring for children whenever possible, and why, when a youngster's case was left on his desk, he passed it on to colleagues who specialized in pediatric cardiology.

A little bit of him wished he had passed on Emily's file.

And a little bit of him was grateful he hadn't. Wade pictured her tiny blue-eyed face, the unruly golden locks, the sweetly innocent smile. An angel, he thought, come to earth to show them all what the seraphim and the cherubim looked like.

"Why?" he whispered to himself. *"Why!"*

Sadness and grief rolled over him like an ocean wave, drowning him in sorrow and helplessness and a feeling of utter futility....

And he wept.

The instant she arrived home, Patrice peeked in on Gus.

"C'mon in, Treecie," he called weakly. "I'm not asleep."

After dumping her coat and purse in the chair beside his bed, she kissed his forehead. "So how was your day?" she asked, perching on the edge of the chair.

He held out his hand, and waited until she put hers into it. "If you consider lying around all day like a lazy bum a good day," Gus said on a weak grin, "this one topped the list."

She patted his hand. "Oh, don't be so hard on yourself. You deserve to take it easy once in a while."

"I've been taking it easy for *years.*"

Patrice heard the dejection in his voice but chose to pretend she hadn't. "Guess who's coming to dinner?"

He gave a flimsy chuckle. "Now, lemme see...who could it be, who could it be?"

Laughing, she said, "He bought me lunch today."

Gus scooted up a bit in the bed and met her eyes. "Did he, now?"

She nodded. "I met his partner, too."

"Next thing y'know, he'll be introducing you to the family...."

Patrice took a deep breath. *If only,* she thought.

"I've been inhaling that sauce all day long. What time is the great doctor supposed to grace us with his presence?"

"I told him we'd eat at six." She studied his face. "But if you're hungry, I can fix you a plate now."

He waved the offer away. "Nah. I'd rather eat at the table, like a normal human being. Besides," he added, giving her hand a gentle squeeze, "do you have any idea how hard it is to eat spaghetti in bed?"

Rising, Patrice smoothed back his hair. "No, but that's quite a picture, I have to admit!" Grabbing the thermos-type pitcher on his nightstand, she refilled his water glass, then shook two aspirins into the palm of her hand.

When he opened his mouth to protest, she quickly said, "If you take them without complaint, I might be convinced to fix you a light snack to hold you over till suppertime."

Grumbling and frowning, Gus downed the pills without a word. "Cheese and crackers would hit the spot...."

She picked up her coat and purse and said, "Comin' right up."

Gus grabbed her hand, gave it another gentle squeeze. "Did I ever tell you what a good kid you are?"

Smiling, she said, "Only about a million times."

"That I'm a lucky man to have a daughter like you?"

Yes, he'd said it before, too many times to count. And every time he said it, Patrice cringed. Because, would a good daughter cause an accident that put her father in a wheelchair for life? She licked her lips. "I'm the lucky one," she admitted. And before he could object, she quickly added, "Has Molly left yet?"

"Don't think so. I heard her answer the phone just before you came in."

Nodding, she handed him the remote. "There was a horrible traffic jam on I-95. See if you can find out what happened."

"Will do," he said, turning on the evening news. "Hope it wasn't an accident. I'll say a prayer for the people involved, just in case." Immediately, his focus turned to the TV screen.

How like him, she thought, to think of a thing like that. She *was* lucky to have a dad like him, and nothing he could say or do would ever change her mind.

"Your doctor friend called a few minutes ago," Molly said, when Patrice walked into the kitchen. "Said he can't make it to supper tonight. 'Patient emergency,' he said. Told me to tell you he'd call you from home if he didn't get in too late."

"Sorry to hear that." She lifted the lid to the saucepan. "Care to join Dad and me for supper?"

Molly sniffed the air. "Much as I'd like to, after smelling that all day long, I'm afraid I'm on duty tonight."

Patrice replaced the lid. "Well, I'm sure there will be leftovers."

"Especially if Gus leaves as much on his plate at supper as he did at lunchtime."

"He skipped another meal?" Patrice frowned. "That's not like Dad at all."

"I wouldn't worry too much," Molly said matter-of-factly. "He's come down with bugs before, and always manages to fight 'em off." She winked. "I don't see any reason to believe this time will be any different."

Except that this time, the fever had lasted for days instead of hours. And this time, Gus's weakness showed in his eyes. "You're probably right," she said. "Maybe there's something to that positive thinking stuff."

"We'll find out soon, won't we."

Before Patrice had a chance to comment on Molly's dull tone and worried expression, the woman hurried into her jacket. "Well, gotta run if I don't want to be late—Channel thirteen says traffic is snarled up everywhere."

"Drive safely, Molly."

"Will do." One hand on the back doorknob, she hesitated. "Have a good night, kiddo. And don't worry too much about Gus. He's a tough old bird."

She nodded. "I know." But she didn't mean a word of it.

An idea popped into her head and she grabbed the phone and dialed Wade's extension, thinking to leave a message telling him she hoped everything was okay.

"Wade Cameron's office."

"H-hello?" she stammered.

"Adam Thorne, here. Can I help you?"

"Adam, hi. It's Patrice. I was just calling to leave a message for Wade."

"He had an emergency."

"Yes, he called, left word with my dad's nurse. I just wanted to let him know it'd be okay if he dropped by late. I could reheat the spaghetti for him...."

"Lucky guy," Adam said. "But I wouldn't count on it. He lost a patient this afternoon and—"

"Oh, Adam. That's terrible! I'm so sorry."

"Yeah, it is."

A moment of silence punctuated his admission.

"Last I heard, he was on his way to break the news to the kid's mother."

"No. Not Emily Kirkpatrick!"

"'Fraid so."

Poor Wade. It was obvious to anyone with eyes that he'd grown quite fond of that little girl. Surely his heart was breaking over this. If only she could go to him, offer a word of comfort.

"You want me to leave him a message?"

She hesitated, uncertain what to say at a moment like this. "If you see him, will you tell him my thoughts and prayers are with him, and that if he needs to talk...."

"I'm sure he knows that already, but I'll tell him, anyway."

"Thanks."

"No. Thank *you*."

"Thank me? For what?"

"You're the best thing to happen to Wade in a long, long time, Patrice. He might not know it yet, but he's been waiting for you his whole life."

Stunned speechless, Patrice swallowed. "He's...he's a good man."

"You can say that again. Trouble is, I don't think *he* knows that yet." Chuckling softly, Adam added, "But I have a feeling you're going to teach him everything he doesn't know about himself."

Confused, Patrice remained silent.

"Took Kasey to wake me up," he explained. "Before

she came into my world, I was more mixed up and lost than Wade is.''

Adam had all but said she was the woman for Wade! And he'd known Wade most of his life. Patrice held her breath and prayed for the right words to respond.

"Tell you what," Adam said. "I'll hunt him down before I head on home, pass your message on in person. Okay?''

"Okay." She was more than a little surprised she could speak past the lump in her throat.

"See you soon."

"Yes, soon," she said as Adam hung up.

Slumping onto the seat of a kitchen chair, Patrice folded her hands on the tabletop. She could only imagine how Wade must be feeling now, after having lost little Emily. A little powerless, she decided, and maybe a whole lot sad.

She closed her eyes. *Lord Jesus,* she prayed, *be with him now and give him strength. Find a way to prove to him how valuable, how needed and necessary he is in so many lives.*

She thought of Gus, upstairs watching the news, weakened by God only knows what. Somehow, she believed that whatever was ailing her father, Wade would find a way to fix it.

"He's so important to so many people," she added, "especially me."

Chapter Eleven

Wade heard footsteps and glanced up enough to see the toes of a pair of wing tips planted on the floor in front of him. "Didn't you hear...nobody's wearing wing tips these days."

There was a grating chuckle, and then a voice said, "How'd you know it was me?"

"I'd recognize those size elevens anywhere." He heaved a deep sigh. "What're you doing here?"

When Adam didn't answer, Wade looked up, into his friend's face. "So," he said, "it's all over the hospital, is it?"

"What, that you lost a patient?"

He stared at the floor again and said through his teeth, "That I fell apart. Blubbered like a weak-kneed—" He balled his hands into fists and punched his knees. "I think maybe I'm in the wrong business, bud."

"Why? Because you get a little attached sometimes?" Adam pulled up another chair, sat down beside Wade and placed a hand on his shoulder. "This thing they talk about out there," he said, using his chin as a pointer to indicate the world that existed outside the hospital, "it's malarkey. Especially for docs like you and me."

Wade knew exactly what Adam was talking about. Day after day, doctors made life-and-death decisions on behalf of their patients. In the wrong hands, that kind of control could easily be abused. Too often, it was, and medical professionals, from GPs to proctologists, wielded their power like a weapon, doled out advice as if their words had been handed down by Moses himself. Not surprising, then, that laypeople and other hospital personnel dubbed the high-and-mighty attitude the God Complex. Adam was right. He and Wade had never succumbed to the know-it-all mind-set because, simply, they cared too much.

"Depending on your viewpoint," Wade said, "that's not necessarily a good thing."

"That's baloney." Standing, he waved Wade to his feet. "Come on back to the office with me. I have something for you."

A souvenir from the islands, no doubt, that Kasey had talked Adam into buying while on their honeymoon. Didn't matter what she'd brought home from some quaint little shop; the gift hadn't been bought that could ease what Wade was feeling now.

But he got to his feet and fell into step beside his longtime friend. "You talk to Kasey about that dinner invitation?" he said, trying to sound jovial.

"Matter of fact, I did. Went home a while ago, and she sent me back."

Wade met Adam's eyes. "Why?"

But Adam only smiled. "You'll see."

He'd hated guessing games, even when he was a kid. And Adam, knowing it, persisted on playing them. "It's for your own good," he'd say, jabbing his shoulder, "to toughen your resistance!'' So Wade went along, pretending the gift that waited was worth trudging all the way back to his office for.

They walked the rest of the way in companionable quiet. It was one of the things he liked best about Adam—that he didn't feel the need to fill every silence with the sound of his own voice. That said a lot about their friendship, Wade thought—the fact Adam had the confidence to say nothing when there was nothing to say.

''Sit down,'' his friend said when finally they reached their shared offices. He moved a stack of files from the chair in front of his desk. ''Take a load off.''

Wade flopped onto the chair seat and propped the heel of one shoe on the corner of Adam's desk. ''So what's Kasey gonna cook…when I come to dinner, that is?''

For a moment, Adam looked puzzled, and then he smiled. ''Oh. Dinner. Well, I imagine she'll fix whatever you like, as usual.'' Laughing quietly, he added, ''I'd be jealous of you—if I didn't know she already got the best-looking of the two of us.''

Wade grinned as his partner sat behind his desk. But the grin vanished when Adam sat Wade's mother's Bible atop a teetering stack of mail. ''Remember when your mom gave this to me?''

''Yeah, I remember.''

As if he could have forgotten! The night she died, Wade's mom had asked Adam to come to her hospital room, and when he got there, she'd booted Wade and his sister Anna out, saying she needed a moment alone with her ''adopted'' son. It wasn't until months later that Adam admitted that night—and that gift—had been a major turning point in his life.

''You need this more than I do, pal,'' Adam said now, sliding the book closer to Wade and sending several envelopes fluttering to the floor. "Something tells me your mom would want *you* to have it back." He held up a hand to forestall Wade's protest. "At least, for a while...."

Eyes locked on the worn gold script, Wade felt a tremor pass through him as he reached for the book. It had been one of his mom's prized possessions, so it surprised him when, hours before her passing, she'd asked his permission to give it to Adam. "He's going through a bad time," she'd said, her weak voice filled with sympathy. "You don't mind, do you?" He couldn't have refused her anything, especially at a time like that. Besides, what did he need with her Bible when he'd never believed a word printed on its flimsy gilt-edged pages?

The heft of it surprised him, considering it was barely bigger than a paperback novel. The smooth black-leather cover, like each tissue-thin page, was turned up at the corners, proof it had been read many, many times. Wade opened to the first page, where in his mother's fanciful, feminine script, the names of her loved ones filled the boxes that made up the Cameron family tree. She'd drawn two hearts, like leaves clinging to the tree. In one, Anna's husband's name; the other said "Adam."

"I remember something she told me once," he said, cracking the quiet that had settled between them. "We couldn't have been more than twelve at the time."

Wade couldn't tear his eyes from the book.

"I asked her why she kept it in the living room, smack in the middle of the coffee table, when *my* mom probably had no idea where our family Bible was."

Wade looked up in time to see a tear form in the corner of Adam's eye.

He quickly knuckled it away. "She said, 'When

things look darkest, God's word brings me light, and I feel like I'm stepping out of the shadows.'''

With the Good Book balanced on one palm, Wade ran the fingertips of the other across the cover, trying to ignore the knot that had formed in his throat. "Yeah, that sounds like something Mom would've said."

"She was one of the finest human beings I ever had the pleasure of knowing."

"She was one great lady, all right," Wade agreed.

"Ever think maybe you oughta pay a little more attention to what made her that way?"

He met Adam's eyes, watched as his friend nodded at the Bible. "Any questions you have, m'friend, you'll find in the pages of that book. I've been where you are now, don't forget, so I know what I'm talking about."

True enough. Adam had wasted a lot of years beating himself up, blaming himself for what had happened that night at the cemetery. As for Wade, it had been only too easy to believe what the newspapers had said: that the engineer was already in the middle of a major heart attack when the boys' pumpkin-headed dummy hit the railroad tracks. Still, despite his highfalutin excuses, there was no denying why he'd chosen cardiology as his life's profession.

Could he have spared himself some of life's miseries if he hadn't hardened his heart to God's word? *Too late now,* he told himself.

And on the heels of the thought, he could almost hear his mother's voice: *"It's never too late, Wade m'boy."*

He heaved a sigh and put the Bible back on Adam's desk. "Thanks, buddy," he said, staring at it, "for the trip down memory lane. It's been a long time since I thought about—"

"You're not leaving here without that book."

Adam's no-nonsense tone made Wade look up. "But Mom wanted you to have it."

"So we're in agreement—it's mine to do with as I please?"

"Yeah, I guess so."

"Then I repeat—you're not leaving here without that book."

Frowning, he picked it up again, tucked the spine into the junction where his palm met his fingers. For a reason he couldn't explain, it fit. Fit as if it had been made for his hands alone.

But he didn't believe in God, except as an unmerciful, power-wielding Being who seemed to delight in slapping sparrows from the sky. What did he need with His word?

His mother's advice to Adam echoed in Wade's mind: *When things look darkest, God's word brings me light, and I feel like I'm stepping out of the shadows.* Well, he supposed, it couldn't hurt to bring the Book home....

"Oh, by the way, Patrice called while you were out," Adam said, standing.

"I left a message with her father's nurse that I couldn't make dinner tonight."

"Idiot."

"What?"

"As I live and breathe, your bullheadedness never ceases to amaze me. How'd you graduate in the top one percent of our class?"

He didn't have to put up with that, not even from the man who'd been his closest friend for as long as he could remember. "Adam...."

"She's nuts about you."

He knew that. At least, he thought he did. Which made them even, because he was nuts about her, too.

"She told me to tell you there'd be a plate of spaghetti waiting, if you felt like eating when you left here."

Yeah, that sounded like something Patrice would say. Wade could almost picture her, arranging meatballs neatly beside the noodles, covering the dish with plastic wrap, then peeking at the clock every ten minutes and wondering—

"She's worried about you."

His head snapped up at that. "Why? I can take care of myself."

Adam stared him down.

"She doesn't need to worry," he said quietly.

"Why don't you tell *her* that?"

"Because if I go over there, I'll have to tell her about her dad's condition." He drove a hand through his hair, then stuffed his hand into his pocket. "I need to get home, get my head straight first. Otherwise, I'll just botch it."

On his way to the door, Adam stopped, laid a hand on Wade's shoulder. "Do yourself a favor and open that Book when you get home." He gave the shoulder an affectionate squeeze. "Trust me, your self-pitying thoughts will disappear like that." He snapped his fingers.

Self-pitying? Funny, he hadn't seen his behavior that way until Adam pointed it out.

"I'm going home to my newly pregnant wife. See you in the a.m.?"

"Yeah." He ran a fingertip along the Bible's spine. "In the a.m."

Alone in Adam's office, Wade let the Good Book open to an undetermined page. "'Through faith we understand,'" he read from Hebrews 11:3.

There wasn't much he understood these days.

* * *

Just as he had suspected, Wade found Emily's mother in the chapel, head bowed, on her knees. She'd been there ever since he'd broken the news to her earlier. "Mrs. Kirkpatrick," he said softly, "I hope I'm not disturbing you."

Turning, she smiled through her tears. "Dr. Cameron," she said, getting to her feet.

Gesturing to a pew near the back, Wade invited her to sit.

Taking her hand in his, Wade said, "Once again, I want to say how sorry I am. The team worked for over an hour, but—"

"I know. Of course I know. Everyone here at Ellicott has been so wonderful." A trembly smile tweaked the corners of her mouth. "We've spent so much time here, Emmi and I, that we came to think of you all as family."

She nodded quickly, so quickly that a tear flew from her face and splashed on the back of Wade's hand. He watched as it slowly slid from his thumb, where it was quickly absorbed by the smooth fabric of his trousers.

"Yes, I'm sure everyone did everything possible for her." After rummaging in her purse for a second, she withdrew a wrinkled tissue. Dabbing her eyes, she exhaled a pent-up sigh and, staring straight ahead, said in a wavering voice, "I knew it was coming. I could see it in her eyes. Today, especially...." She sniffed. "I just didn't want to believe it would happen quite this soon."

Should he put an arm around her? Pat her hand? *Go with your gut,* he told himself. *It's always worked in the past.*

Turning on the seat, he held out his arms. It surprised him a bit, the way she melted against him when he wrapped her in a comforting embrace.

"She's with the angels, now." Her voice, muffled by the lapel of his jacket, wavered. "No more pain, no more suffering, no more operations, no more hospi—"

And then the sobs overtook her, shaking her so hard that they shook Wade, too. He held her tighter, telling her without words that she wasn't alone, hoping to show her that someone cared. "She was a trouper, that girl of yours," he managed to choke out. "She touched a lot of lives, a lot of hearts. I have a feeling she'll be remembered by everyone who knew her for a very long time."

Yes, he'd made similar speeches before, but something was different this time. Oh, he'd shed tears; he'd have to be inhuman not to experience some of the loss his patients' families felt. But cry? *Sob?* No, that had never happened before.

You're some piece of work, Cameron, he chided. Twice in the same afternoon, he'd fallen apart, broken down. *Get a grip,* he thought, *be strong, for Mrs. Kirkpatrick's sake, at least.*

She sat up, leaned against the backrest and exhaled heavily. "Thank you, Dr. Cameron."

For what?

"It's consoling to know you genuinely cared, cared enough about Emily to shed a tear at her passing." She gave him a weak smile, and lifting her chin a notch, cleared her throat. "When you first told me about Emily, I was too overwhelmed to ask. But now I need to know. Tell me," she said, meeting his eyes, "were you with her when it happened? It'd be so nice, knowing that someone who cared this much was with her at the end."

He considered telling her the truth, that he was scrubbing up for surgery—for an operation that wouldn't have saved Emily life, anyway. But one look into her mother's red-rimmed, bleary eyes made him say, "She wasn't in any pain." He hoped this half truth would be enough to convince her that her baby hadn't spent her last moments on earth in the arms of strangers. "She simply fell quietly to asleep and didn't wake up."

At least, that's what the duty nurse had reported to him. Even if Emily had come to, the emergency team had pumped her so full of drugs, she wouldn't have felt a thing.

Mrs. Kirkpatrick grabbed Wade's hand, gave it a hearty squeeze. "I suppose you know that Emmi and I lost her father a year ago." She shrugged. "So, since I wasn't there for her, either, you have no idea how relieved I am, how very, very glad..." Her lower lip trembled, and she bit down to still it. "It'll be so much easier, remembering, now that I know *you* were there."

He watched as she clamped her teeth together in a last-ditch effort to gather her composure. What a brave young woman, he thought admiringly. *This* was the reason he'd never give up cardiology—people like Mrs. Kirkpatrick, and Emily.

And Gus.

The young mother stood and moved woodenly toward the chapel doors. "There's so much to do," she whispered. And turning slightly to face him, she added, "I wondered, when my husband died, what lesson I was supposed to learn from having to plan his wake, his funeral, single-handedly." A sad giggle popped from her lips, and she said on a sigh, "And now I know...."

Wade hurried to catch up with her. "Would you like me to make a few phone calls? Get some of the arrangements started?"

Mrs. Kirkpatrick took his hand again. "No, no, of course not. You've done so much already." Patting his hand, she said in a strong, firm voice, "Don't think I'm not aware how much extra time you gave Emily and me. If not for you, she'd have been gone months ago." And squeezing his hand, she concluded, "You gave me a chance to say goodbye. I'll always be grateful for that."

He hugged her for the last time. "Well, if you can think of anything, *anything* I can do, promise me you'll call, all right?"

"Actually, there is something."

He waited, knowing he'd try to lasso the moon if she asked it of him.

"Would you let Patrice know? She spent so much time with Emmi, especially these past few days."

"Of course I will."

"Thank you, Dr. Cameron. We were very lucky, Emmi and I, finding you when we did. You've been a wonderful doctor, and you're an even more wonderful man. I can see it in your eyes. I can honestly say it's been an honor knowing you."

With that, she left him alone in the chapel.

Humbled by her speech, Wade stood for a few moments in dumb silence. Then he walked to the front of the tiny chapel and stood where Mrs. Kirkpatrick had knelt such a short time ago. He looked up at the crude wooden cross, hanging from the ceiling, at the candles that flickered in their red-glass holders, at the painting beside the altar that portrayed the serene face of Christ.

Looking into the Savior's gentle eyes, Wade shook his head, wondering why nothing made sense. Not fathers who abandoned their families; not mothers forced to work themselves into early graves to provide for their children; not youngsters who died of heart ailments; not nice, middle-aged men who suffered from almost unheard-of diseases.

He waited in the empty room, listening to nothing but the sound of his own shallow breaths, half expecting—no, *hoping*—that an answer would pop into his head, because he wanted to have faith, needed its soothing calm every bit as much as the next guy.

When no answer came, he shrugged, feeling foolish for having given even a halfhearted attempt at finding a reason to believe. Why had he expected God would speak to him this time, when no prayer he'd ever aimed heavenward had been heeded before?

"Hey," Anna said, opening the door, "what a nice surprise."

As Wade stepped into her foyer, she called out, "Hey, kids, look who's here!"

Two young children came thundering down the hall. "Uncle Wade! Uncle Wade!" they yelled in unison.

"How goes it, old man?" asked his brother-in-law. "Long time no see."

Anna closed the door. "There's plenty of time for nagging later." Standing on tiptoe, she kissed Wade's cheek. "When was the last time you had a decent meal? You look terrible."

"You sure are good for a guy's ego," he shot back.

"Uncle Wade," Frank Jr. interrupted, "did you bring us anything?"

Allie clapped her hands. "Yeah, yeah!" she agreed, jumping up and down, "what did you bring us?"

"Just me this time, kids. Sorry."

"Honestly, you two," Anna scolded. "You sound like a couple of little beggars."

Wade squatted to make himself child-size and held out his arms. In no time, they were filled with a five-year-old girl and a seven-year-old boy. "It's okay, Uncle

Wade," Allie said, pressing a juicy kiss to his cheek, "we like you even when you don't bring us nuttin'."

"*Nothing,*" Frank Jr. corrected. He rolled his eyes at Wade. "Sisters. They can be so dumb."

Standing, Wade smiled as Anna wagged a finger under his nose. "Don't even think about agreeing with him, brother dear."

It felt good to be here, among loved ones. So good that he felt generous enough to say "Wouldn't dream of it, sister dear."

"You kids go into the family room," Frank instructed, "so your mom and I can find out what your Uncle Wade has been up to."

"Will you eat supper with us?" his niece asked.

"Oh, you *hafta*," said his nephew. "Mom made your favorite!"

Wade looked at Anna. "Lasagna?"

Nodding, she said, "Thank your brother-in-law. He's been nagging me for weeks to make it."

"Not 'nagging,'" Frank corrected, sliding an arm around his wife's waist. "Nagging is what *wives* do." He kissed her temple. "Husbands 'badger.'"

Laughing, the kids headed for the family room while the adults retreated to the kitchen. This had always been Wade's favorite room in Anna's house. Not as tidy as Patrice's organized kitchen—what with all the colorful drawings and cutouts made by the kids—but cozy and warm all the same. Sitting at the round oak table, they drank decaffeinated coffee while they brought Wade up to date on the kids' comings and goings. He'd been smart to come here. Maybe, by the time he was ready to leave, he'd also be ready to pay a visit to Patrice and Gus....

When the lasagna was ready, Anna stacked plates and

napkins beside Wade. "Make yourself useful, little brother."

Smiling, he started distributing the dinnerware.

"You're not dealing cards," Frank joked, "you're setting a table!" He grabbed the utensils and did the job himself, while Anna, hands on her hips, smiled and shook her head.

"What?" Frank asked.

"I'm just standing here wishing there was film in my camera, is all."

Their laughter attracted the kids, and before Wade knew it, the cheerful family atmosphere had seeped into him. "Gonna hafta get me one of these," he said later, helping Anna load the dishwasher.

"One of what?"

"A family."

"You have a family, right here."

"I mean a wife and kids of my own…."

"You're outta your ever-lovin' mind," she teased. "Do you hear all that racket?" She pointed into the family room. "See that mess in there? You want this 24/7?"

Wade nodded. True, a couple of times he could've sworn Allie and Frank Jr. had broken the sound barrier, and yes, they could turn a tidy room into something that resembled the aftermath of a tornado, but he wanted all of it—the noise, the chaos, the love that filled this house to overflowing.

"Yeah," he admitted, "I do."

"Then, I guess you're gonna have to take down your Lifetime Bachelor shingle and start looking for a proper young lady."

"I've already found her." The words were out of his mouth before he realized he'd said them.

"Frank, come in here!" Anna called. "Frank! Hurry!"

Her husband ran into the room, newspaper in one hand, TV remote control in the other. "What's wrong?" he gasped.

"Honey, you're never going to believe this, but Wade has a girlfriend!"

Shoulders slumped, Frank rolled his eyes. "Anna, the way you were screaming, I thought you'd cut off a thumb with the bread knife or something." Suddenly, what his wife had said sunk in, and Frank looked at Wade. "Did I hear her right? Did she just say you have a...a *girl*friend?"

Grinning, Wade put his hands in his pockets. "Well, more or less."

Anna dried her hands on a dish towel. "What kind of male double-talk is that, little brother? Either you have a girlfriend, or you don't."

"I said I think I've found—what did you call her?—'the proper young lady.' But since I haven't discussed this with her, I have no idea if she feels the same way."

"Well, then," Anna said, "seems to me you have some serious talking to do!"

Then she and her husband exchanged a glance and, speaking what Wade could only define as some kind of curious, marital language, began moving toward the front door.

"Here's your coat," Frank said, jerking Wade's sports coat from the closet. "Honey," he said, handing it to Wade, "get the door, will you?"

The rumble of footsteps echoed in the hall, and the kids came to a screeching halt at Wade's feet. "Are you leaving already?'' Allie asked. ''We haven't even had dessert yet.''

''Yes,'' her father answered in Wade's stead. ''Uncle Wade has work to do.''

''What kind of work?'' Frank, Jr. wanted to know. ''I didn't hear your beeper go off. Did the hospital call?''

''This isn't medical business,'' his mother explained, shoving Wade onto the porch. ''Your uncle has a girl-friend, you see, but she doesn't *know* she's his girlfriend yet, so he has to—''

''A girlfriend? Say it ain't so, Uncle Wade!''

Frank struck a prayerful pose. ''Alas,'' he joked, ''the last hero has fallen.'' Then in a more serious voice, he added, ''Why should he be allowed to dodge the bul-let?''

Anna narrowed her eyes. ''Fra-ank...''

The boy held his stomach. ''A girlfriend.'' He shook his head. ''Yuck. I think I'm gonna throw up.''

Hands clasped under her chin, Allie sighed. ''I think it's so ro*man*tic.'' Suddenly, she began hopping up and down. ''Can I be the flower girl in your wedding? Can I, Uncle Wade? Can I, huh?''

Laughing, Wade said, ''Have you guys ever heard the old saying 'Don't put the cart before the horse'?''

''Bye, little brother.''

''Yeah, see y'Wade,'' Frank added, waving.

Wade couldn't help laughing. ''Here's your hat, what's your hurry, don't let the screen door bang your behind on the way out....''

''I couldn't have said it better myself,'' Anna an-nounced, nudging the kids inside. And smiling, she closed the door.

Wade was halfway to his car when she jerked it open

again. "Call me when it's official," she whispered loudly.

Funny, but he hadn't thought about Emily or Gus all evening. One thing was sure, he thought, a family had a way of keeping a guy's mind off his problems. Yes, he wanted—*needed*—that.

The clock on the dash read 8:45. And Patrice had asked Adam to tell Wade she'd keep a plate warm for him. Maybe, just maybe she felt exactly the way he did.

He'd stopped for the traffic light at Centennial Lane and Route 40 when it hit him: If he went over there tonight, he'd either have to tell Gus and Patrice what he knew, or pretend he hadn't seen the test results yet. Every upbeat thought, all the warm feelings built up during the hours he'd spent with Anna's family, fizzled like a Fourth of July sparkler stuck glitter end first into a cold glass of water.

Well, he decided when the traffic light turned green, he'd never been one to put off till tomorrow what he could do today.

Why start now?

He drove around for nearly an hour, passing her house three times before parking on a dimly lit side street. Opening his cell phone, he dialed her number.

"Hello?"

The mere sound of her musical voice was enough to lift his spirits. "Patrice, I hope I didn't wake you."

"Wade! I'm so glad you called. Is everything all right? Adam said there was an emergency, but he wasn't specific."

Knowing how fond she'd grown of Emily, Wade knew it wouldn't be fair to tell Patrice what had happened now, not on the telephone. "I was wondering if it'd be okay for me to—"

"Are you hungry? I saved you a plate of spaghetti."

Despite his foul mood, Wade smiled. "No, I'm not hungry, but I'd like to stop by, if it isn't too late."

"Of course you can stop by. You're always welcome. Always."

She meant it, too. He could hear the sincerity in her voice.

"Are you still at the hospital?"

"As a matter of fact, I'm about a block away."

"A block? But…"

He heard her sigh, then take a breath to start fresh. "Then I have just enough time to turn on the kettle, brew us a cup of herbal tea."

"Okay," he said, "see you in a few minutes, then. I won't ring the bell, in case Gus is sleeping."

He closed the phone, dropped it into his shirt pocket and put the car in gear. In the minute it took to drive to her house from where he'd parked, he decided to tell her about Emily tonight, and save Gus's test results for tomorrow. He didn't know about Patrice, but Wade knew he'd dealt with just about all the bad news he could stand for one day.

He stood on the porch, hands in his pockets and head down, and pictured his mother's Bible, resting on the passenger seat of his car. *When things look darkest…*

"Lord," he began, "don't get the wrong idea…I'm not coming to You on my own behalf. For Patrice's sake, just give me the strength to get through the next few minutes without blubbering, okay?"

Straightening his back, he knocked softly.

Patrice opened the door wearing a white sweat suit

and sneakers—and the warmest, most welcoming smile he'd ever seen. "You're a sight for sore eyes," he said.

She reached out and took his hand, tugged him gently into the foyer. Without letting go, she looked into his face. "Looks like you've had a pretty rough day. C'mon, let's get you into the kitchen. I'll fix you a nice, soothing cup of tea."

Wade was only too happy to follow.

"Have a seat," she instructed gently. "How 'bout some cherry pie to go with the tea?"

He nodded, grinning. Anna had stuffed him full as a tick, but he said, "Sure. Why not?"

Watching her bustle around the kitchen, doing things for him, getting things for him—for *him*—touched him as few things ever had. He waited until she sat across from him, then said, "I can't tell you how good it is to see you."

Her tender smile made him want to reach out and touch her, and so he grabbed her hand.

"Tell me about your day," she said, stroking his fingers.

"First, do me a favor?"

"Sure, if I can...."

Scooting his chair back, he patted his thigh. "Come sit over here, will you?"

She blinked, clearly wondering about his request. Wade hoped she wouldn't ask *why* he wanted her in his lap. Thankfully, Patrice barely hesitated before doing what he'd asked.

"So here I am," she said, wrapping both arms around his neck. "Start talkin', mister."

He gathered her close, closer than he had a right to, considering he'd never bothered to admit he loved her like crazy, and for a moment, just held her. "Ah," he whispered, "you feel good in my arms."

Her fingers playing in the hair at his temples, she said in a soft, soothing voice, "So you had a bad day, huh?"

Wade nodded. Actually, it had been one of the worst.

"I know about Emily, Wade. Adam told me earlier."

Wade sighed heavily.

"Oh, Wade, I'm so sorry. I know how fond you were of that little girl."

Now, wasn't that just like her, he thought, laying his hands atop hers, to put his feelings ahead of hers when she'd clearly cared as much about the kid as he did. As he looked into her tear-filled brown eyes and shook his head, it took all his willpower not to blurt out the truth about what he felt for her, here and now.

Tilting her head, she massaged his cheekbones with the pads of her thumbs. "How did Mrs. Kirkpatrick take it?"

"Pretty much as you'd expect," he said dully.

Her eyes welled with tears. "That poor woman." Laying a hand over her heart, she bit her lower lip. "If it hurts me this much, knowing Emily is…is gone, imagine how Mrs. Kirkpatrick feels, having lost her only child!"

He tucked a stray curl behind her ear. "Did you know her husband died a year or so ago?"

"She told me, early one morning, while Emily was sleeping. It was her husband's favorite time of day, she said. He loved to watch Emmi sleep…." She grabbed a napkin and blotted her eyes. "In her shoes, I'd be a basket case," Patrice admitted, tossing the napkin back onto the table.

"No. You're wrong. You're the strongest woman I've ever known." A good thing, too, he thought, considering the news he'd have to dump on her tomorrow.

Brow furrowed, she said, "What?"

He blinked. "What 'what'?"

"You looked…you looked, I don't know, *funny* just now. Like you were about to deliver bad news, and changed your mind."

Swallowing, Wade gathered her close again, more to keep her from reading what was written on his face than anything else. "It was nothing," he said. "So how's Gus?"

"Still has a bit of a fever. And he didn't have any appetite at all tonight. Not even for cherry pie, and that's his favorite."

"Well, we'll know more tomorrow."

"I certainly hope so. This waiting is enough to drive a person nuts."

He studied her face. Looked to him like she needed one more good night's sleep a whole lot more than she needed the details about Gus's condition.

Patrice planted both hands on his shoulders. "Your tea is getting cold."

He felt as though he could look into her pretty face forever. "I don't care."

One side of her mouth lifted in an impish grin. "And so is your pie."

"It was cold when you gave it to me."

"Well, then, it's colder now."

"So?"

"So don't you want—"

Wade pulled her close for a third time, and she rested her head on his shoulder. "I'll tell you what I want," he breathed into her ear, "I want to kiss you like there's no tomorrow so I can forget completely about today."

I want to marry you, keep you safe from bad weather and bad news and people with bad attitudes, forever. I want us to have kids together, and plant tomatoes together, and grow old together....

The only sound in the room was the steady *tick, tick, tick* of the schoolhouse clock on the wall above the sink...and the thudding of his heart echoing in his ears.

It was Patrice who spoke first. "Well?"

He grinned. "Well, what?"

No answer.

He looked up to find her sitting there, her eyes closed and her mouth puckered, awaiting his kiss.

Only too happy to oblige, pretty lady, he thought. As his lips touched hers, his mother's words echoed in his head yet again: *When things look darkest, God's word brings me light, and I feel like I'm stepping out of the shadows.*

And for the first time in his life, Wade felt the radiant glow of real, abiding love.

Chapter Twelve

After leaving Patrice's house the night before, Wade had gone home and plugged in to the Internet. He'd searched every online site for more information about Chagas' disease. Though a bit tired from his first all-nighter in years, he felt he'd traced Gus's problem—and a viable solution.

Now, at last, it was time to break the news to Patrice's father. The moment Gus wheeled into his office, Wade closed the door. He dispensed with the usual pleasantries.

"Were you ever in the military, Gus?"

"You betcha." Chest puffed up with pride, he added, "Spent fifteen years in this man's army."

"I'm proud to know a man who spent that much time putting his life on the line for his country."

"Aw, it was peacetime, mostly. I never saw any action."

Maybe not, Wade thought, *but you came home with major damage, all the same.* Sitting behind his desk, he riffled through the man's file. "Where were you stationed?"

"Oh, they moved us around a lot. Different base every few years." Gus ticked them off, one by one, ending with Panama.

"Panama," Wade echoed. "How long ago?"

He shrugged. "Hmm, during the seventies. Why?"

Leaning back, Wade shook his head. "The explanation for your condition is rather convoluted. See, it started out as one thing, ended up something else."

Grinning, Gus made himself comfortable. "Figures. I never was one to do things the easy way...."

"First, let me assure you that we ran your tests four, five times, to rule out any chance of error."

"Okay...."

"The blood work tells us you have Chagas' disease. It's—"

Gus groaned. "I was afraid of that."

Wade was mildly surprised. "You've heard of it?"

"Wish I hadn't." Gus sighed. "Good ol' American trypanosoma cruzi," he spouted, as if to prove what he knew. "Just my luck, comin' down with something incurable."

Wade frowned. "I wouldn't say it's incurable, exactly."

"Aw, don't give me that. You and I both know the best I can hope for is some kind of prescription medication that'll control whatever damage has already been done." He looked Wade in the eye. "Am I right?"

More or less, Wade thought. But in place of a direct answer, he said, "I would've expected the government to educate you guys on prevention."

"In a perfect world, that'd be true enough, but you know as well as I do, the army isn't a perfect world.

What I know about Chagas', I learned on my own after I overheard some natives talking about creepy-crawlies that get their start in cracks and holes of substandard housing." He hesitated. "Want me to go on?"

Gus probably knew as much as or more than Wade did about the disease. So he said, "Sure."

"Those nasty li'l bloodsuckers pass their infection through feces deposited on a person's skin. 'Course, animals are affected, too, but I digress." He chuckled a bit. "Anyway, the Panamanians also call these parasites 'kissing bugs,' because they'll crawl right into a person's mouth, usually while they're sleeping, to do their business." He paused. "So how'm I doin' so far?"

"Disgusting," Wade admitted, grinning, "but right on target. I'm impressed."

"Well, the trouble with Chagas' is, the first symptoms aren't severe enough to cause any real alarm. Folks usually mistake it for a routine case of the flu—fatigue, fever, chills, minor swelling at the bite site…. The real problems don't show up for ten, twenty years or more. That's when the ol' Rhodnius bug takes its victims. Enlarged liver or spleen, swelling of the lymph nodes, digestive disturbances, difficulty swallowing…."

Wade took over from there. "And cardiac problems, like enlarged heart, cardiac arrest, heart failure, and in your case, bradycardia."

"Bradycardia," Gus repeated. "What is *that?*"

"Low heart rate, to put it plainly. My heart beats at a rate of between seventy and one hundred times a minute, depending on what I'm doing. And you, my friend, are lucky to register fifty beats. That's why you've been feeling dizzy and sluggish lately, why your appetite has fallen off."

"Aha. So it caused my fever, too?"

Wade nodded. "I expect so. But we won't know for sure until we try treating it."

Gus brightened. Seeing that look on the man's face alone had made every sleepless minute worthwhile.

"Treating it? You mean you really *can?*"

"We're gonna do our best, starting with a pacemaker and following up with medication."

Gus shook his head. "Pacemaker, eh?"

"Don't worry, I've assisted in a couple hundred of these operations. For your surgery, I'll partner up with an electrophysiologist. Chances are, you won't even need to spend the night in the hospital."

"That simple, huh?"

"Well, not simple, but certainly not as difficult as I'd anticipated when I first saw your test results."

Gus pointed at the folder on Wade's desk. "That big fat thing mine?"

"It sure is."

He whistled, then clucked his tongue. "You keep adding to it, you're gonna need a chair like mine just to cart it around!"

Getting to his feet, Wade laughed. "Hopefully, we'll only need to add a few more pages."

"So have you told Patrice?"

"No."

"Ah, doctor–patient confidentiality?"

"Exactly." Then Wade said, "Do you want me to tell her?"

He thought for a moment. "Might be better, coming from you."

"Just between you and me, if I have a daughter someday, I hope she'll care about me even half as much as Patrice cares about you. She thinks you hung the moon, single-handedly."

Laughing, Gus said, "Well, don't blow my cover, Doc. It's kinda nice havin' her look up to me—" he slapped the armrests of his wheelchair "—especially considering I spend most of my time in this contraption." Gus sighed. "That girl fusses over me as if I were made of spun glass."

"She blames herself for putting you *in* that contraption. So it's not at all surprising that she acts as if you're breakable."

"What?"

Surely Gus knew—it was written all over Patrice's face, in her actions....

"If I've told that girl once, I've told her a thousand times. She isn't to blame for what happened. It was an accident, plain and simple." Gus narrowed his dark eyes. "What did she tell you, if you don't mind my asking."

"Something about a party on a rainy night," he said offhandedly. "She didn't have her license yet and you didn't think it was safe to drive her, but she raised a ruckus and—"

"Ruckus? All she said was, 'Dad, will you drive me?' and I said no. She'd been through so much, losing her mother and brother...never gave me a whit of trouble...took right over running the house like a full-grown woman. And without a word of complaint, I might add."

Gus shook his head. "I hated denying her anything, so when I saw that disappointed look on her face, I caved." Sighing, he added, "Like I told her over and over again, it wasn't her fault. She was the kid, I was the parent. If I had stuck to my guns, the accident never would have happened. I wouldn't be in this chair, and she wouldn't have that miserable reminder of it on her beautiful face."

"Has she considered plastic surgery?"

"I brought it up once or twice, but the suggestion gave her some crazy idea that I thought she was ugly, so I quit talking about it. She's the prettiest thing on feet, if you ask me, scar and all."

"And I agree."

Gus nodded sagely. "I kinda figured you'd say that." Chuckling, he tacked on, "Would you think I'm an old-fashioned fool if I asked again what your intentions are toward my daughter?"

"Not at all." Perching on the corner of his desk, he looked Gus straight in the eye. "She doesn't know it yet—at least, I haven't told her so—but I love her more than life itself. And if she'll have me, I want her to be my wife. Someday. If I ever get around to telling her how I feel."

"Well, then, when the time comes, you'll have my blessing." Gus wiggled his eyebrows. "Provided the operation is a success, that is. You botch the job, and I'll retract that blessing so fast it'll make your head spin."

"Glad to have the incentive to do a good job," Wade said, laughing. Standing, he opened the office door. "I'll try to get together with Patrice sometime today, bring her up to speed on your condition. You want me to call you once she's been told?"

"Nah. I'm sure she'll be more than happy to fill me in." He wheeled into the hallway. "Thanks, Doc," Gus said, extending his hand.

Wade clasped it, gave a hearty shake. "Don't thank me just yet. We have a wedding riding on the outcome, don't forget...."

Patrice pushed the play button on her answering machine and smiled when she recognized Wade's voice.

Wasn't it weird, she asked herself, that the mere sound of his voice could increase her heart rate more than a half-hour aerobics workout! *"Hey, kiddo,"* he said, *"Give me a call when you get a minute. There's something I want to tell you about Gus's case."*

Eleven-thirty, said the clock on the wall. Would he be in the cafeteria, having an early lunch? Grabbing the phone, Patrice decided to give it a shot. Seconds later, she was more than a little surprised when he answered the phone.

"Where's your secretary?" she asked him.

"We have an arrangement," he told Patrice. "She takes the early lunch shift while I cover the phones." He paused. "Between you and me, it doesn't ring much this time of day, which is why I chose this one. But don't let on, because she thinks hers is the cakewalk."

Laughing, Patrice sat at her desk, tossing loose paper clips into an open drawer. "I thought for sure I'd be leaving a message because you'd be in the cafeteria, scarfing down a burger and fries."

"Nah. Tryin' to lay off the greasy kid stuff for a while." Another pause. "So, did you get my message, or are you just calling because you missed me?"

Patrice held the receiver away from her ear. Maybe she'd dialed the wrong number, because this sure wasn't like her serious, stoic Dr. Cameron.

Her Dr. Cameron. She rather liked the sound of that....

"The results of your dad's tests are back. You want me to come down there to talk about it, or would you rather meet me here?"

Her thoughts about Wade's upbeat demeanor were quickly forgotten at the mention of Gus's condition. "I'll be there in ten minutes," she said, and hung up.

He was sitting behind his desk, paging through a three-ring binder, when she bounded into his office. "Got here fast as I could," she said, breathless from her jog.

Calmly, Wade pulled back his sleeve and looked at his watch. "I believe you just set a record." And smiling at her, he added, "You made it in four minutes, thirty seconds."

Patrice took a seat in one of the chairs facing his desk. "Helps to know a few shortcuts." She couldn't help but wonder why he was looking at her that way—as if she were the love of his life and he hadn't seen her in years. Grinning, she shrugged.

"Maybe someday you'll be kind enough to share a few with me?"

"Maybe." But she couldn't continue sitting there, giddy as a shy schoolgirl in the presence of the team's star quarterback. There were far more important things going on in her world than her hopeless devotion to Wade. Squaring her shoulders, Patrice pointed at the thick folder on his blotter. "Is that Dad's file?"

"Hefty, isn't it."

"*Scary* is a better word. Why is it so fat? The others aren't half that bulky. What's going on? He's all right, isn't he? What did the tests—?"

Wade chuckled. "Easy, easy," he said, hands up in mock surrender. "Gus has a problem—pretty serious one at that—but I think we've found a solution for it."

She took a deep breath. "A serious problem? Oh, I was afraid of that."

"Sweetie, didn't you hear a word I just said? Things could be problematic, but there's a solution."

Sighing in relief, she whispered, "Thank You, God."

But wait. Had Wade just called her…*sweetie?*

Patrice didn't know why it had surprised her so, considering their little tête-à-tête in her kitchen the night before.

First things first, she told herself, in order of importance. "So what's Dad's 'problem'?"

She watched Wade lean forward, balance his elbows on the edge of his desk. He looked so knowledgeable, explaining Gus's illness. But as he went into more detail about the disease, its onset, its symptoms, the bradycardia, Patrice's fears escalated. "Sounds like the Ebola virus, and that's deadly."

"Actually, it's a related malady, very similar in many ways. Except Chagas', if caught in time, can be controlled and even cured."

"Thank You, God," she repeated. Then, "You don't really mean there are *bugs* living inside him?"

"Parasites," he corrected gently.

Patrice shivered. Like it made a difference to Gus's insides! Then it dawned on her. "Good grief, you're *not* joking, are you."

He shook his head somberly. "I'm afraid not. But I believe medication will eradicate the problem in a week or so, and when we're sure it's taken care of, we'll implant a dual-chamber pacemaker to take care of the bradycardia."

"Bradycardia," she echoed. "Sounds so serious."

"Can be, if left unchecked." He leaned forward a little more. "But we've got it checked."

Nodding, Patrice attempted a smile. "So, surgery, huh?"

"Uh-huh."

Tears stung behind her eyelids, and she struggled to keep them at bay. "Are you sure…sure that he's strong enough?"

"Wouldn't be suggesting this course of action if I wasn't. The meds should bring him back to his old self. That's one of the reasons we're waiting a couple weeks to do the implant surgery."

"One of the reasons?"

"Caution, sweetie. I always like to err on the side of caution."

She blew a stream of air through her teeth. "So he's really going to be all right?"

"He's really going to be all right." He paused. "But something else is wrong. Very wrong."

Her heartbeat doubled, and she nearly lost her precarious hold on her emotions. "Oh, what now?"

"Well, for starters," Wade said, pointing at her, "you're way over there, and I'm way over here."

Memory of their kisses last night flashed in her head—and in her heart. Smiling, Patrice said, "Which means one of us has to move?"

He grinned.

"Hmm," she said, "how do we decide?"

"Mind if I make a suggestion?"

"You've been doing pretty well so far...."

"My chair is bigger than yours."

Rolling her eyes, Patrice feigned lack of interest—not an easy task, considering the way her pulse was racing—and trudged to his side of the desk. "There," she said, standing beside his chair, "are you happy now?"

"Well, that's better. But not quite good enough."

"You're not an easy man to please, Wade Cameron."

"That's where you're wrong, Monkey Lady. Takes little or nothing to make me happy." And taking her hand, he said, "Someday I'll have to show you my so-called bachelor pad. My sister Anna calls it the Great Gobi Desert."

"Why?"

"Because it's barren and boring."

Patrice laughed softly.

"And small. *Very* small."

"I've never been in a real bachelor pad before...."

"Just one of your many attributes."

She raised her eyebrows.

And he wiggled his. "I like my women gorgeous and guileless."

Women. Plural. She couldn't help but wonder, standing there beside him, how many there had been, how many he'd truly cared for, and how many had been...sport. Is that how he saw her—as the pawn in a game of some sort? Was his main interest in her as a "win"? Maybe she should be playing hard to get— *harder* to get, at least, so if Wade was in it for the thrill of victory, the game would at least last longer. But if she did that, what trophy would *she* claim?

Heartache. And she had had enough of those on her shelf to last the rest of her days. Patrice grit her teeth, determined to harden her heart, intent upon protecting herself. She hadn't been unhappy, after all, taking care of Gus. And what with this...bradycardia thing that had cropped up, he'd need her now more than ever. *Focus,* she'd always told herself. *With focus, anything in life is possible.* She could live without a husband and children, without a home of her own, with the proper focus. And the key, experience had taught her, was to aim her focus outward, on anything but herself, her dreams and desires....

Wade pulled her onto his lap just then, drew her into a hug.

She looked into his eyes, searching for a sign—any sign—that in a week, a month, she'd be another notch on his belt. Seeing none, her heart softened. If only what she *thought* she read on his beautiful face could be real.

"Now *that's* better."

He'd said it with a warm, loving smile that sent shivers up her back. She loved the feel of his muscular arms around her, loved the sound of his voice so near her ear; the way she only had to lean her head slightly to rest it on his broad shoulder. *A good fit,* she said to herself. *A real good fit.*

"Something else is wrong."

She sat back, waiting for the truth, for the "this is going faster than I can handle" speech.

"There are no pretty lips pressed up against mine."

A nice surprise. He was different, she had to give him that. But then, why wouldn't he be, when he'd likely racked up more hours wooing women than she had entertaining kids with Mort! So no one was more surprised than Patrice when she said, "Are there supposed to be lips pressed to yours?"

"Definitely."

So she obliged him, kissing him ever so softly at first. In no time, what she felt for him began to bubble up from her heart and through her lips, and she found herself telling him the truth about her feelings...with her kisses.

There was no turning back. Not even her strict self-disciplinary rules and good intentions could save her now, because she'd let herself fall in love—the feet-over-forehead kind of love—with him.

Would he break her heart?

Quite likely, considering his past.

But at the moment, Patrice was willing to risk it.

Would he come to the Lord if she set a good enough example?

Possibly.

But here and now—though she was ashamed to admit it—the state of Wade's soul was the last thing on her mind.

Would he ever profess his undying love for her?

Well, miracles happened every day, didn't they?

"Got any of that spaghetti left?" he asked, breaking the delicious connection.

Spaghetti! How like a man to be thinking of food at a time like this. "Yes" was her breathy answer. "There's plenty of spaghetti left."

He brushed the backs of his knuckles across her cheeks, and, staring deep into her eyes, said, "How would you feel if I invited myself over for supper?"

Good thing he was holding her so tightly, Patrice thought, or the headiness of his touch, his look, would send her floating off into space, maybe even tumbling onto the floor. It amazed her that she had the presence of mind to say, "Saves me the bother of inviting you."

"So what time should I be there?"

Cuddled against his chest, she sighed dreamily. "Suppertime, of course."

"You li'l nut." Chuckling, he kissed the top of her head. "Is it any wonder I love you like I do?"

Every muscle tensed, every nerve end tingled. Holding her breath, Patrice waited, hoping he'd say it again. Praying the words hadn't been part of her silly, schoolgirl wish.

If only it *were* a crush. She could easily get over a crush.

Lord, she prayed, eyes closed tight, *if this is a dream, don't let me wake up....*

"Funny," Wade said, breaking into her thoughts, "but I never figured you as rude."

She sat back, looked into his face. Rude? It was the last thing she'd expected him to say. "What?"

He smiled in his easygoing, heart-stopping way and said, "When a man tells his woman he loves her, she's supposed to say she loves him, too."

Lucky for you he's a cardiologist, she thought, grinning to herself. Her heart seemed swollen three times its normal size, and was beating three times faster than usual.

She felt playful, flirty—thrilling new emotions, feelings she had little to no experience with. *Oh, go with the flow!* she told herself. "But...what if the woman doesn't love the man?"

For an instant, shock and pain glittered in his golden eyes, telling her he'd expected her to admit she loved him, proving he'd needed to hear it every bit as much as she had, and making her regret she'd made the ridiculous remark. "Oh, Wade, I'm sorry," Patrice said, kissing his cheeks. "I didn't mean it, honest. I was just teasing." And throwing her arms around his neck, she added, "I *do* love you. I really do!"

Wade held her at arm's length and studied her face. "Well, I don't mind admitting, that's a relief." Then he added, "I have a confession to make."

Nothing he could say now could possibly matter. "You're married?" she teased.

He laughed. "'Course not."

"Engaged?"

"Not anymore."

That reminded her of the photograph. "What happened?"

He shrugged. "Lots of things."

"Name a few."

He squinted. "For starters, she met a guy willing to buy her a bigger ring."

She'd suspected all along that horrible blonde had hurt him! "Oh, Wade," Patrice said again, "I'm so sorry."

"I'm not."

From the look on his face, he'd meant it. "But you loved her, didn't you?"

He shrugged. "Thought I did at the time, but I'm smarter now."

"Smarter?"

"Whatever I felt for her, well…" He looked away for an instant. When his eyes met hers again, they glimmered with raw emotion. "Let's just say it wasn't love." He hugged her closer still. "I know what it is now."

Dare she hope? "'It' being love?"

He nodded. *"You,"* Wade began. *"This* is love."

She said a quiet prayer of thanks, for the good news about Gus, for Wade's profession of love. Snuggling against him, she sighed. "So what's this confession you wanted to make?"

"I asked Gus for your hand in marriage."

Startled, she sat up. "You *what?"*

He nodded. "It's true. When he was in here earlier, I told him how I felt about you. I said if you'd have me…"

Tears filled her eyes and she swiped them away. "You'd what?"

"I'd be the proudest man born if you'd do me the honor of becoming my wife, that's what."

Biting her lip to still its trembling, she shook her head.

He frowned. "Is that a no?"

"Yes. I mean, no. I mean…" Laughing past her tears, Patrice hid behind her hands. "Oh, Wade, I just can't believe this!"

"Why?" He forced her to come out of hiding, to meet his eyes. "Because I'm thirty-one and still single? Because people think of me as a playboy?"

"No, not because of *you*..." She turned slightly, so he couldn't see her scar.

But it was as though he could read her mind, for he took her in his arms and kissed it, gently, tenderly. Lovingly. "I've said it before and I'll say it again—you're the most beautiful thing I've ever set eyes on. That scar of yours doesn't make a whit of difference to me, and I mean that."

For a moment, she only stared into his eyes. Then, nodding, Patrice said, "I believe you."

"It's about time."

She smiled happily. "So what did Gus say?"

"About what?"

"When you asked for my hand in marriage, silly!"

"Well, it wasn't a simple yes or no answer."

Patrice frowned.

"No, I'm afraid your father put some restrictions on me...."

"Restrictions?" Her frown intensified. "What kind of restrictions?"

"If I botch his surgery, the deal's off."

Reading the teasing glint in his eyes, she laughed. "*Now* who's the nut?"

"Well," Wade began, "I have to admit...I'm nuts about you."

Patrice had never been happier in her life. She had a wonderful job, Gus was going to be all right, and Wade loved her. *Wade loved her!*

"So what do you say?"

"To what?"

Wade slapped a hand to his forehead. "Can I have cheese on my spaghetti tonight?" he joked.

"Well, if you want—"

He groaned. "I was kidding!" he interrupted. "What do you say to *my proposal?*"

Tilting her head, Patrice memorized every inch of his face, from the sparkling hazel eyes to the little-boy grin. "You call that a proposal?"

He stood, gently coaxed her into his chair, then got down on one knee. "Patrice," he said, taking her hand in his, "will you marry me?"

Nodding, she started to cry.

"So is that a yes?"

"What do you think?" she blubbered.

"I think you're hedging, so later when you come to your senses, you can back out on a technicality."

What did he expect her to say to that? The truth, she decided, plain and simple: "Nothing I've ever done in my life made more sense."

And nothing could have surprised her more than the tears that puddled in the corners of Wade's eyes. "You've made me very happy, Patrice, and I swear to you, I'll spend the rest of my life trying to make you happy, too."

More unadorned truth: "I don't doubt it for a minute," she said, smiling.

Gus's eyes fluttered open and he groaned quietly. "What's a guy gotta do to get a drink of water around this place?" he complained good-naturedly.

Patrice, who had been dozing in the chair beside his bed, leaped to her feet and poured him a cup of water. "Hey, sleepyhead," she said softly. "I was beginning to think you decided to go for a Guinness record."

Gently, she slid a plastic straw between his parched lips and watched as he sipped.

"So what's the prognosis?" he croaked out.

Patrice hadn't seen Wade in hours, not since he'd met her in the waiting room to tell her the operation had been a success. "A-okay," she said, remembering how handsome and important he'd looked, dressed in his green scrubs. Grinning happily, she gave Gus the thumbs-up sign, then glanced at her watch. "Wade had another operation to perform after yours, but he said he'd be in to see you when it was over."

"What time is it?"

"Nearly five."

He licked his lips. "Good." Then he said, "You think they're gonna feed me?"

Shrugging, Patrice admitted, "I have no idea. Guess that depends on whether or not Wade gives you the green light to go home tonight or decides to keep you, for observation."

Frowning, he grabbed the bed controls. "What does that mean, anyway?" he asked, raising the head of the bed. "What do these people observe, exactly?"

"Y'got me by the feet," she said, laughing as she plumped his pillow. "You feeling okay?"

"Ask me in an hour, when the anesthesia is totally worn off," he said, smirking.

She sat beside him again and took his hand. "I can't tell you how relieved I am that things went well, Dad."

"That makes two of us!"

"We have to do everything we can to make sure you stay healthy, because I honestly don't know what I'd do without you."

He met her eyes. "With a little luck and a whole lot of assistance from the Big Guy," he began, looking at the ceiling, "you won't find out for a couple of decades yet."

She patted his hand. "At least."

"I want to stick around long enough to roll a couple of grandkids around in my chair."

Grandkids...

The comment made her smile. And as Gus nodded off again, Patrice contemplated her many blessings. Admittedly, the list was long, and growing by the day. "God's been very good to us," she whispered, tidying Gus's covers.

Wade walked into the room just then. "You can't give *all* the credit to God," he said, laying Gus's chart at the foot of the bed. "You deserve to take some of the credit for what's good about your life, y'know."

She wanted to scold him, to rattle off the many reasons *he* should be thanking God. But Patrice held her tongue. This was neither the time nor the place for a lecture on faith.

"And you deserve some credit for something else, too."

"Like what?"

He scribbled something on Gus's chart. "Like showing me that God *does* answer prayers." He tucked his ballpoint into his jacket pocket. "I'd almost forgotten the lesson Adam's mother told me, years ago."

"Yoke ye not to unbelievers," the Bible said. Happy as she was that Wade had professed his love for her, Patrice couldn't help but wonder if *this* conversation had been an answer to her prayer last night, asking for God's guidance, asking Him to show her a sign if He wanted her to spend a lifetime married to Wade. "And what lesson was that?"

"'Ask and ye shall receive.'"

Patrice didn't have to ask what he'd prayed for; his loving smile made it clear: he'd prayed to win her heart!

Gus stirred, grunting slightly. "What's a guy gotta do to get a bite to eat around this place?"

"'Ask and ye shall receive,'" Wade said again, grinning.

Epilogue

Wade stood at the front of the church, tugging nervously at his cummerbund.

"Stand still," Adam said from the corner of his mouth. "You're fidgeting worse than your nephew."

He looked out into the congregation and saw Frank Jr. sitting there in the front row like a proper little gentleman. He winked at the boy and admitted that Adam was right. He *was* fidgeting an awful lot. And as if to prove his inability to stand still, he ran a finger under the starched white collar of his tuxedo shirt.

"May as well relax, pal," Adam added. "These things never get started on time."

Tucking in one corner of his mouth, Wade wished Adam would dispense with the brotherly advice; rather than calming him down, it was having the exact opposite effect.

"Think of something pleasant," Adam said as if on cue. "Like, the reason you asked Patrice to marry you in the first place. I remember that helped time pass faster for me."

At last. Some advice he could sink his teeth into!

Wade took a deep breath, then stared at the gleaming toes of his black rental shoes. He'd asked Patrice to marry him because he loved her. But it was more than that. Much more. She'd given his life purpose, stability. He had an incentive to get up in the morning, now— one not motivated by obligations to his patients, but propelled solely by how she claimed his presence had improved her world. Quite a chest-puffing notion, knowing a woman like that respected and admired him that much!

Quite a responsibility, too. Precisely why he'd started viewing just about everything in life with different eyes. She'd made him feel like a man, a real man, for the first time in his life. So was it any wonder he felt obligated to start acting like one?

When he'd told her about his part in the train accident, she'd said he'd punished himself long enough. She'd taken his hand in hers and prayed aloud that he'd come to believe that God had forgiven him. Wade believed that now, and finally, he knew real, blessed peace.

The organ music suddenly grew louder, its notes bouncing from every door and window, from every wall and pew in the tiny old-fashioned church. The powerful chords seemed to seep through the soles of his shoes to the marrow of his bones, reverberating in his hard-beating heart. He knew from having attended the weddings of relatives and friends that the music was a signal.

The bride would soon appear.

He looked up, saw the faint outline of her, standing proudly in the shadows beside her tuxedoed, wheelchair-bound father.

She was everything to him. The girl of his dreams. His wife to be. The woman who had completed his life.

Patrice Cameron. It had a nice ring to it, and Wade knew who he had to thank for making it all possible.

As "The Wedding March" began, he watched her stand a little taller, throw her shoulders back, take a deep breath.

Patrice had been determined to have a small, intimate wedding, with only their closest friends and loved ones present. Wade had a feeling his whole life would be that way—intimate and loving—thanks to Patrice.

When she took that first step toward him from out of the shadows, Wade remembered what his mother had told Adam so many years ago, and he murmured the line to himself now: *When things look darkest, God's word brings me light, and I feel like I'm stepping out of the shadows.* It's what Patrice had done for him, by inspiring him to meet God and believe in the power of faith, as one reborn. If it hadn't been for her, he wouldn't have a growing relationship with the Lord now. And he wouldn't have had the courage to work through his fears and doubts about his ability to be a good husband. Turns out he was nothing like his father, after all.

A bold ray of sunshine slanted down from the skylight and he watched, openmouthed, as Patrice stepped into it. She'd made no attempt to hide her scar, he noticed. "Out of the shadows," he whispered.

"What's that, buddy?" Adam whispered.

"Nothing," Wade answered as she took her place beside him.

And looking into her beautiful smiling face, he added, "'Ask and ye shall receive.'"

* * * * *

Dear Reader,

Tragedy...

Sooner or later, each of us has a head-on collision with it. If we're strong when it hits, we pick up the pieces and move on. If not, we throw up our hands and demand "*Why*, Lord?"

But Christians are taught "Don't ask why. Just have faith." Easier said than done! Because suffering tests more than our mettle, it burrows into the foundation of our faith, making us question God's promise: "Let all those who put their trust in Thee rejoice; let them ever shout for joy, because Thou defendest them." (Psalms 5:11)

There's a line in an old song that goes something like "into each life a little rain must fall." As Wade and Patrice discovered, the Creator defended them from the rain when He said, "I do set my bow in the cloud, and it shall be a token of a covenant between Me and thee." (Genesis 9:13) Alone, each was blinded by life's briny storms, but when He brought them together, their eyes were opened to the rainbow that led them *out of the shadows*...to the soft, warm light of enduring love.

May you bask in that same tender radiance, all the rest of your life!

All my best,

Loree Lough

P.S. If you enjoyed *Out of the Shadows*, please drop me a note c/o Steeple Hill Books, 300 East 42nd Street, New York, New York 10017. I love hearing from my readers and try to answer every letter personally!

Next Month From Steeple Hill®'s

Love Inspired®
Change of the Heart
by
Lynn Bulock

When an accident landed Carrie Collins in the
emergency room, the feisty redhead didn't exactly
hit it off with the handsome—and bossy—
Dr. Rafe O'Connor. But when they were thrown
together during a church-sponsored mission trip, they
just might realize they were meant for each other!

Don't miss
CHANGE OF THE HEART

On sale August 2002

Take 2 inspirational love stories FREE!

PLUS get a FREE surprise gift!

Mail to Steeple Hill Reader Service™

In U.S.	In Canada
3010 Walden Ave.	P.O. Box 609
P.O. Box 1867	Fort Erie, Ontario
Buffalo, NY 14240-1867	L2A 5X3

YES! Please send me 2 free Love Inspired® novels and my free surprise gift. After receiving them, if I don't wish to receive anymore, I can return the shipping statement marked cancel. If I don't cancel, I will receive 3 brand-new novels every month, before they're available in stores! Bill me at the low price of $3.99 each in the U.S. and $4.49 each in Canada, plus 25¢ shipping and handling and applicable sales tax, if any*. That's the complete price and a saving of over 10% off the cover prices—quite a bargain! I understand that accepting the books and gift places me under no obligation ever to buy any books. I can always return a shipment and cancel at any time. Even if I never buy another book from Steeple Hill, the 2 free books and the surprise gift are mine to keep forever.

100 IDN DNU6
303 IDN DNU7

Name	(PLEASE PRINT)
Address	Apt. No.
City	State/Prov. Zip/Postal Code

* Terms and prices are subject to change without notice. Sales tax applicable in New York. Canadian residents will be charged applicable provincial taxes and GST. All orders subject to approval. Offer limited to one per household and not valid to current Love Inspired® subscribers.

INTLI_02   ©1998 Steeple Hill